CITY OF MIRRORS

CITY

OF

MIRRORS

MELODIE JOHNSON HOWE

PEGASUS CRIME

NEW YORK LONDON

CITY OF MIRRORS

Pegasus Books LLC
80 Broad Street, 5th Floor
New York, NY 10004

First Pegasus Books cloth edition August 2013

Interior design by Maria Fernandez

Library of Congress Cataloging-in-Publication Data is available.

ISBN: 978-1-60598-468-1

10 9 8 7 6 5 4 3 2 1

Printed in the United States of America
Distributed by W. W. Norton & Company

In fond memory of Jeff Corey

If you want a friend in Hollywood,
get a mirror.

—Nora Poole, movie star

CHAPTER ONE

M other never owned a house. If she was living in one for any length of time, it meant she wasn't making a movie. It meant she was out of work. My early life consisted of boarding schools and, depending on where mother was shooting her latest film, rented houses. On my vacations I would join her in these strange impersonal places. Sometimes there was a strange impersonal man living there, too.

When I was fifteen she was stuck with me for Christmas vacation in one of those houses. She pointed to the indoor swimming pool. "You can swim when it rains!" she beamed.

I would paddle around in the giant pool while the raindrops and the acorns dropping from the oaks pounded the glass ceiling. In a corner of the room stood a white-flocked tree tilting precariously and shimmering with yuletide decorations. Next to it Brent or Burt or Bart—I never quite got his name—wearing an early version of a Speedo sat in a deck chair, watching me.

On the wet hard floor I offered up my virginity, and he took it with brutal efficiency. After Christmas he got tossed out with the tree, and Mother viewed me as a competitor from that moment on.

Maybe that's what I had wanted, I thought now, stripping off my clothes and walking down the steps into the water. It was as warm as I remembered. Outside the oak trees spread their branches over the glass ceiling, dropping their acorns on the roof. *Plonk. Plonk.* I smiled and began to swim.

Twenty-five years later, I had come back to this place that was never ours, to say good-bye to Mother.

Taking long easy strokes back to the shallow end, I came up for air, blinking chlorine from my eyes.

"Jesus Christ, Diana, you're naked." Stunned, Celia Dario stood on the deck above me in five-inch heels, calves tight, black chiffon blouse tucked into a short tangerine-colored skirt. Her long raven hair was twisted into a chignon, making her look professional and chic. A man in a black jacket, white dress shirt, and jeans, stood next to her staring at me with deep brown solemn eyes.

Oh, hell. I crouched low in the water, trying to cover myself.

"This is my client, Mr. Ward," she said, trying to regain her equilibrium.

"Sorry, I thought you said he wasn't going to be here for another half hour. That I had time to . . ."

"Not to take all your clothes off! Just to look at the house where you lived for fifteen minutes of your life." Taking a deep breath, she turned to her client. "I'm sorry . . . for all this." She waved manicured fingernails in my direction; her client still hadn't taken his eyes off me.

He was about six feet tall, firm body but not heavily muscled. His bent nose seemed to have taken a few punches. His dark brown hair, graying at the temples, waved back from his lean face. He had a matter-of-fact self-possession that was beginning to irritate me.

"You could turn your back," I told him.

"Why? I've seen everything there is to see." His somber lips slid into a smile. And suddenly he was charming, which was even more irritating.

I pushed my determinedly blond hair back from my face. "Do you have a towel?" I asked Celia.

"No, I don't have a towel," she snapped.

"You look familiar," the man said.

"Which part of me?"

Celia shifted into her best realtor mode. "This is the actress, Diana Poole," she continued, sensing an unexpected sale point. "Her mother, Nora Poole, the famous movie star, just died last week. She rented Bella Casa." Yes, the house had a name.

"She died here?" he asked.

In most house sales, death is not a selling point. But in Hollywood it's important for homes to have a lurid history of the famous living badly and dying even more badly in their mansions.

"Not exactly in Bella Casa, but . . . nearby." Celia shot me a glance, wanting my help.

"She died in bed in a room at the Bel Air Hotel with a shot glass in her hand and a half-empty bottle of bourbon on the nightstand."

"My father died like that." He paused, rubbing his index finger over the bump in his nose. "But not in the Bel Air Hotel. More like Motel Six."

"I'm getting cold, I'd like to get out of this pool," I announced.

He turned to Celia. "Why don't I see the living room again?"

She started to guide him back to the white louver doors that led to the main house, but he stopped her. "Help your friend. I can wander around on my own." He tossed me a lopsided smile as he took one last look.

After he left, Celia scooped my bra up off the deck and shook it at me. "Do you know how hard it is to sell a twenty-thousand-square-foot mansion that needs a total remodel in this market?" Her dangling gold earrings swayed erratically.

I climbed out of the pool. "I'm sorry." I grabbed my jeans and tried to dry myself off with them.

"Forget it, he's not interested."

I took my bra from her and put it on. "How do you know?" I stepped into my panties.

"I can tell." Her violet-colored eyes darted to the door where Mr. Ward had disappeared. "He is handsome, though."

"Almost handsome." I picked up my jeans.

"Even better. I can tell he liked you."

"I was stark naked. He's a man. What's not to like? Stop trying to fix me up." My jeans stuck to me as I wiggled into them. "Are you okay?" I'd noticed her face was drawn.

"Why?"

"You seem worried. I mean, beyond my taking a swim."

"I'm fine. Aren't you working today?" She handed me my blouse.

"One o'clock call." I ran my hand through my wet hair. "Thank God, I wear a wig." I managed to button myself up.

"Say hello to Robert for me."

"I will." Robert Zaitlin was Celia's lover and the producer of the movie in which I had a small but important role. He was married to an old girlfriend of ours.

"He told me he's having problems with a young actress," she said.

"Jenny Parson. She can't get through a scene without forgetting her lines."

She nodded. "I'd better go see what Mr. Ward is up to. Want to have dinner tonight?"

"Great." I paused. "Celia, I just want to thank you for helping me get this part."

"You gave a great reading. Besides, Robert has always had your best interest at heart, you know that."

Only a woman in love with a movie producer could say that and mean it. But I wasn't worried about Robert Zaitlin; it was the young actress, Jenny Parson, who troubled me.

In my Jaguar, so old it had five ashtrays and no airbags, I headed east on Sunset Boulevard then turned down to Santa Monica Boulevard toward the old Warner Bros. sister studio, which was once the old Samuel Goldwyn studio and is now called The Lot. But what's in a name?

The heater, which never turned off, blew hot against my wet jeans. My silk blouse clung to my damp body like an unwanted lover. I began to laugh at the absurdity of the situation I'd just created, and then suddenly I burst into tears. Mourning for a dead mother I didn't like and a dead husband I loved can do that to you.

Colin Hudson, my husband, died a year ago of a heart attack. We had been married for eight years—an eternity in this business. He left me with what is euphemistically called a teardown in Malibu, the old Jag, two Academy Awards for Best Original Screenplay, a bank account in the red, and an emptiness I couldn't fill.

In order to earn a living, I'd gone back to what I knew best— acting. Of course, I was eight years older and the parts for women in their early forties were few and usually lousy. And to be honest, if I had not been the daughter of Nora Poole my name would have been forgotten. Hollywood has all the attention span of a coked-up executive producer.

The bold-striped awning of the Formosa Bar came into view. It was one of the few great watering holes from the Golden Age of Hollywood that was still standing. The others had become photographs in coffee-table books reminding us of how great movie life had been and would never be again.

I turned right and pulled up to the gate of the studio. Recognizing me, the guard waved me through, and I drove slowly past the enormous, gray stucco soundstages that looked like vast warehouses where all the Hollywood dreams and nightmares were stored. I parked in front of the makeup and wardrobe building and stared up at its benign facade. I would go in there looking like myself, a little bedraggled, and come out looking like the role I was playing: a mother who was a drunken slut.

CHAPTER TWO

The camera aimed at Jenny Parson and me. The key light felt warm on my skin. Jenny crossed to her mark—a piece of blue camera tape stuck to the carpet. She glared at me. Her auburn hair curled around her oval face and down to her shoulders. I held a glass of scotch (colored water) in my hand. Using the acting technique sense memory (conjuring the past to give reality to the present), the odorless liquid reminded me of the smell of bourbon in my mother's shot glass. My blouse was buttoned haphazardly, and the tail end of it hung out from the waist of my too-tight, too-short miniskirt. The red wig felt heavy on my head. "Don't you dare talk to me like that," I slurred, staggering on my high heels, while making sure I didn't block Jenny's light.

"Why, because you gave birth to me?" she snapped back. Her green eyes flared in a defiance that felt real to me, and for the first time I thought we'd make it to the end of the scene. I fed off her anger, using its power to say my next line.

"Who says I did?" I let my mouth turn ugly.

Her full lips tensed. "You . . . you gave birth . . . didn't . . . give. . . ." Her lively eyes grew vague. She froze. I knew the look. God, did I know it. She'd gone-up again. Forgotten her lines.

I held my expression, trying to will her to remember. My makeup felt tight on my skin, like a second layer of flesh. Jenny clenched her fists, groping for her dialogue, then turned away from me and stared angrily out into the shadowy darkness of the soundstage.

"Cut!" The director, Beth Woods, ripped off her earphones, jumped away from the monitor she'd been viewing us on, and emerged from the dim light onto the set.

Spiked henna-red hair cut short, Beth wore a leather jacket that looked as if she'd borrowed it from a Mossad agent. She had the worried look of a director who knew her film and maybe her career were going down the toilet.

"Diana, you could help her out by just continuing with your line," Beth chided.

I was about to remind her I had done just that on a previous take, and she'd told me not do it again. But I said nothing. We were all tired, and tempers were flaring. The grips moved restlessly. My head ached from the damn wig.

Beth took a deep breath and put her arm around Jenny. "What's the problem, love?"

Jenny shot her a cat-like look, and Beth removed her arm.

"I can't remember my stupid lines. It's kind of obvious, isn't it?" At least she didn't say *duh* to her.

Jenny was twenty years old and playing sixteen. She had that jarring quality young girls have today: a youthful innocence mixed with a slutty in-your-face seductiveness.

Robert Zaitlin, the producer, walked slowly onto the set. He pulled thoughtfully at his perfectly unshaven chin. The lights reflected off his perfectly shaved head. "I think we should call it a day."

Astonished, the director turned on him. "We're behind."

"Wrap it," Zaitlin ordered.

With an abrupt turn, Jenny ran dramatically out of the sound-stage. I couldn't help but think tears should have accompanied her grand exit. But there was none.

Beth let out a long disgusted sigh, and called out "It's a wrap!"

The crew converged on the set, taking down lights and wrapping up cords. The boom mike disappeared from overhead, and the prop man took the glass out of my hand while the wardrobe, hair, and makeup people waited for me. The set no longer belonged to the actors.

Stepping over cables, I started to leave, but Zaitlin put a hand on my arm and walked me to a quiet corner.

"I was the one who told you to go ahead and get married, but don't give up your career." Robert always started a conversation as if the person he was talking to was inside his head and on the same wavelength. Prologues wasted too much time. "So did your mother," he continued. "Even your husband. We all tried to convince you. But no, you didn't listen to me. Or them."

As I waited for him to come to the point, he leaned close and I got a whiff of his sweet cologne mixed with the smell of a very long disappointing day.

"I didn't think you had a chance at a comeback. But you're damn good in this role. I really think it could be a springboard for larger roles."

Zaitlin's copious belly pushed against his tailor-made blue-striped shirt. Sweat had gathered under his loose heavy chin. He was not a physically attractive man, but his energy, intelligence, and intensity lit up his blue eyes and made him appealing. He also had the producer's ability to focus on a person as if they were the only one who mattered. Maybe that's how you end up with a wife *and* a mistress.

I smiled, understanding what he was really saying. "You want something, don't you?"

Gripping his heart, he feigned being hurt. "I only want the best for you, Diana."

"And what else?"

"I've got Jake on my ass."

Jake Jackson was the hot new star and the reason the movie was able to get made.

"He wants me to replace Jenny Parson," he continued.

"Replace her."

"You're as ruthless as your mother."

I doubted that, but let it go. Now Zaitlin looked helpless and vulnerable. "I can't," he said. "I'm too deep into the movie to change horses, to mix a metaphor. Besides when she gets it right she's great, and that's all I care about. Without her, we'd have to reshoot half the movie." He placed a fatherly hand on my arm. "And who knows, maybe if he gets rid of her he might want me to recast you."

"Are you threatening me? I thought you only had my best interest at heart."

"And I do. If the new actress doesn't look like she could be your daughter, my hand is forced. Diana, you are wonderful in this role. It could put you up there with your mother."

I didn't care about being "up there" with my mother. But I did need the work. "What do want me to do?"

"I've tried talking to her. Now I want you to. Have dinner with her tonight. Get to know her. See if she's on something." He lifted his shoulders. "Drugs maybe. Then spend tomorrow going over her lines with her."

"Drugs? You usually handle this kind of thing. And I'm having dinner with Celia tonight."

"I'll take care of Celia," he said possessively.

"What if Jenny doesn't want to . . ."

"You'll convince her. I can tell she looks up to you. I have good instincts about these things, that's why I'm a producer." He grinned wolfishly, patting my cheek. "Don't forget Gwyn's party tomorrow night for our son. It's his birthday."

Catching sight of the director, he yelled, "Beth! I want to look at the last take. Maybe there's something we can use from it." Finished with me, he strode away.

I wondered whether Zaitlin really thought I was good, or whether he was just saying that to get me to help Jenny. Compliments in Hollywood are handed out by the bagful, like Halloween candy. It's never been easy for me to completely accept them, because I'm always searching for the one that has the poison in it.

CHAPTER THREE

J enny and I had trailers—our dressing rooms—in the alley next to the stage. I knocked on her door, opened it, and peered inside. Already dressed in her street clothes, she wore a short black leather skirt, black tank top, and a lush emerald green cashmere-wrap sweater. She looked not only sexy but also her age. As if she didn't care or didn't want to look at her reflection, she sat with her back to a large mirror surrounded by lights. She was talking on her cell. When she saw me she quickly disconnected.

"Sorry, I didn't mean to interrupt," I said. "May I come in?"

"Are you going to lecture me?" She dropped her phone into a very expensive leather purse that was slouched on the makeup counter.

"I'm not your mother. I only play her." I stepped up into the trailer and closed the door behind me.

"If you can call that a mother." She snorted, baring small sharp teeth. She was oddly beautiful, like a pretty animal. But nonetheless an animal.

Sitting down on the built-in sofa, I glimpsed myself in the mirror. Out from under the set lights, my makeup looked harsh, exaggerating the lines on my face.

I pulled off my wig. "God, this is giving me a headache." My own hair was bound flat to my head with a gauzy net. Jenny eyed me warily as I took that off too and dumped it inside the wig. Then I shook my hair loose and asked casually, "Want to have dinner tonight?"

"Can't. Going clubbing." She shot me a hard look. "And why would you want to suddenly have dinner with me?"

"Is too much clubbing the reason you're having trouble remembering your lines?" I rubbed my scalp and fluffed my hair.

"The assistant director told me I won't be needed tomorrow, and is it any of your business what I do?" Her chin jutted defiantly.

I thought about telling her that making a movie was a group effort, each person dependent on the other for success. But I decided that concept wouldn't have much meaning to her. She seemed to be a very insular young woman. She sat on the set observing, never entering the camaraderie that formed among the actors and the crew.

"Yes, I do think it's my business," I said flatly. "I want this movie to work because I'm good in it and it will help my career so I can get another role and another, thereby earning money so I can eat and live. In other words, I'm a professional actress."

She laughed a surprisingly deep harsh laugh. "I heard you gave up your career to get married. Doesn't sound too professional to me."

Trying to control my temper, I leaned back and stroked my wig as if it were an agitated pet dog I had to calm. "I made a choice knowing I couldn't do both well."

But was that true? I remembered my mother, my husband, Colin, and I sitting on the beach one afternoon. We had watched a pelican high in the summer sky spot a fish, then tuck its long wings to its sides and drop like a guided missile into the ocean.

"Only hunger can teach you to do that," Mother had observed, squinting into the sun, her hair as determinedly blond as mine is now. "I had that kind of hunger. I would've done anything to be a star. And did."

"I never had that kind of hunger," I said.

"No, you didn't." Colin had hugged me.

Now Jenny said, "So you chose the man over acting. And you come in here blaming me for potentially hurting your career? I don't see it."

"You don't have to. Zaitlin asked me to talk to you. Find out if you're on drugs."

"Drugs? Is that what he thinks? Oh, God, something's wrong with Jenny, it must be drugs," she said, imitating a stupid worried parent.

"He's trying to figure out why you, who has a role other actresses your age would kill for, are such a fuck-up." I flung the wig aside

Offended, her lips pursed, and her checks flushed. "Is that what he called me?"

"No. That's what *I'm* calling you." I held her gaze, glad that I didn't have children of my own.

"Why isn't he here telling me all this? Is he afraid of me?" She seemed pleased that a big time moviemaker like Zaitlin couldn't control her.

"I think he's at his wit's end with you. So he asked me to help because he knows I need this movie to go well."

"He's such a manipulator."

"That's what producers do, Jenny. So why are you fucking up?"

Thinking for a moment, she spoke with an unnerving honesty. "Because I don't want to be an actress. I don't get make-believe. I don't get pretending. I don't get any of it. I get reality. I get doing what you need to do to attain what you want. But why play dress-up and imagine you're not who you really are? I mean, I never even did that when I was a child."

"Then why did you read for the part?"

Her expression hardened and she fell silent, staring down at her hands.

"Does your mother want you to be a movie star?" I edged forward, resting my elbows on my knees, trying to create some kind of intimacy between us.

"My father." She didn't look up at me.

I nodded. "Well, the problem is not your father at this point. The problem is, you are in a movie and you happen to be good."

"Really?" Surprised, she lifted her chin.

"Really. You'd be fired by now if you weren't."

"I doubt it." She moved back in her chair, crossing her legs.

I wondered why she doubted it, but I let it go. "Okay, here's the deal. You go clubbing tonight. And I'll see you tomorrow morning at ten o'clock to go over your lines with you."

"No way. I won't be up." She tossed her head, flipping her hair back from her shoulders.

"Eleven o'clock then."

"Three. Sometimes I wish I did want to be an actress." She looked away, momentarily letting her guard down. "It'd make my father happy. He's such a dreamer, at least about me. But I know exactly who I am even if he doesn't." Her defenses were in place again.

"Well, maybe you'll want to act after you know your lines and start behaving like a professional."

She lifted her chin. "Maybe I'm more capable than you think I am."

"Oh, I'm sure you are. Where do you want to meet?"

"My place." She dug around in her bag and came out with a crumpled cocktail napkin and a pen that had specks of face powder and a stray strand of her auburn hair stuck to it. She blew at the pen until she was satisfied that it was clean, then wrote her address on the napkin. We both stood and she handed it to me. "It's a condo on Beverly Drive near the Four Seasons Hotel."

I took the napkin. "Nice shoes." She was wearing black peep-toe pumps with high, shiny, chrome-like heels. They were as pricey as her purse and her clothes. "They remind me of the god Mercury. Silver wings on your feet." I winked at her. "See you tomorrow at three o'clock."

Grabbing my wig and stepping down out of the trailer, I turned back to close the door and glimpsed her standing stock-still, arms crossed against her chest, green eyes narrowed to slits, watching me with a cold calculating suspicion. I didn't exactly feel a chill, but her expression brought me up short.

CHAPTER FOUR

Hollywood is like smog: it moves and settles wherever it wants to. Right now Malibu was the place to be. Once again.

The houses that line Pacific Coast Highway are a buffet of styles: new Spanish, board-and-batten cottages, expensive stone chalets, and some that have all the warmth and style of a bank building. Shoulder to shoulder, like a phalanx of bunkers, they stand against the constant loud rumblings of the cars and trucks speeding along the highway. The back sides of the homes face the beach with only a strip of sand between them and the ocean. It is of course the interiors of the houses and their views that make them desirable and very expensive. My seventies-style, dark-brown wood-and-beige one-story was squeezed among them. In need of repair, it was in Celia's vernacular a teardown.

Unlocking my front door, I stepped into the small pavered foyer. The house smelled damp, and the air hung heavy and undisturbed. From the kitchen a twenty-four hour news cable station blahed, blahed, blahed, filling the stillness that permeated my life. Even after a year, I couldn't make myself come home to deathly quiet. I needed the sound of a human voice even if it came from a TV.

In the living room, I threw my purse on the sofa and opened the sliding glass doors to let in the salty air and the sound of the crashing ocean. Colin's two Oscars on the mantel stared at me blindly, proud in their art deco nudity. I took my iPhone from my bag and checked for messages. I had a text from Celia telling me she couldn't make dinner. Something had come up. Robert Zaitlin, I thought. And then I wondered what I always wondered: Why wasn't I seeing someone? Hell, why wasn't I having sex with someone? Anyone. Pathetic.

Exhausted, I took a shower. Pondering why Jenny didn't fear being fired by Zaitlin, I watched as my heavy makeup mixed with the water at my feet, turned it beige, and swirled down the drain. I was shedding my actor's skin.

Wrapped in Colin's silk paisley robe, I scrounged in the refrigerator for food and wine. I collected some low-fat cheese that tasted like cardboard and some low-fat crackers that tasted like the low-fat cheese and put them on the kitchen table. Then I opened a can of low-fat minestrone soup and heated it in a bowl in the microwave. While it was being nuked, I opened the door to Colin's office, which was just off the kitchen. The air was undisturbed and cold. His computer sat on his desk. Shelves of books that lined the walls waited to be thumbed through by him. The old twin bed he used for naps, which he called "thinking time," was wedged next to a back door. It looked as if nobody had ever laid down on it, or punched the pillow into submission. His chair was swiveled toward me as if he'd just heard me come in. As if he were just looking up from his work to see me.

"My mother died last week." I paused, then I quietly closed the door.

Filled with too much wine and uneatable food, I stood on my rotting redwood deck breathing in the cold night air and feeling the sea wind tugging at my hair. The moon, as big as an actor's ego, draped the sand and water in a silvery glow. A groaning noise coming from the pathway I shared with the house next door startled me. Owned by Ryan Johns, the screenwriter, the massive white cement structure rose high above me like a giant marshmallow with windows: a model to self-aggrandizement and no taste.

I moved closer to the sound. In the moonlight I could make out the form of a man lying half under a giant hibiscus bush. He was wearing Bermuda shorts and Ugg boots. Moving quickly to the corner of my deck, I grabbed the hose, turned it on full force, and aimed it at him.

"*Tsh unami, Fuckn' Tsunami,*" a drunken Ryan bellowed as he struggled to sit up against the blast.

As I turned off the water, he thrashed around, clutched the hibiscus bush, which was dangerously close to snapping from his weight, and clawed his way up to his feet. He was a big burly Irishman who looked as if he was born in a pub, except he came from a wealthy family in Connecticut that didn't understand their son's creativity. Or so he'd told me drunkenly over and over the one night I mistakenly went out to dinner with him. His thick reddish-orange hair formed lovely ringlets when it was wet.

In spite of myself, I smiled. He shook himself like a St. Bernard and almost fell over. Staggering, he grabbed hold of his ornate banister with both hands.

"You're a mean woman, Diana." His drenched Hawaiian shirt sagged on him.

"And you're a drunk."

"You need a man. Then you wouldn't be so bitter."

"And one night I'll just leave you out here and see how you like it."

"I was cel . . . ler . . . brating. Sold another idea for a screenplay."

We lived in a world where ideas were sold as if they were diamonds and then promptly turned into what they really were: rhinestones.

"I wonder what Colin would think of that." He reeled up the stairs to his veranda. "He never sold jush an idea."

"He's dead. Why do you keep competing with him?"

"Nobody's dead to an Irishman."

Wondering if he had even been to Ireland, I left him slumped on one of the many lounges that lined his long veranda.

In bed I clicked on the TV and took a sleeping pill. I watched W. C. Fields stumble down the stairs and announce "I've arrived." David Copperfield directed by David Lean, I thought. The only thing my mother and I enjoyed doing together was watching old movies.

The pill wasn't working. I took another and then let my hand wander over to the cold side of the bed. I was afraid to sleep, and I was afraid to stay awake.

The loud ringing of the phone jerked me out of my pharmaceutical slumber.

"Hello?" I mumbled into the receiver.

There was no reply.

"Hello?"

I could hear rustling sounds, and then a woman's terrified scream.

"Hello!" I sat up, groggy as hell. My tongue felt thick. "Who's calling?" I peered at the display for the caller ID number. It took me a few seconds to focus. God, it was Celia.

"Celia!" I yelled frantically into the receiver. "Celia!"

The phone disconnected.

I called her back and got her voicemail. Could she have turned her cell off that quickly if she were . . . what? I thought of calling the police. But what would I say? I threw off the duvet. Pills scattered. Had I spilled them when I fell asleep? Shit. How many *did* I take?

Unsteady, I forced myself up and into my robe. The room tilted as I took Celia's house key from a china bowl on my dresser. Celia lived about ten houses down from mine. We had exchanged keys so that when we were traveling we could look after one another's place.

Lurching down the hall and into the living room, I opened the door to the deck. The cold wind jarred me. I gulped in air and shook my head, trying to clear my brain. I stumbled down the stairs, out onto the sand, and fell to my knees. I managed to get back up on my feet. Christ, I didn't have shoes on. Staggering along the water's edge, feeling lightheaded and queasy, I somehow made it onto Celia's terrace.

I pounded on the French doors. I pounded again. No response. I let myself in.

"Celia?" I called into the dark, too dazed and confused to think I might be in danger.

Stumbling into the sofa, I made my way around it, into her bedroom, and found the light switch. Her bed was made. Everything was where it should be. Breaking out into a damp sweat, I checked the rest of the house. She wasn't there. In the kitchen I opened the door that led to the garage. Her car was gone. I stared a moment, then closed the door, locked up the house, and left.

My teeth chattered. I wrapped my arms around me against the wet piercing wind. The ice-cold water bit at my bare feet as I trudged home. I noticed Ryan Johns was still sprawled on his lounge.

In my bedroom, I stared at the phone and the pills on my bed. The room began to swirl. I had to lie down. I had to get warm. Just for a minute, I promised myself, until the dizziness and nausea passed. Then I'd think about what I should do. Collapsing onto the duvet, I closed my eyes. The awful sound of Celia's scream echoed in my head as my world spun around.

CHAPTER FIVE

slowly opened my eyes, then quickly closed them against the morning light seeping in around the edges of the shaded bedroom window. Turning on my side to snuggle in, I felt the grit of sand between my toes and on my calves. The nightmarish sound of Celia's scream came back to me.

Sitting up, I grabbed the phone and called her. Again I got her voicemail. Shit. With my head pounding, I threw on a pair of jeans, a sweater, and tennis shoes. I finally found her house key on the floor where I must've dropped it last night.

I ran along the hard wet sand. Celia's house was a sprawling cottage with bougainvillea and roses clambering along her terrace. I knocked on the French door. No answer. Peering in, I saw her lying on the sofa. She was turned on her side, her back to me, wearing the clothes she'd had on yesterday. She was still.

I banged louder. "Celia, it's Diana. Let me in!"

Without moving, she yelled "Go away! I'll phone you later."

No woman screams the way Celia had last night without something being very wrong. Taking her key from my pocket, I opened the door.

"Oh hell, Diana, somebody tells you to do something, and you always do the opposite." With a groan, Celia sat up, keeping her head lowered. Her long raven hair screened her face. Her orange skirt was rumpled, and her black chiffon blouse was ripped at the right shoulder seam. She was holding a bag of frozen organic peas.

Moving closer, I gently pushed her hair back from her face.

"Don't, Diana. Please," she mumbled.

A large bruise spread purple and yellow-green over her right eye and cheek bone. "What happened to you?" I asked.

Sighing, she lifted her head. Her lower lip was cut, the blood dried and brown.

"I don't want to talk about it." She pressed the bag of peas to the discolored area.

"I'm taking you to the emergency room."

"No!"

I sat down next to her. "Who did this to you?"

"Nobody. It was a stupid accident. I . . ."

"Before you go on you should know that your cell phone rang mine last night and I heard you scream. If you don't tell me who did this, I'm calling the police."

"You heard me?"

"Yes. Screaming."

"Oh, God, no."

"Tell me what happened, Celia."

"I can't." Her face was strained, terrified. "It could ruin me and my real estate business."

"Did Zaitlin do this?"

"He would never do such a thing. And you mustn't tell him."

"Then who?"

Her violet-colored eyes darted around the room as if someone dangerous was hiding among the pale blue linen-covered chairs, warmly polished chests, and striped silk drapes. The frozen bag of peas dropped from her hand to the floor and she began to cry. I put my arms around her. She leaned her head on my shoulder and sobbed. Calming, she pulled away, and I dug for Kleenex in my pocket and handed it to her.

"Do you remember how you and I met?" Sniffling, she dabbed at her face.

"I was standing in line waiting to see my mother's latest movie, and you cut in front of me." I picked the bag of peas off the floor and held it to her cheek.

"You didn't say a word. You just let me do it. And I told you that you would never get ahead if you let people cut in front of you. Do you remember what you told me?"

I shook my head.

"You said 'Maybe I don't want to get ahead.' That moment defined us, don't you think?"

"Maybe I just didn't want to see my mother's movie." It made my vacation time with Mother easier if I had seen her latest film.

"No, you wanted safety, and I wanted to be like Nora. You gave up acting, something you were very good at, to get married. To not be like your mother. I gave up acting because I was terrible at it."

Celia and I had been friends since we were sixteen. Back then, she had what I called a "normal" life—living in one home with one mother, one father, and a grandmother they called "big mama." She and her family had been a stabilizing force in my nomadic youth. Later, she, Zaitlin's wife Gwyn, and I were starlets together.

"I worked hard for all of this, Diana." Celia gestured at her room.

As if seeing it for the first time, I realized there were no family photos placed on the expensive bamboo side tables. There was nothing personal in the designer down-laden sofas and color-coordinated area rugs. There was no sign of Celia, of the young girl I once knew, or the woman she had become. But what do you display on your shelves if you're a long-time mistress—photos of Zaitlin, his wife, and their son?

"I don't want one night to destroy my life. Please don't make me tell you what happened to me," she added softly.

"But you've been beaten up, I heard you scream. I can't let that go."

"I'm really sorry, but is your fear important enough to you that you're willing to ruin my career?"

"I don't think that's the point. I would never do anything to harm your career. And it's not fear, it's concern. We're friends, Celia. You can't carry around what happened to you all by yourself. You need to talk about it."

"Then promise me you won't tell anyone. Not the police, not Robert, not anyone."

Staring at her desperate face, I took a deep breath. "I promise, but if it happens again, I'm dragging you to the emergency room."

"It won't happen again." She walked over to her French doors and stared out at the steel-gray ocean, hugging herself.

I joined her, watching the morning fog swirl, and waited.

Finally she spoke: "The man who was with me yesterday when we found you in the swimming pool."

"You mean Mr. Ward? The one who was looking at the house?"

"Yes. He wanted . . . he wanted to meet me for a drink. He said there were some things he needed to discuss if he made an offer on the house."

"You thought he wasn't interested in it."

"I should have listened to my instincts." She pushed her fingers through her hair. "When I got there . . ."

"Where?"

"A bar, that's all I'm telling you. We talked about the pros and cons of the house. Then we just began to chat in general. You saw him. He's handsome in that kind of off-kilter way. I enjoyed being with him. I got a little tipsy. Well, *sloshed* might be a better word. He said I was in no condition to drive and he'd take me home. He was parked on a quiet side street." She let out a weary sigh. "When we got in, he threw me back against the passenger door. His hands all over me. I struggled. That's when he hit me, hard." Tears rolled down over her bruise again.

"Did he rape you?"

She shook her head. "I somehow reached behind me and got the door open and I fell out onto the sidewalk, screaming. He drove off. Left me there like trash. I made it back to my car. At that point I was sober enough to drive." She forced a smile, then winced, touching her lip.

"Christ, Celia. I wish you'd report . . ."

"Diana, you promised. You and I are never going to mention this again." She held my gaze.

"All right. What are you going to say to Robert when he sees you?"

"I was tipsy and stumbled in my five-inch heels and fell flat on my face. He's always predicted one day I would, so he'll believe it. I need to lie down."

I stayed while she showered and got into bed. Her hair fanned out like an ink spill on her snowy white pillows. "Thank you for being a good friend, Diana."

"Get some sleep." I wondered whether keeping quiet about what had happened was really being a good friend. But Celia was right—in real estate an attempted rape by a client could jeopardize her career and reputation maybe more than his.

"Are you going to the party tonight?" she asked.

I stopped in the doorway and turned. "What party?"

"Robert said they were having some kind of celebration."

"Oh, God, I forgot. I think it's a birthday party for their son. I don't suppose you're going."

"Of course not."

"Why do you stay with him, Celia? It's not like you're kept by him."

She stared down at the delicate laced edge of the sheet. "I don't want to end up like my parents did. When my father got home from work he would lie on the sofa expecting to be waited on by 'big mama' and my mother. Both women vying for his attention and arguing over who was in control of the kitchen. God, I hated it."

I smiled. "I loved your life."

"I loved your mother's. Robert comes here to see me because he wants to, not because he has to. And if I don't want to see him, I don't. I'm not dependent on anyone. I like my life the way it is." Then she added, "And I want to keep it."

"I'll call you later to see how you're doing."

She closed her eyes, and I left her looking vulnerable tucked among the mass of her pristine bedding.

Walking back home, I noticed Ryan was still splayed on his lounge, snoring with his mouth open. The golden hair on his legs glistened in the sunlight. He must've slept there all night. God, he's going to get sunburned.

"Ryan!" I yelled up from the beach. "Wake up!"

He kicked his feet and turned onto his side.

Climbing the steps to my house, I thought of Ryan, Celia, and me. Ryan got so drunk he passed out on the walkway, a man battered Celia, and I drank a bottle of wine and took sleeping pills. Just another Monday night in Malibu.

CHAPTER SIX

When I'm acting in a scene and the director tells me to stop and do nothing, I never question it. While the other actors are chewing the scenery and flapping their arms, a good actor can draw the audience to her by simply not moving. I don't mean doing an imitation of a statue. She has to find something real, a true emotion that shadows her face, revealing why she has chosen to stop. But that's in the movies. In real life, we're all afraid of stopping. Even Celia. Even Ryan. Even me.

Now standing in my kitchen, I downed four Advils. It's always the charming ones, I thought. The men your instinct, your gut, tells you to watch out for, tells you they don't like women. But then the charming ones smile, talk you into their world. Your protective instinct falters, and you let them seduce you until they hurt you. I knew guys like Ward well. My mother had a string of them. Christ, what was Celia thinking?

After drinking two cups of coffee and eating scrambled eggs, I went back to bed and slept for three hours. Then I got up and dressed in good jeans and a tailored white shirt. The last thing I wanted to do today was read lines with Jenny Parson, but I'd be damned if she was going to ruin our movie.

Putting on my makeup, I assessed my face in the bathroom mirror with an objectivity that only an actress can have. When you spend your life staring into a mirror trying to be who you are not, believe me, you know exactly what you look like—not to be confused with knowing who you are. My face was still beautiful, but it was becoming set. Less optimistic. Less adaptable. My blue eyes were no longer beguiling. Now they had a matter-of-fact quality to them. I had put on a little weight, but my body was still firm, tending to voluptuous. And the easy soft sexuality I had once exuded had disappeared. Somewhere.

The phone rang and I hurried to answer it, thinking it might be Celia.

"Is this Ms. Diana Poole? Nora Poole's daughter?"

"Yes."

"This is the Hotel Bel Air. There has been an unfortunate mix-up. The crematorium sent your mother's ashes to us. It seems nobody picked them up, and the hotel was the only address they had for her."

God, I'd forgotten. "I'll be there in a half hour."

"Just ask at the reception desk," she said, cheerfully helpful.

I hung up, sat down on the edge of the bed, and buried my face in my hands.

CHAPTER SEVEN

The smog hadn't yet killed the swans at the Bel Air Hotel. They floated regally down the little stream that ran under the bridge that took you into the lobby. I've always loved the swans. As a girl I would hang out with them while mother had drinks with Jeff, Jake, or Jack. The swans had a feathery elegance and arrogant disdain for the guests. For all of us.

Warm and expensively unassuming, the lobby was a Southern California dream of upper-crust country: teatime and T-shirts. I stopped at the front desk and adjusted my sunglasses.

"I'm here to pick up my mother," I said to a young shiny woman who looked as if she'd been polished with a can of Pledge.

"I'll call her. What room is she in?"

I took a deep breath, fighting back the now familiar urge to break out in hysterical laughter or hysterical tears. Or both. Controlling myself, I said, "I'm sorry, I'm Diana Poole. You have a . . . package . . . for me."

She suddenly looked stricken. "Oh, yes." Her voice turned somber and now she spoke in a hushed tone. "They told me to expect you. I'll be right back."

Disappearing, she soon returned holding a regular brown shipping box. I don't know what I had expected, but it wasn't UPS.

"Our condolences." She shoved the box toward me. "I so admired her."

"Do you have some scissors?"

"Of course." She plucked a pair from a drawer.

As she watched uneasily, I took the edge of one of the blades and sliced across the tape binding the box. I flipped open the lids and there was Mother's urn. The one I had chosen. Her name was engraved on a sterling silver nameplate. I lifted it out of the box; it was heavy and handmade of cherry wood. As the funeral director had explained, "The grain of each wood urn is as individual in character as the life being mourned." He sold me.

"Thank you." I walked out of the hotel and waited for the valet to bring my car around. I strapped Mother into the passenger seat, then tipped the valet who discreetly pretended not to notice what I'd done. Mother and I sailed down Stone Canyon Road together for the last time.

I worked my way though the heavy traffic to Jenny Parson's condominium complex just down from the Four Seasons Hotel on Beverly Drive. I drove around the block twice before finding a place to park the Jag. I attempted to lock the car, but like the air conditioning, nothing was working. I contemplated putting the urn in my trunk but I somehow couldn't do it. So I carried Mother with me.

Inside the lobby, a doorman outfitted in a maroon-colored jacket decorated with brass buttons, gold braid, and looking like a banana-republic general peered out from the thick double glass doors as I approached. He opened them for me. The white marble lobby was upscale and austere. Black leather chrome benches were precisely placed near exotic potted palms.

"I'm here to see Jenny Parson. My name is Diana Poole," I informed him.

He looked at some papers on a clipboard. "Take the elevator up to 302, she's expecting you."

Good, I thought, she had left my name. Maybe she actually wanted to be an actress.

Reaching the third floor, the elevator door opened, and the lingering smell of cooking hit me. No matter how expensive the condominium, there is always an odor of food in the hallway strong enough to turn you into an anorexic.

Jenny's door was at the end. I pressed the doorbell and waited. I tried the bell again—I could hear it ringing inside her condo. When there was still no answer, I knocked loudly.

Finally I gave up and went back down to the lobby. The doorman raised his sparse eyebrows when he saw me.

"I guess Jenny went out. Have you seen her?" I asked.

"No. But she can take the elevator down to the underground garage without going through the lobby."

"If you mean Jenny Parson, her car's here," announced a woman, eyes surgically stretched and tilted toward the heavens. Holding a quivering Chihuahua outfitted in a pink turtleneck sweater, she unlocked one of the brass mailboxes that lined the wall near the concierge's desk. "I just drove in and saw it. Brand-new Audi." She peered in the box. It was empty. The dog licked her ear.

"If her car is here then she should answer the door," I said.

The doorman shrugged.

"Well, thank you again." I started toward the entrance, then stopped. Maybe it was holding my mother's ashes that brought out my unexpected maternal feelings for Jenny Parson. I turned around and asked, "What time did she leave my name?"

The doorman rechecked his list. "Six P.M. yesterday."

That was soon after I'd talked to her. So I had made some kind of impact. Jenny wasn't capricious; if anything she was very direct. But she was struggling. Still, she had told me she was going clubbing last night. Maybe she'd had too much to drink and was sleeping it off, or she stayed overnight with a friend—or a boyfriend. Go home, Diana, I told myself. Instead I eyed the doorman. He sucked in his stomach and eyed me back. He was an immovable object. Improvise, Diana.

Glancing down at the urn, I said, "This is her mother's ashes. Jenny's expecting me to bring them to her."

"You can leave them at the desk," he said.

"How would you like to pick up your mother's ashes in a lobby as if she was some package dropped off by UPS?"

"I . . . I . . ." He knew he was trapped.

The woman with the dog gaped at him as if he had just maligned her own mother. Even the Chihuahua raised a disgusted lip showing a tiny fang.

"I hope you wouldn't treat my mother that way," she said to him.

He flushed.

"Please," I said quickly. "I'll just leave them in her living room with a little note."

"All right," he relented. "But I can't let you go in there alone. I'll take you."

We rode up in the elevator, ignoring one another.

He unlocked the door to 302 and stepped in first. "Ms. Parson?"

I slipped past and walked into the living room. "Jenny? It's Diana."

Her corner condo was meagerly furnished, giving the impression comfort didn't matter much to her. The floor-to-ceiling windows looked out to the hills above Sunset and down across the vast gray sprawl that was the city.

"Jenny?" I walked down a hall into a bedroom.

"I think you should just leave the ashes . . . urn . . . ." The doorman was close on my heels.

The queen-size bed was made. A giant flat screen TV dominated a dresser. Her closet door had been left open displaying an array of designer clothes. I peered into a beautifully appointed bathroom— the towels were neatly folded on brass bars.

If I were a young girl who had been out clubbing the night before, there would be clothes strewn on the floor and a bed messed up. Some signs of a life in disarray—the way my apartment had looked when I was her age. Maybe she hadn't come home last night. On the other hand, her car was in the garage. But a friend or a boyfriend could have picked her up here. The plain truth was that Jenny was a no-show. What a waste—and what was going to happen to the movie?

The doorman cleared his throat, trying to hurry me along. "I'll tell Ms. Parson you were here."

Back in the living room, I asked, "Is there any other place she could be in the building? Maybe the laundry room?"

He crossed to the kitchen and opened a door, proudly displaying a washer and dryer. "Not many condos have the space for these appliances. All of ours do."

I felt a warm wind ruffle the back of my hair. Turning, I saw a small window off the dining area had been opened. At the same time, I could hear the sound of a large engine. I looked out the window and down to an alley that ran alongside the building. A truck from the sanitation department was emptying large blue bins.

"They're late again," the doorman announced.

I turned to him. "Thanks for your help."

"Aren't you going to leave her mother's ashes?" He gestured at the urn in my arms, then frowned. "Her father didn't say anything about her mother being ill. He's very protective of his daughter." Suspicious, he stabbed an accusing finger at the urn. "That name-plate says 'Nora Poole.'"

But I was looking out the window again. I realized I had just seen a flash of silver as one of the dumpsters was being loaded onto the truck. There was something about it . . .

The doorman was still talking. "I didn't know Nora Poole was Jenny's mother." He was trying to reason it out. "Wait, I know you. You're Diana Poole. What's going on here?"

Ignoring him, I stared at the shiny object that now jutted out from a large black garbage bag. The blade of a knife? I felt a chill. It was the high heel of a shoe. Silver, like Mercury's wing, like Jenny's beautiful high heels I had admired yesterday in her trailer.

"Stop!" I screamed down at the two men. "Stop!"

They continued working since they couldn't hear me over the grinding noise of the truck's motor. The doorman had taken a step back and was gaping at me.

"Come here," I ordered. "Keep shouting at them to stop. Jenny's in there!"

His face blanched. "What you talking about?"

"Her shoe!" I hurried past him. "And call 911!"

Clutching the urn, I ran down the hallway and kept slamming the elevator's down button until it arrived. Bolting through the lobby and out the front doors, I flew down the sidewalk to the alley. I rushed at the garbage truck with its two operators, yelling at the top of my lungs. The bin was on the lift, tilting dangerously into the maw of the truck.

"There's someone in there." I pointed to the garbage bag on top as it rolled to the edge. "A woman is in there!"

One of the men pointed to his ear protectors, meaning he couldn't hear me.

Stepping forward, I yanked one of them away from his ear. "Stop it!" I yelled.

He glowered at me but pushed down on a lever. The bin froze in midair. I leaned over, gasping for breath.

"*Que paso?*" He took off his ear protectors.

35

I pointed up to the bin. "Shoe. Check the bag, *por favor.*"

"You lose shoe?"

"Yes. A shoe!" Please, God, let it be just a shoe.

Commanding his partner in Spanish, the bin slowly descended to the ground. Then he got up on the lift. "This bag?" He pointed.

I nodded. My heart pounded.

Shaking his head, he pulled himself up into the bin and ripped open the bag. His mouth fell open and he lurched backward crossing himself, saying a prayer in Spanish. The doorman loped down the alley, epaulets flapping, waving his cell in the air. "I called 911. The police are coming."

As he scrambled down, I stood on my toes trying to see into the bin. I glimpsed blood-matted auburn hair and one green milky eye looking directly at me. I wish I hadn't.

Staggering back, I slumped against the building's white marble wall. It felt warm on my back from the sun. I slid down it into a sitting position and leaned my forehead against my mother's urn.

CHAPTER EIGHT

'␣ve always thought it odd that people sometimes refer to a
moment in life as if it were a scene in a movie. Real life doesn't
have a camera, lights, and a boom mike hovering around you.
It doesn't have a time limit defined by the length of the dialogue.
It doesn't have a corpse leaping to her feet after the director calls
"Cut!" and asking "How did I do?" And it doesn't have the set
laughing at her unintentionally funny question.

Mother would always remind me that in acting, reality was no
excuse. "Only the hack," she explained, "says 'But that's how it
happens in real life.'"

Yet when the black-and-white patrol cars arrived, rooftop beacons
flashing in the twilight, the unnecessary ambulance parked beside

the truck, and the yellow crime-scene tape encircled the area, it did look like a movie. And I was beginning to think reality was no longer an excuse in my own life.

Detective Dusty Spangler introduced herself in a voice as flat as Kansas: "I know, it sounds like a stripper's name."

I had the feeling she used this line to put people at ease or gain more information. Her pale hair was pulled back into a stub of a ponytail. She wore almost exactly what her male partner wore. Blue blazer, a shirt, and gray slacks. Her sizable belly hung over her belt and leather hip holster. I wondered how she reached her weapon in an emergency.

After I'd told her exactly what had happened, she checked her notes and said, "So you used your mother's urn to get into the condo. You're a very resourceful woman." She made it sound like one of the Seven Deadly Sins.

I asked her if I could leave, explaining that I didn't want to deal with the media. I knew that once they found out Jenny and I were both in the same movie, it would turn into a circus. She let me go with the assurance that I would give her my complete statement at the West Los Angeles Station.

Now I drove up the long driveway to Zaitlin's house. I had called him at the crime scene to tell him what had happened. Beyond upset, he had wanted to see me immediately.

Zaitlin and his family lived in a grand French château, always referred to without irony as "the farm house," atop a hill in Brentwood. Three stories high, with a steeply pitched slate roof, dormers, turrets, and four useless towers, the stone mansion had spectacular views west from the Pacific Ocean all the way east to the San Bernardino Mountains, which towered over Pasadena.

When I arrived at the crest, expensive cars were parked in a driveway built to hold many expensive cars. I pulled up to the front entrance, and a valet appeared and opened my door. Rap music pounded viciously from the side yard.

I leaned my head back against the seat and remembered tonight was the birthday party for Robert and Gwyn's son. I closed my eyes. A party was the last thing I needed. Then I grabbed the urn and let the valet help me out.

"I won't be long," I told him.

The two-story foyer was empty except for a security guard in a black suit standing in front of a massive carved-wood door. A round marble table filled the center area of the limestone floor.

Approaching the guard, I caught a glimpse of my stunned hollow-eyed reflection in a floor-to-ceiling wrought-iron framed mirror. I looked like a blond ghost holding an urn.

"Diana Pole, I'm expected," I told him.

He repeated my name into his Bluetooth, nodded, then opened the door.

Shrill laughter and the loud voices of people trying to be heard over the relentless music hit me like a blow to the head.

The partygoers filled the enormous room, which was decorated with antique area rugs, seductive sofas obese with down, and a walk-in fireplace. Gilt-framed French paintings depicting turn-of-the-century women leisurely reading, pouring tea, taking baths, or strolling with their parasols glinted from the walls. More or less famous guests spilled out open French doors onto a veranda that led down to the gardens and a rented pavilion from which the music blared. Young attractive waiters, hope still in their eyes, circled with trays of martinis, mojitos, and expensive red and white wines. Others displayed small filet mignons on bite-size hamburger buns, caviar, iced crab, and Dodger Dogs. Everyone here was the chosen, the connected, the sought-after.

Grabbing a martini, I downed it and placed it back on the tray. The alcohol streamed through me, burning the edge off what now seemed to be a permanent chill.

"Diana, so good to see you," Barbara Quinn, a producer who had never hired me, grabbed my shoulders and looked intently into my face. This was a new thing in Hollywood—looking intently into people's faces, creating a false intimacy. I liked the old way better—staring at the forehead.

"Last year Colin, and this year your mother," she continued. "You look devastated. A great writer. A great actress. Both gone. Is there going to be a memorial service for her?"

Memorial service? "I . . . haven't had a . . ."

"Hold that thought. I'll be right back." She swooped away to chase after an up-and-coming actor whose name I couldn't remember.

Ryan Johns loped toward me. He had on a fresh pair of Bermuda shorts and another loud Hawaiian shirt topped off with an expensive cashmere blazer, and his Uggs. His crimson legs and face clashed with his orange-red hair.

"Look what you did to me," he said. "You left me out on my deck until I burned to a crisp. Where have you been? I was hoping you could drive me here. I had to take a cab. Too many DUIs. Do you know what it's like to take a cab in Los Angeles? We got lost in Mar Vista. Where the hell is Mar Vista? Can you drive me home?"

"I'm leaving right away."

"Great, it's a dull party."

"Have you seen Zaitlin?"

"No . . ." His eyes came to rest on the urn. "That's not . . ."

I nodded.

"Nora!" His blue eyes shined with glee. "You brought your mother to the party?" He was as delighted as if I were a school chum who'd brought a live frog to class.

A sliver of a blonde sidled up to him. "Remember me?"

"I . . ." He was trying to think fast.

"Hot pink leather coat? Back bedroom of your agent's house?"

"I had trouble with the buttons."

"You passed out. We have unfinished business." She ran a fingernail along his bottom lip, then turned and slipped away. He winced at his burnt skin being touched.

"What do women see in me?" he asked, honestly amazed.

"I have no idea."

Ryan grabbed a drink from a passing waiter and stalked after the Blond Sliver.

"I don't know how a man can drink as much as Ryan does and be such a successful writer. But he'll never be in Colin's league." Zaitlin's wife kissed me on the cheek.

"He has high-concept ideas," I said.

Tall and thin, Gwyn Zaitlin had a sad elegance about her. She wore her mink-brown hair pulled severely back from her tired face. It was as if she wanted to show us every deep line and erosion that burying her soul had cost her. Some women don't have a soul to lose but she did. Of the three of us, Celia, Gwyn, and myself, she was the one who had my mother's kind of talent. But she had suffered a breakdown and began hearing voices and cowering in bushes. During that period she got pregnant; to this day she says she doesn't know who fathered her son. Her parents put her in a sanitarium in Switzerland where she was to have an abortion and get her sanity back. In that order. But even in her deepest despair it never occurred to her not to keep the baby.

I always thought the sanitarium was where her soul and talent got buried, not because of Ben, her son, but because she had returned so utterly unwaveringly normal. Hollywood normal, that is. It was as if she had been given a script and she was playing the same role over and over. Three years later she met Zaitlin, and they married. Many people thought he married her for her family's money. But as Gwyn reminded me, "Someone was going to marry me for my money, so why not the man I wanted?"

And now she was one of the town's major hostesses and a force for charities, especially rape victims. But in the land of plastic surgery, she moved through Hollywood with a raw aging face, a warning symbol that no one heeded.

"Robert's waiting for you." She took my arm and guided me back through the party. "It's terrible about Jenny Parson. You haven't told anybody have you, Diana? I don't want my Ben's birthday ruined."

As I shook my head, we returned to the quiet of the foyer.

Her hazel-colored eyes, like a chameleon's eerily changing their shade to fit her surroundings, fell on the urn. "What's that?"

"My mother."

"Nora? Give it to me. I'll put it in the guest closet."

"No." I said too loudly, causing the security guard to glance toward us. My own vehemence surprised me. Then I realized Mother's ashes had become my mooring, something safe to hold onto in an otherwise horrific day.

She touched my cheek. "Are you all right, Diana?

"I'm really *not* losing it, Gwyn."

"You mean as I did?" Her hand dropped away.

"I'm sorry. I didn't mean that at all." I squeezed her hand.

"I know you didn't. I don't know why I said it. I guess the death of that young actress has made me anxious. Was she any good?"

"She could've been if she'd wanted it."

"Like you. I know you always thought I was the one with the talent. But it wasn't true. I'm glad you've gone back to acting. And I'm glad Robert is here to help you." We paused by his closed office door. "How is Celia these days?"

Gwyn was the sort of wife who could live knowing that her husband had a mistress. The problem was that Celia had once been a dear friend to her in the pre-Zaitlin days. She had even gone to Switzerland to visit her. But now they saw each other only by chance. Since I was still Celia's friend, I never knew when Gwyn wanted to talk to me about her as Robert's mistress or as my friend. Conversing with her could be a minefield.

"She's fine," I said simply.

"Really? I heard Robert on the phone telling her how to take care of a swollen eye."

"She took a spill, fell off her five-inch heels, and got a little bruised. That's all." I regretted telling the lie, feeling I was betraying Gwyn while protecting Celia.

"She never liked being shorter than us." She smiled, opening the door to Zaitlin's overly decorated office.

Robert was wearing an expensive silk jacket, jeans, a striped shirt, and no tie. Looking exhausted, he sat behind his desk, talking on the phone. He waved us in. Beth Woods, the director, still wearing her leather Mossad jacket and cargo pants, slumped on a dark green velvet fringed sofa, her elbows resting on her knees and her head hanging down. She looked as if she'd just vomited. On the wall behind her hung a Chagall painting of a voluptuous woman floating through the sky with a horse.

"Diana." Beth glanced up, acknowledging me. "This is awful."

As I nodded, Zaitlin snapped into the phone, "How the hell do I know what we have to be careful of? I want to be ready in case we do have to be careful. Try to get this through your head—an actress in my movie is found dead by another of my actresses whose very famous mother has just died. This will be all over the media." He slammed down the phone. Nobody says good-bye anymore in Hollywood. Jenny certainly wasn't given the chance to, I thought.

"The cake is going to be served soon," Gwyn announced.

Zaitlin stared at her. We all did. "You're worried about the god-damn birthday cake being served while I'm trying to save a sixty-million-dollar film?"

"No, I'm worried about our son."

There was always the tension of Ben between them. Ben who carried a total stranger's DNA.

Zaitlin let out a long sigh. "I'm sorry, Gwyn. This won't take long. I'll be there for the presentation of the cake." The only times I ever heard Robert apologize for anything was when speaking to his wife.

After Gwyn left, Zaitlin's eyes narrowed in on the urn. "What's that?"

"My mother." I sat down, facing his desk and resting the urn on my lap.

He placed his hand over his shaved head as if to keep the top of it from exploding. "You weren't carrying that around when you discovered Jenny, were you?"

"Actually, I was."

"Oh, shit," Beth moaned, running her hands through her already disheveled spiked hair.

"It's bad enough you found Jenny. But to find her while carrying around Nora Poole, for God's sake? This is a media wet dream." Zaitlin's face grew red, and a vein protruded on his forehead. Struggling to regain his composure, he asked, "What did you tell the police?"

"Just what I knew. Not much." Then I explained what had happened, including how I got into Jenny's condo by using the urn as a ruse.

Despite herself, Beth laughed. "You are a natural actress, Diana."

"Why didn't you just leave when she didn't answer the door?" Zaitlin demanded.

"You asked me to go there and help her with her lines. But then I became worried about her."

"She wasn't your problem!" he snapped.

"You made her my problem!" I snapped back.

"Could she have committed suicide?" Beth asked, trying to break the tension.

"Not unless she jumped out of a window from the third floor then put herself in a garbage bag and threw herself into a dumpster," I told her.

Blanching, she collapsed back into the depths of the sofa.

"Murder could mean a long investigation. You never know what the cops will dig up." Zaitlin's fingers tapped his desk nervously.

"What could they dig up?" I asked.

"What do you usually dig up in a horror movie? The unexpected. Like learning you used Nora's ashes as a ploy. How do we get in front of that?"

"I wasn't thinking about the media at the time. Is there something I don't know? Or should know?"

"We're just trying to preserve what's left of our film, Diana," Beth spoke softly, as if giving me an acting direction. "You know how the media distorts everything. And there's Jake Jackson to consider. If he feels his star image is going to be harmed by being associated with this project now, he may pull out. It'll all collapse around us."

I realized that Beth needed this movie as much as I did. It's not easy for women directors.

"She's right." Zaitlin let out a long sigh, then said "Sorry if I sounded unfeeling." He was now in fatherly mode.

But he hadn't sounded unfeeling. He'd sounded panicked. And I wondered if it was only the movie he was worried about.

"Are you all right?" he asked me.

"No. I had to pick Mother up at the Bel Air Hotel, and then I found a young woman's murdered body. No, I'm not all right."

He stood and came around to me. "Let's get you something to eat." He helped me to my feet. "You can wish Ben a happy birthday, go home, and get some sleep. I just want you to know that I'll do everything not to shut down the film."

"Why did you put up with so much from Jenny?" I asked him.

"I told you, we were in too deep to fire her."

"Why did you hire her?"

"Because she was good. I thought she had it. Star quality."

My eyes met Beth's, and she quickly stared down at her motorcycle boots.

"What's with all the questions?" Zaitlin said. "You're lucky to have gotten this part, Diana. That reminds me—Pedro Romero, the director, is here. I want you to meet him. He has a new script."

"I'm not up to meeting anyone."

"This is an opportunity. Take it. Nora would. She had a wonderful brutal strength." There was longing in his voice, and I wondered if Zaitlin had gone to bed with my mother. "But I think you should leave her here with me," he added gently.

"I can't."

The office door opened, and a man in jeans, black T-shirt, and an army-green windbreaker stepped into the room. I froze, recognizing the dark hair graying at the temples and the tough crooked nose. It was the man who had been looking at Bella Casa yesterday. The man who saw me in the pool. The man who Celia told me had beaten her up. His dark eyes looked straight through me as if I didn't exist.

CHAPTER NINE

"Sorry, I didn't realize you had company. I'll wait outside," the man said to Zaitlin.

"No, no. We have a problem on our hands. We need to talk." Zaitlin gestured in my direction. "Leo Heath, this is Diana Poole."

"We've met," I said. "Except you gave a different name. But maybe you don't remember."

"How could I forget?" His smile slipped sideways as his dark eyes grew bemused.

Afraid I wouldn't be able to control my anger, I said nothing more. I didn't want to compromise Celia in front of Zaitlin.

Zaitlin turned to Beth. "Take Diana and introduce her to Pedro Romero before he leaves. He's too artistic to stay for any length of time at a party."

As we walked out the door, the clamor of the guests assaulted me again. Beth and I made our way through the throng and out onto the veranda. "What does this Heath do?" I asked.

"He owns a security firm. Does a lot of work for Zaitlin. These are his men working the party now. He also helps Zaitlin get things done that need to be done." She rolled her lips inward, pressing them together.

"So he's a fixer."

"You can look at it that way."

I gazed out over the rolling lawn, the glittering pool, the tennis court, the rented pavilion, and in the distance a guesthouse, lamplight burning in its paned windows. More security guards looking like stern funeral directors with buds in their ears and cords running down their thick necks patrolled the grounds. In Hollywood, a party without security was like a premiere without limos. What was it about us that we needed so much expensive protection? Maybe it was for our threatened egos.

"Is Heath going to fix Jenny Parson?" I asked her.

"Maybe ease the situation. Did you have any personal dealings with her?"

"Such as?"

"I don't know." She shrugged, and for a moment her square, defiantly unfeminine jaw appeared soft and weak. It was as if her strength had been drained from her. "I don't believe in good and evil. But if I did, Jenny would be evil."

"How?"

"She sensed people's weaknesses. Knew how to use them."

"Did she know yours?"

"My fear of never working again? That's my weakness. Who doesn't have that fear in this town?"

Her gaze settled on a man lurking in the shadows of a large potted palm, surrounded by his walking-around guys. It was as if he was too sensitive to come out into the light.

"Pedro!" She waved, nudging me toward him.

My hand automatically went up to smooth my hair. And for the first time in the entire day, I thought about my lack of lipstick, blush, mascara, and powder. But it was far too late for any of that.

"Pedro Romero, this is Diana Poole, the actress Robert told you about," she announced.

"I know who she is." A small, thin man with dark slicked-back hair took a few tentative steps toward me, then bowed slightly.

"I'll leave you two to chat." Duty accomplished, she hurried back toward Zaitlin's office.

"You carry death with you." Romero's eyes twinkled darkly.

"My mother's ashes."

"Ah, Nora Poole. I always wanted to meet her."

I couldn't help notice that he didn't say he'd always wanted to work with her.

"It is very Latin of you to be so intimate with death," he said. "In my country we celebrate it, we make fun of it, and we defy it." Raising a fist, he pulled his legs together and thrust out his chest. He was a matador.

"No, I'm afraid it's very American of me. The door locks on my car don't work, and I was worried someone might steal her."

He chuckled. "You mean 'American' in that you always have a more pragmatic reason?"

"Yes."

"I like that you do not apologize for being American. Most everyone here does." He flipped a small hand indicating the guests. Then his eyes burrowed in on me, and I watched him studying the planes of my face with the impersonal eye of a camera.

"I enjoyed our conversation very much," he said, as if he had just finished editing a film. He took my hand and kissed it so softly I barely felt his finely trimmed mustache. Patting the urn, he added, "I finally get to meet Nora Poole." He slipped away toward the living room, his guys miraculously appearing around him again.

"Diana!" Ben Zaitlin pushed his way through a group pretending to listen to a newly axed but still famous news anchor pontificate. "My mother sent me out here to give you this." Ben held out a plate piled with food. "And I'm not to mention the ashes." His smooth pale skin was flushed from too many drinks. Black hair flopped around a lean pointed face.

"Thanks for the food but I'm not hungry, besides I don't have enough hands to hold the plate. Happy birthday, Ben."

Ben balanced the plate on the balustrade. He had the same elegance as his mother, and the same aura of sadness. He was dressed in a stylishly hip suit with a pink rumpled shirt hanging, untucked.

"I haven't seen you in a long time. How's Princeton?" I asked.

Putting their children in Ivy League colleges was still important to Hollywood royalty. After all the years on the West Coast they were still looking for East Coast acceptance.

"I flunked out. Mother was pissed." He shoved his hands into his pants pockets and swayed as if he were trying to balance on a rowboat.

Surprised, I said, "So you're living at home again?"

"I have my own place. Please don't ask the next question, Diana."

"And what would that be?"

"'So what are you going to do now?' I'm so sick of talking about my future. I wish I didn't have to think about one."

"All right, I won't ask." I couldn't help smiling just a little.

Glancing around, he lowered his voice. "I just heard someone say they got a message on their cell that Jenny Parson was murdered. Is it true?"

"Yes. I suppose you're going to know soon enough. I found her body."

His eyebrows shot up and his head went back. "Wow. What was that like? Sorry, I didn't mean to sound like a jerk."

"I know what you meant. It was awful."

He shifted uneasily. "I guess that's why Robert hasn't come out of his office yet. How come you found her?"

I briefly told him why I had gone to her condo and where I'd seen her corpse.

"God," he murmured, taking his hands from his pockets and resting one on the balustrade to steady himself. "I always wondered why Robert hired Jenny. He was always bitching about her. But why would someone want to kill her?"

It was then I realized that only Ben had asked that question. Not his mother, not Zaitlin, and not Beth Woods. Not even me. "I don't know."

"I saw her," he said flatly.

"When?"

"Last night. I was at this club called The Den. She was drunk and arguing with some guy."

"Did you talk to her?"

"No. I don't even think she knew who I was, meaning Robert Zaitlin's stepson."

"You didn't introduce yourself?"

"I try to stay away from what's Robert's business."

A waiter paused next to Ben, offering a drink from his silver tray. He grabbed a mojito, spilling some. I declined.

The waiter moved on as Ben surveyed the white party tent. "Looks like a meeting place for a bunch of evangelists. I wonder who this party is really for?" He took a long sip. "None of these people are my friends."

"Your parents don't know how else to do it. Business is personal in this town. It's all the same to them."

He poked a finger at the hot dog turning greasy cold on my plate. "Dodger Dog. Robert took me to one game. He bought me a hot dog. It made him feel like a father. He's never gotten over it. What was your father like, Diana?"

"Like you, I never knew him. He'd died crashing his car into a tree on his way to the hospital to visit his wife and meet his new daughter. Mother turned him into a saint. A young husband and actor who lost his life while desperately speeding to see his new baby daughter."

"Do you believe that shit?"

"No. A woman died in the car with him."

"You're kidding." His onyx-colored eyes were swimming now.

"My mother in her hospital bed with the infant me suckling at her breast contacted her lawyer who paid the woman's family off. The media never knew about my father's other love. But she made sure that I grew up knowing my father had cheated on her. She believed children needed the truth, not fairy tales, though obviously she felt differently about what her public needed."

"God, how do any of us even function?" He downed the rest of his cocktail, smacked his lips, and shoved the empty glass at a passing waiter who took it.

I remembered the young me turning my phantom father, sometimes known as "that bastard" by mother, into my Leading Man. The only male who could be whatever I wanted him to be. Other men faded in comparison to the handsome, kind, always young, thoughtful father I had created. Except Colin. He somehow managed to exceed the fantasy. Exhaustion flooded through me. Too many memories and the discovery of a corpse had taken its toll.

"I better be going. It was nice seeing you again, Ben," I said.

"Wait." He leaned close. "How's your friend Celia?" His long thick lashes, which most women would kill for, shaded his eyes.

"She's okay."

"I know."

I looked sharply at him. "Know what?"

"About her and Robert."

"How did you find out?"

"I began to listen to people. It's amazing when you stop trying to be important and just listen to what people are really saying. Not all the bullshit. It's amazing how many secrets you can pick up."

"Have you talked to your parents about Celia?"

"Why? They never mention her to me. They had no problem telling me Robert wasn't my real father. That my real father raped my mother. And she's created a name for herself fighting for rape victims and their unwanted children. I'm her poster boy. But they couldn't admit Robert's had a mistress for ten years? It was like I was the only one in the universe who didn't know. I felt like such a loser." He glared up at the stars poking through the night sky, and I thought I saw tears in his eyes.

"You're not a loser. Nobody wants to hurt anybody, Ben. Or be hurt. And they certainly didn't want to hurt you."

"Why didn't my parents just get divorced?" he blurted, sounding like a teenager.

"Money."

Surprised at my frankness, he burst out laughing, staggering slightly. "You are *soooo* cool. You're not like the rest of them. You say what's on your mind." He wagged a finger at me. "You'll never get ahead that way in this town."

I smiled. "Of course there's the possibility that despite everything they still love each other and you."

"Now you don't sound like the cool Diana." His expression clouded. "Maybe I don't want to be loved by them. Nobody's thought of that, have they?" Pausing, he moved closer. "I've always wanted to say this to you. But don't get all uptight. It's a compliment."

"What?"

"Watching your earlier films when I was young got me through my adolescence. You were *soooo* sexy." His breath was hot and moist against my check.

I laughed. "Glad to be of help."

Below us on the lawn the caterers rolled out a big birthday cake with twenty-one candles ablaze. My heart sank for Ben. Robert had finally appeared and stood hand in hand with Gwyn. They both extended their arms toward him, beckoning him like two divas competing for the same audience of one.

"This is so fucked." Quickly, he grabbed my shoulders, pulling me to him. With the urn wedged awkwardly between us, he kissed me hard on the lips. Whispering in my ear, he said, "I just wanted to kiss a woman Robert hasn't had. He hasn't, has he?"

"No," I whispered back.

From the lawn, Gwyn stared up at me as Ben lurched down the stairs and across to where they were waiting. By the accusing look on her face, I knew Gwyn had seen the kiss. Misunderstood it. The family and many of the guests followed the cake into the tent. The rap music stopped.

To the dissonant sound of off-key voices singing "Happy Birthday," I stood alone, haunted by Ben's question: Who would want to murder Jenny? Then I caught sight of Ryan Johns sneaking across the lawn with the Blond Sliver at his side. They paused at the guesthouse door, he spoke to her, and she tossed her head back and giggled. Then he quickly shoved her inside, closing the door behind them. Christ, he wanted me to drive him home.

When the birthday song ended, there was quiet for a brief moment, and then a man's voice speaking in a low firm tone floated up to me from the patio below. I peered over the balustrade and saw Heath, who "got things done" for Zaitlin. I watched him talk importantly on his BlackBerry, at ease with the power of his body. Had he thought that Celia needed to "get done"? I wanted to confront him, but I had promised her not to say anything.

I assessed the plate of food that Ben had left on the balustrade. Adjusting the urn in my arms, I grabbed the plate, leaned over the railing, aimed, and dropped it. It landed perfectly—crashing and shattering just behind where he stood. Food flew in all directions.

In one swift movement, holding his cell in his left hand, he reached inside his jacket with the other and spun around looking up toward the balcony. Seeing me, he stopped in mid-action, hand still inside his windbreaker.

His aggressive response startled me. Gathering myself, I said, "I'm so sorry, Mr. Heath, or is it Mr. Ward?"

His hand fell to his side. "You can get hurt doing something like that."

"Do you like to hurt women?"

His forehead wrinkled and he cocked his head to one side, still looking up at me. "I think I liked you better naked." A waiter rushed to him and started to pick up the pieces of plate and food. Heath turned on his heels and strode away.

Son-of-a-bitch.

As applause erupted from the marquee I went downstairs and across the lawn, the grass sucking at my heels. Stopping at the door to the guesthouse, I could hear Ryan muttering "Ouch. Ooooh. Ouch."

"I'm not hurting you," a voice as thin as the blonde whined.

"I'm sunburned."

I pushed open the door. Ryan, his Bermuda shorts and briefs hanging down around his Uggs, gaped at me. The Sliver was on her knees in front of him, mouth open. Ryan clamped his hands over his genitals.

"If you want me to drive you home I'm leaving now," I announced.

"*This* minute?" he gasped.

"I'm sure she can take you home."

"I'm not driving all the way out to Malibu and back," the Sliver whined.

"Do we have to discuss this now? I'll take a cab."

I looked at the Sliver. She was young. Maybe Jenny's age.

"You want to be an actress?"

"Who doesn't?"

"Then get up off your knees."

"What are you trying to do to me, Diana? You're a bitter woman."

Ryan's words stayed with me as I made my way back across the lawn toward the valet. What could be worse than a bitter woman? A beat-up woman. A murdered woman.

CHAPTER TEN

When I was a child I believed Sunset Boulevard could take me anywhere I wanted to go, from the Pacific Ocean to downtown Los Angeles, to New York, even to Paris, where mother had once shot a movie. As I grew more aware of my surroundings, I was shocked to discover Sunset Boulevard had its limitations. And I began to understand the limitations of my own life.

It was 10 P.M. when I curved down Sunset onto Pacific Coast Highway and drove past my house to Celia's. I had called her and told her I was coming. She thought I wanted to talk about Jenny Parson's murder, which was now all over the news. But I didn't. I needed to tell her that Zaitlin was doing business with the man who had beat her up. And I knew it was going to turn her world upside down.

Sitting at the pine farm table in Celia's kitchen, I stared at Jenny Parson's smiling face spread across a wide plasma screen, the sound off. It was the perfect headshot of a hopeful young actress. But then, according to Jenny, she wasn't a hopeful young actress. She had only been doing what her father had wanted her to do.

I glanced at Celia, who was wrapped in a white terry robe, her long hair tied back into a haphazard ponytail. The bruise on her face was darker and meaner-looking than it had been in the morning. I had told her about the call from the Bel Air Hotel and finding Jenny's body. Smelling the homey aroma of the waxed wood surface and hearing the hum of the spotless stainless steel refrigerator, two things happened: I realized I was starving, and my unexpected tears began to flow. Again.

Celia took my hand, this time comforting me. "I can't even imagine what you've been through, having to pick up your mother's ashes and finding Jenny Parson. What can I do?"

"You could get me some bread and cheese," I sobbed.

Along with the urn, there was a Kleenex box on the table next to a half-empty bottle of white wine. She grabbed a tissue and stuffed it into my hand.

"Did you know Jenny Parson well?" She opened the refrigerator, letting its cold light escape into the warm kitchen.

"Just enough to feel what a horrible waste her death is."

"Was she talented?"

"Funny, Gwyn asked the same question. Would it matter less if she wasn't talented?"

"Gwyn? You went to the birthday party for Ben after discovering . . . ?"

"Zaitlin wanted to know what had happened." I blew my nose and tossed the Kleenex onto a pile of other discarded tissues. I looked more closely at Celia's face. "Have you been crying?"

She nodded. "I don't think I'll ever be the same again. Will you? After what you saw?"

"I haven't been the same since Colin died so I don't know what 'the same' is anymore."

Retrieving what she needed, she slammed the refrigerator door and glanced at the TV. Jenny's face had disappeared and now there was a picture of the alley, police cars, and the body bag containing her corpse on a gurney being loaded into the coroner's van. The gurney hit a bump, and the body moved and jerked as if Jenny were kicking, trying to get out. We both turned away from the awful image.

She placed a baguette and some Brie on the table. "The bread is stale." She sat down and poured us more wine.

"I have to tell you something, Celia." I stared into my glass.

She pushed the cheese plate closer and waited for me to continue.

I raised my head. "It's . . . it's about the man who hit you."

Her body went rigid. "What about him?"

"I met him. He was introduced to me as Leo Heath. Not Ward."

"Introduced? Where was this?" She balled up a tissue, tightening her fist around it, her knuckles going white.

I gulped wine. "Tonight at Ben's party. In Zaitlin's office."

"In Robert's office at his house?" Her brow furrowed as she tried to take in what I was telling her. "What was Ward or whatever his name is doing there?"

"He owns a security firm and does some jobs for Robert. His guards were working the party."

"You're telling me Robert knows him?" The fear I had seen in her this morning returned full force.

"Robert had called him about Jenny's death. He's a Hollywood fixer."

Her hand trembled as she tucked a stray strand of hair behind her ear. "Did Ward . . . Heath say anything to you?"

"Not really. I mean, he knew I recognized him. I tried to dump a plate of food on him."

"What?"

"I know it was stupid. But I felt I had to do something."

"You always have to do something. I never should have told you."

"Could Robert have sent him to Bella Casa?"

"And have me show him the house without telling me? It doesn't make sense." She threw the wadded tissue onto the same pile. Her expression darkened. "What are you implying, Diana?"

"Nothing." I sat back. "I'm just telling you what happened."

"Well, don't." Standing, she walked the length of her kitchen, terry slippers scuffing on the planked floor. "I asked you to stay out of it."

I tore off a piece of bread. She was right—it was stale.

"Oh, my God," she blurted, pointing to the screen.

There was a photo of me slumped down against the alley wall, clinging to my mother's urn. Eyes half closed, lips drooping, I looked as if I'd been drinking rotgut out of the urn. Who had taken the picture?

Celia clicked the remote, turning on the sound, sitting down again.

"We now have more information on the murder of Jenny Parson," said the news anchor. "This is a picture of the actress Diana Poole soon after the discovery of her friend's body."

"Friend? She wasn't my friend."

"What is that she's holding?" the co-anchor asked.

"It's apparently the urn containing her mother's ashes. According to Al Bailey, the doorman at the Beverly West condos, Ms. Poole used the urn to trick him into gaining entry into Ms. Parson's condo."

"Oh, God, in the alley the doorman must've taken the picture with his cell phone."

"This case is getting more and more bizarre," the co-anchor smiled broadly.

"Diana Poole's mother, the famous actress Nora Poole, died last week of natural causes at the Hotel Bel Air," the anchor said, as if that piece of information cleared up everything.

"Turn it off." I sat up and downed the last of my wine.

Clicking the remote, Celia slid it angrily across the table, then stood. I peered up at her. Her mouth was set firm, her face pinched. "I want you to go."

"What?"

"I told you to leave this alone. And you went and got involved."

"I didn't search out Heath. He walked into a room where I was standing."

"I can't trust you anymore, Diana."

"I know this has been a shock for you. We've both been through a lot in the last twenty-four hours."

"You never approved of my relationship with Robert."

"You keep bringing that up. This has nothing to do with what I feel about you and Robert."

"It has everything to do with it! I don't want to lose him. To lose everything."

"Did you want me to lie? Not tell you what happened?"

"I'm not sure I believe you." Her voice rose, angry and hurt. "You're using this to create some kind of . . . I don't know . . . distrust between Robert and me."

"That's not true. What's going on? Does Heath have some kind of hold on you? Or is it Zaitlin?"

"You honestly think that Robert has . . ."

"Why was Heath using an assumed name at Bella Casa?" I paused and asked in a softer voice. "Why did he beat you up, Celia?"

Tears streaming down her face, she screamed at me, "Maybe because I looked like a woman who needed to be beaten up!"

"You don't mean that." I reached for her hand.

She recoiled from my touch. "Get out." She swept past me and into the hallway. Stunned, I gathered the urn and my purse.

The front door was open. Celia glared down at the floor.

Stepping outside, I turned back to her. "Let me help you . . ."

She slammed the door in my face. Celia and I had never had a major fight. But there was a disturbing finality to that closed door.

Acting is a series of emotional adjustments or beats, as they are sometimes called. But the adjustments have already been made before the scene is played. The actor knows how the story will end. I know this is my cue to cry or to laugh, so I have already prepared my feelings because I'm aware this moment is coming. Now driving down the street to my house, unlocking the door, and turning on the lights in my living room, I was at a loss. I was not prepared for Celia's reaction, for the possibility of losing her as a friend. I told myself we were both overwrought and I just needed to give her time. I hoped I was right.

From the TV in the kitchen I could hear my name being tossed around by two female anchors.

"Shut up!" I yelled at them. They didn't.

I set my purse and the urn on the coffee table. My gaze shifted to Colin's Oscars. There was room on the mantel for another successful ghost. Picking up Mother, I placed her between his two awards.

"We're back together again after all these years." I leaned my forehead against the hard stucco mantel. I wanted to cry but I was too tired.

Tensing, I became aware of someone outside on my deck. I whirled around. Pressing his face against the sliding glass door, Ryan Johns peered in, looking like an aging lost boy. I let out my breath and opened the door. He rolled in with the salty cold air.

"I feel sobriety coming on. How about a nightcap?" He wriggled his eyebrows at me.

"I'm going to bed."

He lingered, hands in his jacket pockets, beer belly hanging over the waist of his Bermuda shorts. "Diana, I vaguely remember hearing, in my sexually unfulfilled drunken haze thanks to you, somebody at the party say that Jenny Parson was murdered. Did you hear about it?"

"It's all over the TV. I discovered her body. You can go into the kitchen and learn all about it. I'm still going to bed."

"You found her body?" Confused, he ran his large hands through his red unruly hair. "How well did you know her?"

"You don't need to know someone well to find their corpse. We were working together on a movie, that's all. We talked alone in her trailer yesterday evening."

"What about?"

"She couldn't remember her lines. Why? Did you know her?"

"This'll bring her father down here." He edged crablike back out onto the deck and toward the stairs.

"You know Jenny's father?" I followed after him.

"In a way." He loped down the steps to the common pathway.

"In what way?" I yelled after him.

"I owe him money." He ran up his steps and disappeared inside his house.

My landline rang. Closing and locking the sliding doors, I answered it.

"Don't you ever answer your cell?" Zaitlin bellowed.

"I turned it off."

"You're all over the television holding your mother's ashes, for God's sake."

"I know. I think it was the doorman who took . . ."

"Our insecure star, Jake Jackson, is chewing my ass out about it. He asked me if you'd gone fucking nuts." Before I could respond, Zaitlin continued, "I'm sending a car for you tomorrow at eleven in the morning. Jackson wants a meeting to discuss if we go forward with the movie or not. And he wants to make sure you're okay."

"In what way?"

"'Okay' as in not fucking *nutso*."

"You know I'm not. And why a car? You think I'm so crazy I can't drive?"

"In case there are reporters outside your house. I don't want any more mistakes, Diana."

63

"Mistakes? You mean like finding Jenny Parson in a garbage truck?" I was yelling now.

"No, I mean your reaction to it."

"If you had done your job as producer I wouldn't have been put in this position."

"All right. Let's calm down. We're all on edge. Just don't bring your mother to the meeting." He hung up.

I slammed the phone down and stared at the urn dominating the mantel. The cherry wood looked substantial. Her nameplate shone. Maybe I should unpack her Oscar for Best Actress in a Starring Role and put it up there. Except I wasn't sure where it was stored. I wasn't sure where anything or anyone was.

In bed, I took a sleeping pill and turned out the light. The TV flickered a bad black-and-white film. They weren't all great.

I thought about Ryan owing Jenny's father money. He didn't ask how Jenny was murdered. Nor did Celia. Nobody seemed interested in how she died or why. Except Ben. And why would the head of a security firm, a fixer, use an alias to look at Bella Casa? And then there was Beth Woods, our director, who thought Jenny was evil. Why did she think that?

My mind wandered to tomorrow's meeting with Jake Jackson. He had star power and an image to protect, a dangerous combination. Was he going to kill the movie? Or just kill me by recasting my part when they recast Jenny's? One way or another we were all in danger. Somehow. I reached out my hand to the empty side of the bed. It was a futile attempt for comfort.

The sound of a woman screaming bolted me out of my sleep. My heart leaping, I blinked at the TV. Joan Crawford, her mouth opened so wide you could park a truck in it, was screaming herself into a nervous breakdown. I didn't blame her.

CHAPTER ELEVEN

By nine o'clock in the morning, the fame suckers were gathering outside my house. Cameramen and reporters with microphones were focused on my front door with all the intensity of a group of sharpshooters. On the ocean side, a few photographers took pictures of my rotting deck and yelled for me to come out and talk to them about Jenny Parson. I ran around pulling shades and curtains.

In the kitchen I drank my coffee and ate my breakfast huddled low over the table so they couldn't get a good shot of me through the window above the sink. The onslaught brought back all the old fears I'd experienced with my mother as we were rushed through hotel kitchens to avoid the paparazzi that always waited for her.

Instead of feeling special, I had felt trapped and vowed never to live like that. Yet here I was, not because I was one hell of an actress, but because I'd discovered a dead one. And the fame suckers wanted a piece of that.

The limo driver whom Zaitlin had ordered to pick me up at eleven arrived thirty minutes early. When I looked out my peephole, he yelled above the pandemonium that he was here to get me. Letting him into the house, I slammed the door before they could take a picture.

"I'm Gerald, ma'am." He was a big guy with dyed brown hair.

"Wait here." Before he could answer, I left him standing.

In my bedroom, I gulped more coffee and put on makeup with a shaky hand. Then I struggled into my LBD (little black dress), which I thought would make me look less "nutso" to Jake Jackson. Slipping into high black heels, I ran around trying to find my cell phone. It was in my purse. Grabbing a short gray leather jacket (a little edge always helps in Hollywood), I hurried into the hallway.

The driver came to attention.

"I'm ready, I think," I said.

"Do you want me to hold your jacket up in front of your face or anything?"

"I'm not a suspect. Let's just get to the car as fast as we can."

"It's parked about fifteen houses down. I couldn't get any closer, sorry." He put his hand on the doorknob. "Ready?"

"As I'll ever be." I slapped on my sunglasses.

But you are never ready. Reporters with mikes rushed at me, mouths flapping, screaming questions. I could smell their rancid coffee breath and the sweat of the paparazzi, which was permanently distilled into the zip-up jackets they wore.

"Diana! Did you see her die?" shouted one man.

"How close were you and Jenny?" added another.

"Will her death hurt the movie?" a third bellowed.

"Did you kill her?" a woman called out.

Lights flashed. Video cameras crushed in on me. I dipped my head, trying to turn away from the prodding lenses.

"Look this way, Diana. Do you know who did it?"

"What did her body look like?"

Elbows and the sharp edges of equipment jabbed into my shoulders and back. I tripped over feet and someone stepped on my toes.

"Did your mother know her?"

"Smile, Diana!"

A woman jerked at my hand and stuck a cell phone in my face. "Talk into this, Diana. Why were you carrying your mother's ashes? Was it a ritual murder?"

The driver grabbed my arm and pulled me through the mob. "The car is down this way. Run!"

Cursing my choice of high heels, we ran for the limo as vehicles speeding on the highway came dangerously close. The asphalt was uneven and slippery with sand and gravel. The photographers and reporters chased after us.

"Diana! Diana!"

I stumbled as we reached the glistening black car. The driver caught me, grabbing my purse as it slipped from my shoulder. Quickly he opened the rear door and pushed me in. I fell flat on my face onto the black leather seat as he slammed the door shut.

Breathless and unnerved, I righted myself, flipped my hair out of my eyes, and saw the back of a man sitting in the front passenger seat. There was something familiar about him. The driver slipped in behind the wheel and threw my purse into the man's lap. The locks on the doors slid down just as one of the paparazzi reached my side of the car, angrily striking at the darkened window with the palm of his hand. Tires screeched and I sank back into the seat as we sped off.

The passenger turned his head. Leo Heath's solemn dark brown eyes stared at me from his lean rugged face. I stiffened.

"What are you doing here?"

"Security. Zaitlin wanted me to keep an eye on you. Put your seat belt on." He faced forward.

"Sorry about shoving you so hard," the chauffeur offered as he rapidly cut in and out of the traffic. "Hope I didn't hurt you."

"I'm fine." But I wasn't. I was rattled by the run through the gauntlet of the fame suckers. And the presence of Heath wasn't helping.

"May I have my purse?" I asked.

"When you're finished, I'll give it back to you." Heath didn't bother to turn around.

"I beg your pardon? I'd like my purse. Now."

He put it on the floor.

"What do you think you're doing?" I demanded.

Both men acted as if I hadn't spoken. Jesus, what was going on? I looked more closely at the car. The burl wood on the side panels and the dashboard was rich and expensive, the leather soft as a baby's ass. I peered out the front window at the shiny Mercedes Benz emblem on the hood. Zaitlin was careful with his money. He never would have sent such an expensive car to pick me up. This was no rented town car or SUV, it belonged to someone. And it wasn't Zaitlin.

I peered at the heavy chrome molding lining the doors and listened to the silence. There was no road noise—other cars, the wind. I could feel the heavy smooth grip of the tires on the pavement, but not hear them. This was the kind of car presidents used: soundproof, bulletproof, maybe even missileproof. Except that Heath with his bashed nose and the chauffeur with his dyed hair were no secret service.

I reached over and pulled at the door lock. It didn't move. Then I tried my window. I couldn't open it

I took a deep breath, calming myself. "I need some air. Unlock my window so I can control it."

Heath turned up the air conditioner. "Let me know it if it gets too cold." He was as accommodating as a maitre d' with a hundred-dollar tip in his pocket. The air ruffled his hair.

So they weren't going to give me my purse and they weren't going to let me operate the window. I pressed my lips together as I fought back the fear that was crawling through me. When I stumbled, had my bag really slipped from my shoulder, or had the driver purposely taken it? There was nothing in it except my lipstick, hairbrush, wallet, and cell phone. My cell. My contact to the outside world.

The driver swerved left onto Malibu Canyon Road. We were going in the wrong direction for Zaitlin's house. My fear was no longer crawling, it was at full gallop.

"This isn't the way to Zaitlin's!" I leaned forward, gripping the top of the driver's seat.

"The meeting's been canceled," Heath said.

"By whom?" I demanded.

"Zaitlin."

"He would've told me."

"He told *me*."

"Is that why you won't let me have my purse, so I can't call him?" Silence.

"I thought you were supposed to protect me."

"I am."

We began the long climb up the twisting canyon road.

"So where are you taking me against my will? If anything happens to me, the photographers and TV people saw this car. Saw me get into it." I stared into the rearview mirror and met the driver's dull penny-shaped eyes. "Gerald, your name is Gerald, right? They saw you. They have you on tape."

"Will you tell her to shut up!" he snapped at Heath. "She's giving me a headache."

Heath glanced over his shoulder at me. "Nothing's going to happen to you. Trust me."

"Trust *you*? A man who likes to batter women?"

The driver's eyes slid sideways, regarding him curiously. "What's she talking about?"

Heath swiveled fully around so fast I had to jerk my head back to keep our chins from colliding.

"I know what you did, you bastard."

He had that empty expression of not knowing me again. Turning forward, he hit a button on the dashboard. A window rose up cutting me off from them. I pounded on it. The driver laughed at something Heath said, but I couldn't hear it. I could hear only my heart thumping against my ribs as the limo sped down the canyon and into the west valley.

Soon, the car raced up the on-ramp to the Ventura freeway and headed north. My permanent chill was back. I slipped on my jacket, but it had lost its edge.

CHAPTER TWELVE

As we raced north up the 101, I stared out my darkened window, watching rows of car dealerships turn into rows of condos turn into rows of outlet stores turn into rows of planted fields.

Everything I looked at was shaded in black as if all of California were in mourning. As if it were all noir. Then the ocean appeared, as bleak as a nightmare. Surfers in wet suits, sleek as seals, waited on their boards for the next murky wave. These two men couldn't be stupid enough to hurt me. After all, my abduction was captured on tape for everyone to see. But why take me in the first place? Did it have something to do with what I knew about Celia? Or was it

Jenny Parson? I dug my fingers into the lush leather. I felt like I did when I was in bed at night. Very alone, very scared.

As we reached Santa Barbara, I watched the driver lift his cell phone to his ear, say a few words, then put it down. The limo curved off the freeway onto Cabrillo Boulevard, a street lined with hotels and palm trees on one side, and the ocean, volleyball courts, and palm trees on the other. I watched mothers and fathers pedaling, with Herculean effort, rented surreys filled with their kids along the pristine sidewalks. Though the windows were too dark for me to define colors, I knew the parents' faces would be red from their endeavor. And I envied these tourists their sunburned skin, their tired legs, their cranky children. They might go back home and get divorced and selfishly rip out the hearts of their kids, but right now they were pedaling with all their might for them.

Soon we turned into the Santa Barbara Harbor and Marina. Using a key card to open a barrier gate, the driver guided the car into a private lot. My body grew alert. I knew this was when I had to do something.

The driver opened the door for me. The minute my feet hit the pavement I screamed and tried to run. But Heath was out of the limo, grabbing my arm. With one hand he swung me around to him, then clamped the other hand on the back of my head and shoved my face into his chest, muffling my voice. I could smell his freshly ironed white shirt and the soap he'd used. To anyone passing I'd look like a woman crying or laughing intimately into her boyfriend's body. Son-of-a-bitch.

I struggled, trying to push myself away.

Lowering his head, lips brushing my ear, he said, "Shut the fuck up, please."

I raised my right thigh, preparing to kick him in the groin.

"And if you're thinking of kneeing me, I'll knock your standing leg out from under you so fast you won't know how you ended up on your ass."

The driver moved in on me, and I felt a hard jab in my lower back. I'd done enough cop shows to know the feel of a gun muzzle.

Heath removed his hand from my head. "Nobody is going to hurt you, I promise. So relax." He was so sincere.

I glared up at him. "Relax? With a gun in my back?"

"Jesus Christ, Gerald, put the pistol away," he ordered the driver.

"You don't have to deal with *him*. I do," the driver growled. "I was told to deliver her, and that's what I'm doing. Walk." He jabbed me harder.

"If you don't put it away I'm taking her back to Malibu, now."

Gerald thought about this, then holstered his gun.

At least I knew they didn't want to kill me. For now. But why should I trust Heath? And who was '*him*' Gerald had to deliver me to?

With my purse slung over his shoulder the chauffeur stood on one side of me, Heath on the other. They walked me past the Yacht Club, a gray weathered building that looked like a ship marooned on the sand. The teal-blue ocean shimmered with the noon sun. As we reached the public boardwalk, seagulls dipped and soared under the piercing blue sky. Boats of all shapes and sizes bobbled in their slips. Tourists, children, the homeless, and old salts mixed together. A tan woman, about my age, wearing a T-shirt, long skirt, and flip-flops grinned at me. I saw an opportunity. I flashed her my best eat-the-camera smile.

"Do I know you?" she asked.

"Yes. Would you like my autograph?"

Gerald shuffled his feet like a nervous horse. Heath was amused.

"Oh, I thought I knew you from high school. We're up here for the Camarillo High Reunion." She looked more closely as if inspecting a piece of produce. "Are you somebody?"

"Yes, I'm . . ."

Before I could finish, Heath said in an easy seductive voice, "Excuse us. She's had a little too much to drink." Draping his arm over my shoulder, he winked at the woman, who actually winked back at him.

His fingers slid down and dug into my elbow. I gasped as pain shot through my arm and the two men forced me farther down the boardwalk.

"What were you going to do, write 'help me'?" A sardonic smile played on his lips.

"Something like that." I tried to pull away, but his fingers pressed deeper into my skin and bone, and I stopped trying.

"You don't give up, do you?"

"Maybe you're just not used to women who fight back."

"You don't have to fight me."

We paused at another gate that led inside the marina. The driver unlocked it, and we started down the long dock. The water smelled of salt and gasoline. I peered around to see if there was anyone relaxing on their boats. But there were only pelicans ogling me from the tops of pylons, looking like old drunks, and sunburned FOR SALE signs tucked into portholes.

We came to a yacht, a little smaller than a Princess cruise ship, docked in a slip far from the other boats. At the top of the deck-stairs stood a man wearing a baby blue windbreaker with the sleeves rolled up, showing off his biceps and a tattoo running down his right arm. I kept telling myself that no harm could come to me in the Santa Barbara Marina—unless my captors decided to sail out of the marina.

The man reached down to take my hand, and now I could read his tattoo. It said: One Night With You. His jacket fell open revealing a gun tucked into his waistband. I whirled around. Heath pressed in on me.

CHAPTER THIRTEEN

The gunman helped me up onto the yacht. Heath followed. The driver, my purse still slung over his shoulder, remained on the dock.

A bar with stools, lounge chairs, and built-in banquets filled the spacious deck.

"She goes in alone." The man blocked Heath's way.

"No, I go in with her." Heath glanced down at the One Night With You tattoo on the guard's muscular arm. "Finally got lucky, uh?"

The guard's neck stiffened, and his biceps flexed as if he had no control over them.

"He's waiting," Heath reminded him.

Fierce resentment oozed from the man as he ushered us into a mahogany-paneled salon about the size of my house. The floors were dark wood, and rich Burgundy-colored drapes were pulled over large rectangular windows blocking the sun and the water from view. A crystal chandelier glowed from the beamed ceiling. Old oil paintings of someone's royal ancestors and their dogs hung on the walls. A dining room table surrounded by twenty matching Chippendale chairs took up the end of the room. I felt as if I had walked not onto a yacht but onto the set of an old Merchant Ivory film about the English upper class.

A man in his sixties sat on a paisley velvet sofa. Tall and thin, ash-gray hair swept back from a face as bony and grim as a skeleton's. His long narrow chin ended in a goatee. Staring with red-rimmed, stone-colored eyes at a heavily draped porthole, the man seemed to not to know we were there. Heath leaned against the wall near the salon door. I remained standing, trying to control my fear, which was fighting for dominance with my anger. The tantrum-squawking of the seagulls outside punctuated the tense silence. The thug waited, his thick arms hanging down, fingers twitching.

Finally the man said to him, "Leave."

As he did he bumped Heath's shoulder. Heath pretended not to notice.

The man continued, "You found my daughter's body."

"You're Mr. Parson?"

"Sit down, please." He gestured to a burgundy leather club chair opposite the coffee table.

My anger beat out my fear. "Look, I'm very sorry for your loss, but you had no right to have me abducted, to scare the hell out of me, to drag me up here . . ."

He raised a hand up, stopping me.

"I'm meeting two detectives at my house in Montecito in about an hour. They're going to explain what happened to Jenny. I know how the police operate, Ms. Poole. They won't give me the complete picture even if they knew it, which I doubt they do. So I brought you up here to tell me exactly what you saw before I talk with them."

"There is such a thing as a telephone. You could have called me. Or at least your driver or Heath could've told me where they were taking me."

"If they told you that it was I you were to meet you'd naturally begin to plan what you were going to say. I've found over the years I gain more information from spontaneous discussions. I haven't slept much, so let's get this over with." He rubbed his long fingers against his thigh as if trying to massage life into it. His navy blue slacks matched his polo shirt. Black velvet slippers with gold embroidered crests added a hint of Old World decadence to his outfit.

A door opened near the dining room table and a young man with teak-colored skin and glistening black hair entered. He wore a white polo shirt and khakis.

"What would you like to drink after your journey?" Parson asked me.

"Nothing."

"Same here," Parson said to the young man, then turned to Heath. "You?"

"No."

"Please, sir, eat something."

"I can't, Luis. Leave us."

Frowning with concern, Luis drifted out, closing the door.

"Do you still wish to stand, Ms. Poole?"

"I wish to be taken back to my house."

"Not until we talk."

"He just wants to know what happened to his daughter," Heath said. "Make it easy on yourself."

I relented and sat down, crossing my legs. Parson stroked his goatee, a ghost of a connoisseur's leer playing on his dry lips as he took in my body. Heath shifted his weight.

I focused on the red garden roses exploding from a vase on the coffee table and wondered what kind of power this man had that he was able to force Zaitlin to cancel our meeting, if there really had been one. There was no doubt Parson was a grieving father. But he was also surrounded by armed thugs, and that made him a very dangerous grieving father. I decided to ask a few questions myself.

"How were you able to get Zaitlin to cancel my meeting? Do you control him in some way?"

"I like an intelligent woman. Don't you, Heath?"

"Not always."

I ignored Heath as Parson leaned forward. "You might say Jenny was murdered on Zaitlin's watch. He's only trying to accommodate me. And your meeting has been postponed, not canceled."

"Yet he felt the need to send Heath with me. Why?"

"Heath owns one of Los Angeles' best investigative security firms. He is looking into Jenny's death for Zaitlin. Zaitlin will share any information he learns with me."

Seemingly unaware he was being talked about, Heath pulled a strand of blond hair from his lapel and flicked it onto the floor. It was mine.

"I thought it might be because of all the heavily armed men you have surrounding you." Not waiting for an answer, I continued. "Where is Jenny's mother? Doesn't she want to know what happened to her daughter?"

The deep lines around Parson's mouth twitched. "You really want to make this difficult, Ms. Poole?"

"After what you've put me through, it's only fair you should answer some of my questions first."

He let out a heavy sigh. "My wife, her mother, is at our Montecito home. She's devastated and under sedation. When I married her she was just twenty and I was forty-five. Now she's forty-five. Jenny was our only child. My wife blames me for her death because I let her move to Los Angeles to work." He paused, considering. "Are you worried about your friend Ryan Johns?"

I tensed. "How did you know we were friends?"

"It's what I do. Knowledge of people is important in my business. But I never harm people who owe me money. What's the point? Unless, of course, he's involved in my daughter's death."

"What is your business?"

"I'm an investor."

He tapped the crown of his diamond-encrusted Rolex. Even Parson with his self-created, Old World, upper-class trappings couldn't resist some major bling. "It's getting late. There won't be any more questions unless I ask them." Like a bony pasha, he settled back into the abundant pillows and stretched his long thin arms across the back of the sofa as if to receive grapes or sex or both. "I'm waiting for my information, Ms. Poole."

If he had been another kind of father I would have been kinder in my assessment of Jenny. But I decided for him I would be brutally honest. "Jenny couldn't remember her lines, so Zaitlin asked me to go over them with her."

"Are you saying my daughter came to the set unprepared?"

"Yes."

"That doesn't sound like Jenny."

"Maybe you don't know much about her. The night before she was murdered . . ."

"That would be last Monday?" Heath asked.

"Yes. The day I met you," I said pointedly, then I turned back to Parson. "I talked with Jenny in her trailer. She couldn't make it through her scenes without forgetting her lines. She ran off the set. Zaitlin had to call a wrap. Jenny was costing the production time and money."

He shook his head. "Jenny would never behave that way."

"But she did."

Parson paused. "What did you two talk about in her trailer?"

"She told me she didn't care about the movie or her obligation to it. She was more interested in going clubbing. She confessed she didn't want to be an actress, that you'd forced her into it, that she was doing it for you." As I watched his face flush and the tendons on his neck protrude, I continued. "She said you were a dreamer, but she was the one who was the realist. She told me she didn't believe in pretending. Even when she was a child."

"Stop talking," Parson commanded, in a low threatening voice.

I did. Heath's muscles tensed but he stayed where he was.

Except for the seagulls, it was quiet as Parson mulled over what I had just told him.

Finally he spoke in a calm voice. "When I was child I used to sneak into the one movie theater in our neighborhood. Not because I cared about the movies being shown, at least at first, but because in the dark with no one watching me I could eat the popcorn and candy stuck on the filthy floor. And if I didn't get kicked out, I'd sleep there overnight. I was starving on the streets, and that's one way I survived. But that also began my love affair with the movies. They saved my life." His voice deepened with pain and anger. "They should've saved Jenny."

I suddenly realized that Jenny had grown up in a world of fantasy, her father's, right down to the décor on his boat. But the guns were real.

"Did she appear to be afraid of someone?" he asked.

"Quite the opposite. She struck me as being a tough, singular young woman who delighted in not letting Zaitlin tell her what to do. Or anyone else. Except . . ."

"Yes?" He leaned forward licking his lips, greedy for more information.

"When I told her I thought she was a good actress, she let down her defenses for a moment and became a vulnerable young woman who needed to hear just how good she was."

"I knew she wanted to act." He sat back and pounded his fist into the palm of his other hand. "I knew it! She was her father's daughter." Then he asked, matter-of-factly, "Describe how you found her body."

I told him about conning the doorman to get into her condo. Looking out her window, seeing the garbage truck, and then the sun reflecting off the silver heel of her shoe. How I ran into the alley screaming for the sanitation workers to stop dumping the bin. As I talked he listened with an eerily distant expression, as if I were recounting a nightmare I'd had that didn't relate to him.

When I finished he closed his eyes. "I bought her those shoes." Tears ran down his sunken cheeks, and I felt both loathing and sympathy for him. Taking a white handkerchief from his pocket, he wiped at his face. "Why were you so intent on getting inside her condominium?"

"I was worried about her. She had left my name with the doorman. That meant she wanted to see me and go over her lines."

"Once you got into her condo, why did you look out the window?" It was Heath.

"What?"

"Something must've prompted you to."

"What else do you do with a window but look out of it? And I was vamping for time. The doorman couldn't understand why I wasn't leaving the urn, which was why he'd let me into her condo in the first place. I was trying to come up with a plausible answer. Then I saw the glint of her high heel."

"So you didn't see the actual murder scene?" Parson asked.

"No. I mean there was no blood or upset furniture in her condo, so I doubt she was killed there."

"She wasn't." Heath removed a battered leather notepad from inside his jacket. It was stamped with a military insignia of some kind. "One of my contacts in LAPD told me that they think Jenny was murdered in her car, an Audi, while it was parked in the condo's underground lot. They've impounded it."

"What else did you learn?" Parson was now fixed on Heath.

"Do you want to discuss this in front of her?"

"Ms. Poole seems to know my daughter quite well. No reason she shouldn't know more. It may help her memory."

Heath shrugged and flipped his notebook open and read from his notes. "I was told she died of blunt-force trauma to the back of her skull."

"How many times was she struck?" Parson asked sharply.

"Don't know. They haven't been able to start the forensics yet. Too much backlog of waiting cases. She may have been slammed against the passenger side of the car window. Or someone could have been hiding in the back seat, rose up, and struck her from behind."

"You said passenger side?"

"Jenny wasn't driving. The police have her car on the garage security tape coming in at 12:33 A.M. But a man is behind the wheel."

"Can they identify him?" He sat forward.

"The images are shadowy," Heath continued. "So far they can't make an identification on the male. But it's early yet. There is equipment that should be able to resolve the image well enough—and if the cops don't have it, then you can afford to pay some company to do it for them."

"There has to be a security tape of them stopping, of the man getting out of her car," Parson said.

"Her parking space is out of range from the cameras."

"Christ. What happened to the driver?" Parson snapped. "He had to leave the garage somehow."

"About fifteen minutes after they drove in, there's an image of a male wearing a hooded sweat shirt walking into camera range from where her car was parked. He ducked his head as if he realized he was being taped. There's an exit door to the alley. You can leave through it without using a key, but it locks behind you automatically, so once you're outside you can't get back in unless you have a key. The door isn't in camera range either."

"Is he the same man who was driving?"

"At this point the police can't say."

"What about the plastic bags she was wrapped in? And how was she transferred from the garage to the . . ." he paused, then said, "Refuse area."

"Nothing on that so far."

Parson shifted his body toward me. "Do you know who my daughter was with the night of her murder?"

I remembered Ben Zaitlin had told me he was at the same club that night, but I wasn't about to give Parson his name.

"No."

He inhaled sharply, nostrils twitching. Leaping to his feet, he picked up the vase of red roses. And threw it over my head against the wall behind me. I ducked. He shifted his body and kicked the coffee table. It crashed into the empty chair next to me. I jumped up.

With one long stride, Heath stood between Parson and me.

CHAPTER FOURTEEN

Heart pounding, I stood with glass shards around my feet. Facing Parson, Heath remained standing between us. He balanced lightly on the balls of his feet, shoulders tensed as if he were about to swing a punch. Doors slammed as Luis and the tattooed man bolted in from the back of the yacht and from the deck.

"Get outta here!" Parson barked at his guys.

Both vanished.

"Nobody withholds information from me." Parson stared at me over Heath's shoulder. His rage had turned his face a violent red and spittle had formed at the corners of his mouth.

"Hey man." Heath held up his hands, palms toward Parson, his voice low and reasonable. "She has no reason not tell you what she knows. She's here to help you. She's the only one who cared enough about Jenny to make sure she was all right."

Parson's body trembled, then he collapsed back onto the sofa. Heath held his ground for a few more moments, turned, and moved toward me. I let out my breath as he kicked the pieces of the vase away from my feet. He went back to his place against the wall. I sat down.

With his long fingers, Parson wiped at the saliva on his lips. "Heath is right." His voice was measured. "You were the only one who tried to help her, and I appreciate that. But that doesn't mean you might not want to protect someone."

I made sure my voice was firm when I spoke. I didn't want to show this man any vulnerability. "I don't know who killed your daughter. You must have enemies. Maybe they wanted to get back at you through her. Your portholes are draped . . . are you afraid someone might shoot you?"

"I find mourning in the brilliant sunlight unbearable," Parson said.

I swallowed hard. I had felt the same when Colin died.

"Nobody I know, least of all my enemies, would dare to hurt Jenny. And if anyone is in danger, I would say it was you, Ms. Poole."

"Why me?"

"Jenny's body was meant to be pressed into a landfill, never to be seen again. But you found it. If I were her killer I'd be worried about what you knew or didn't know, what you saw or didn't see. You might suddenly remember some little thing I'd forgotten, some insignificant detail that could lead back to me." He smiled grimly. "No, I'd have to take you out."

Furious, I rose up out of the chair. "I'm tired of being threatened by you and your thugs. Let me go now or I'll tell the police you held me here against my will."

"In my world the police have little power." Parson stroked his goatee. The bony pasha was back. "You remind me a lot of your mother."

Christ, my mother again.

"'No bullshit allowed,' that's what Nora would always say when we were in bed together."

Was there *anybody* she hadn't had sex with? "I really don't want to hear about your affair with my mother."

"It was a long time ago. I thought since you were carrying her ashes, you must still love her."

"Mr. Parson, I'm ready to leave. And you don't want to keep the cops waiting."

He looked at me thoughtfully. "Your husband, Colin, was a wonderful writer. I'm sorry he died."

My mouth went dry. "So am I."

"I have fond memories of talking to him about the creative mind."

"You knew him?"

"You were newly married at the time. That would be, what? Eight, ten years ago? If I remember correctly you were on location finishing shooting your last movie. Too bad. You were becoming as good as your mother when you decided to quit. Colin and I had interesting discussions. He told me the creative mind could plot and deceive and dazzle just as brilliantly as the criminal mind, except that the criminal mind had no conscience. I disagreed with him on that point. I told him it was writers who had no conscience." A thin dry laugh escaped his lips.

"How would my husband know you?" I didn't bother to keep the contempt from my voice.

"I used to throw parties on this boat. Hollywood loves to rub shoulders with those of us who have, how shall I put it . . . a darker kind of star power." Parson contemplated me. "It might be best for you and the memory of the ones you've loved to think of any names you've forgotten to give me."

"What are you trying to say?"

"Oh, and if asked by the police or anyone else, I want you to say you were willingly picked up by my limo driver as recorded by the media. You came here of your own volition to help a grieving father learn more about his daughter's death." He flashed me his skeletal grin. "If you think about it, the paparazzi were far more dangerous to you than I've been."

"What could be so damaging to my husband? He's dead, for God's sake." My voice broke.

"The last thing I want is for you to be hurt by the actions of one who has died."

"Do you ever speak without it sounding like a threat?"

He waved a hand at Heath. "Drive her back to Malibu."

"Your chauffeur isn't taking me?" I said.

"Gerald is driving me to Montecito for my appointment with the detectives. Come and visit sometime. It's high on a hill with sweeping views of the Channel Islands and the Pacific. Hollywood people are moving into the area in droves. Colin thought you'd love it there." He stood, his thin body drooped. "I'm very tired. It's been a trying day." He walked softly in his velvet slippers to the door that Luis had used and left the salon.

"Son of a bitch."

"Yes, he is," Heath said.

"I was referring to you." I swept past him and out onto the deck.

CHAPTER FIFTEEN

"What's your problem?" Heath called after me.

I was hurrying ahead on the boardwalk, weaving through the tourists and the locals. Gerald had returned my purse. I was searching through it when I stopped and whirled around. Heath came to a sudden halt.

"I'll tell you what my problem is. I don't like the way you treat women. You've done nothing but maul me . . ."

"Only because you wouldn't listen to what I was saying."

"Women don't listen to me so I have to beat them up?"

His head snapped back. He adjusted his sunglasses. "Whoa, how'd we get to me beating up women? And what about you trying to drop a plate of food on my head?"

"What were you doing using an assumed name at Bella Casa?"

His smile slid sideways, and his head cocked. "Maybe seeing you naked in the swimming pool made me forget my real name."

"Don't try to charm me. My mother and I used to eat up guys like you and spit them out."

"Vivid image. I'm not sure what to do with it."

"Do you really want me to tell you?" I dug around in my purse some more. "Where is it?"

"What?"

"My cell. I need to call a taxi." I tossed my hair out of my face.

"To take you back to Malibu?" His brow furrowed.

"There's no way I'm getting into a car with you. And I'm going to give the taxi bill to Zaitlin. Where's my cell!"

"It's probably in Gerald's jacket pocket. A precaution in case you grabbed your handbag from him and made a run for it. He must've forgotten to give it to you."

I started back toward the yacht. He grabbed my arm, stopping me. "The gates are locked. You can't get in, and I don't have a key. What's wrong with you? Do you always act like this?"

I shook my arm. "Let go."

He released me. "I'll see that your cell is returned to you."

I suddenly felt helpless. A feeling I try to avoid at all times. Trying to compose myself, I breathed in the smell of burgers and fish 'n' chips wafting through the salty air from the lunch shacks and restaurants. Fishing boats bobbed in their docks; metal rigging rattled and clinked against the masts. The ocean gleamed.

"Everything seems so damn normal, so beautiful. And it isn't," I said.

He drew his hand through his hair. "Look, we've gotten off on the wrong foot. Of course you were frightened this morning, and I apologize for that. I told Parson and Zaitlin they should tell you where you were being taken. But Parson won out. Zaitlin went along with him."

"You were just following orders."

"If you want to put it that way. On the other hand, why are you constantly saying that I like to beat up women?"

"Don't you?"

He pushed his sunglasses up to the top of his head and shoved his face close to mine, forcing me to look directly into his eyes. "No. I have never hit a woman." Then he added, "Except when I was forced to."

"You are so full of it." I turned away, but he pulled me back. "Get your hands off me." I jerked free.

"If you would just stand still and be quiet a moment, I can explain."

"All right, tell me about all the exceptions."

"One of my clients had a girlfriend who was stalking him. She came at me with a knife. I decked her." He rubbed the bump on his nose, staring out at the ocean.

"That's it? That's the exception?"

When he spoke next his expression was somber. "There was another time in Afghanistan." His gaze shifted back to me but it was distant. "The woman had a baby in one arm, a hand grenade in the other."

"And you decked her, too?"

"No. I shot her right between the eyes. Any other questions?" His face was as hard as stone.

"No."

He slipped his glasses back down over his eyes, and we started walking again. Heath's serious directness had hit a nerve, and I thought of Celia's sudden anger last night. She had asked me to leave her house as if she wanted to get rid of me, as if she was purposely pushing me out of her life for good. And all of that happened after I'd told her the man named Ward was really Heath, and that he worked for Zaitlin. Had I caught her in a lie? Did she choose to end our friendship so she wouldn't have to tell me the truth about who struck her? At the same time I couldn't shake the feeling I needed to protect her. I didn't want to tell Heath or anyone that it was Celia who accused him.

"What were you really doing at Bella Casa?" I asked.

"Would you believe I'm tired of renting? That I need a place to call my own?"

"A little big for one person, isn't it?"

"You and your mother lived there. There were only two of you."

"Movie stars always live in houses that are too big for them."

"What makes you think I'm not married with a couple of kids?"

"You're a loner through and through."

He adjusted his shoulders. "You're right, I am."

"And the assumed name?"

"Working on a case. That's all I can say."

"Did you know Celia Dario before she showed you the house?"

"No."

"With all the work you do for Zaitlin, you had to know she was his mistress."

"I did."

"Is that why you used the assumed name?"

"I can't tell you. Client privilege. Your turn. Tell me why you think I like to abuse women."

"I might have been acting under a misconception. I'm not sure."

"That's it? That's your only explanation?" His brows rose.

"Client privilege."

Shaking his head, we continued to the car park in a moody silence. Soon Heath took out his keys and beeped open the doors to a brand-new silver-gray Mercedes convertible.

"Expensive car."

"I have to blend in with my surroundings. Makes me look like an executive producer."

He got into the Mercedes. I didn't. In seconds the dark blue soft-top folded back into the rear of the car.

He looked up from behind the wheel, his head back, his black sunglasses staring at me, an arm draped casually over the passenger-side bucket seat. "My company has a small fleet of autos, all different models and years. Makes it easier to tail people. I had one of my employees drive it up here this morning. She went home by Amtrak."

I looked down at him. "Parson and Zaitlin must pay you very well."

"I don't work for Parson. He's not the kind of man you want to do business with. Aren't you going to get in?"

"Put the top back up."

"You don't strike me as the kind of woman who's afraid to get some wind in her hair."

"I don't want the two of us driving in a Mercedes convertible along the happy freeway of life looking like the perfect narcissistic couple in a car commercial. Especially when I'm an actress and not getting paid for it."

He let out a deep warm laugh. The top curved up and into place.

I slipped into the passenger seat. "If you don't work for Parson why are you sharing information with him?"

He started the car. "Parson is a father whose daughter has been murdered. He may be an asshole, but he has every right to try to find her killer. And Jenny, no matter what or who she may have been, has every right for her killer to be brought to justice." He threw the car into reverse, backed out of the parking space, and drove toward the exit gate.

"You said, 'no matter what or who she may have been.' Did you know Jenny?"

"Never met her."

I leaned my head back against the seat. I thought of my husband attending a party on Parson's yacht. He'd never told me about it. Then there was Celia, who may have been lying to me. And finally there was Heath, who could be the greatest liar of them all.

I closed my eyes. "I don't know who to believe anymore."

"Welcome to my world," he said.

CHAPTER SIXTEEN

D riving smoothly and confidently, Heath took us back along Cabrillo Boulevard. The tourists were still pedaling for all they were worth, and the boats were swaying on the glistening water. I thought of what Parson had said about not being able to mourn in the brilliant sunshine. It was true, the dazzling perfection of a beautiful California day was a fist-punch right into your wounded heart.

"What does Parson know about my husband?" I asked.

"I don't know."

"Would you tell me if you did?"

"Depends."

"On what?"

"On the information. Who it can hurt, and how important it is."

"Who are you to judge? Don't your clients pay you for all the information you discover?"

"You're not my client. They also pay me to keep their secrets. Think of me as a priest. One that doesn't like choirboys," he added.

He guided the car into a roundabout and followed it onto Coast Village Road in the wealthy enclave of Montecito. Expensive shops, galleries, and cafés lined the street. I looked up toward the Santa Ynez Mountains and wondered which mansion held Parson's sedated wife. The village ended at the 101 on-ramp. Heath sped onto the freeway, and I was finally headed back home.

Adjusting my sunglasses, I studied his profile. With his graying dark hair, strong chin, and crooked nose he was more elegantly unhandsome than handsome. I've acted with many great-looking men, and I've learned it's the ones who aren't so good-looking that have a better sense of themselves, which made them more attractive.

"Like what you see?" He was staring straight ahead at the highway.

"I'm trying to see you as a priest. It's bad casting. What does Parson do exactly? Or do your vows not allow you to reveal that either?"

"He told you. He's an investor. He owns real estate, some islands, and people."

I thought of Ryan Johns owing him money. "How does he own people?"

"He collects information on them. You've already discovered he's not a nice man, Diana."

"So he does have something on my husband." I felt a small rip in the tether that kept me moored. The tether that kept me from being my mother, with a collection of unwanted and discarded men in her life. The tether that held me to the one person I had been certain loved me.

"I know you don't want my advice," he said, "but I'm going to give it to you anyway. Sometimes it's better to leave the dead alone. Let them have their secrets."

"I wish I had left Jenny Parson alone instead of talking my way into her condo. I wish my Jag worked and that my house didn't need a new roof and deck. And I especially wish Colin hadn't died."

"I had a girlfriend once that did nothing but wish for things. She used to cut out pictures of expensive handbags and shoes from fashion magazines and tape them on the refrigerator door. A sort of if-you-visualize-what-you-want-you'll-get-it bullshit. In her case it worked. She married a wealthy man. But every time before I opened that damn refrigerator for a beer I saw Prada, Fendi, and Channel."

"Doesn't sound like you and your girlfriend had a lot in common."

"We had mindless sex. She liked wearing these Gucci stiletto heels she bought on sale . . ."

"I can figure the rest of out for myself. Thank you." I peered out the window, watching drivers cutting each other off, and thought of Colin and me making love, our hot sweaty skin pasting our bodies together, and me hoping we would never be able to separate ourselves.

"What did you and Ben Zaitlin talk about at his birthday party?" Heath asked.

Heath's question jarred me back to reality. "You're a good inter-rogator. Chat about other things like your girlfriend and sex and then zero in with *the* question."

"Practice. Ben kissed you."

"Did his mother tell you that?"

"No, I was watching. That's a big part of my job . . . to watch."

"He's a lonely kid who discovered his stepfather has had a mis-tress for half his life. He wanted to kiss a woman that Zailin hadn't gone to bed with."

"And did he kiss a woman who hadn't gone to bed with his stepfather?"

"Is this for your own personal file? because I don't see how it's pertinent to the case."

He shrugged.

"Yes, he kissed a woman who hasn't had sex with Zaitlin."

"Did Ben want it to go further than the kiss?"

"I'm not going to take advantage of a twenty-one-year-old."

"I don't think he'd see it that way. Was he at The Den the night of Jenny's murder?"

"I'm sure the club has a security tape."

"I'm going to take your answer as a yes unless you tell me otherwise. Did he say who else was there?"

I sighed. "Jenny. She was drunk. And I think Ben said some guy drove her home."

"Does this guy have a name?"

"Ben didn't say."

"Did he mention whether he was wearing a gray sweatshirt with a hood?"

"You mean like the man on the security tape in Jenny's garage?"

He nodded.

"I've found over the years that most men don't think about what other men are wearing. In fact, they can hardly remember what their wives were wearing," I said.

"I'll remember what you wore today. Tight sexy black dress. Gray leather jacket for toughness. Which I've discovered you have in spades."

"Do me a favor. Forget the dress. Remember the toughness."

Grinning, he said "I'll try. How well did Ben know Jenny?"

"He said he knew she was causing her father problems on the set, but he didn't really know her personally. He implied that she ignored him."

"You believe that?"

"Yes, I do. Besides, what's his motive for killing Jenny? Zaitlin has more motive than Ben. I've never seen him put up with so much from an actress who wasn't a star." Hearing my own words, I now realized why Zaitlin had put up with her. "Is Parson backing the film?"

"You won't see his name anywhere."

"God, all an actor wants is a job. No one thinks about where the financing comes from to make the movie."

"You've probably helped launder a little money in your career and never knew it." He swerved off onto a freeway exit ramp.

I tensed. "Where are we going?"

"Lunch. Or are you one of those actresses who doesn't eat?"

I thought of the nonfat food in my refrigerator that never rotted, just turned rigid. "Actually, I'm starving."

He pulled into a shopping center lined with big square-shaped warehouses that didn't look much different from soundstages, except for their enormous signs announcing Target, T. J. Maxx, Best Buy, and Nordstrom's Rack. Hollywood doesn't have a monopoly on selling dreams at cost.

CHAPTER SEVENTEEN

The Red Pepper was a pseudo-Mexican food chain restaurant with ropes of plastic red peppers hanging from the walls and waitresses stuffed into pseudo-Mexican fiesta skirts and blouses.

I slid into a booth.

Heath remained standing. "I'll be right back." A cell phone rang in one of his pockets. It was a familiar ringtone. In fact it was my ringtone. He took my iPhone from the inside of his jacket and handed it to me. "It's for you."

Anger gave my adrenalin a jolt. "You bastard."

"You weren't going to drive back with me. I had to think of something." He strolled off toward the restroom.

Glaring after him, I answered the call.

It was Zaitlin. "What did Parson say to you?"

"Robert, how could you let Parson have me driven to Santa Barbara without telling me where the hell I was going, who I was going to meet, or why? I thought I was being abducted."

"Nothing I could do. Parson wanted it handled his way."

"You could've said no."

"It wouldn't have changed anything. There are some things you don't know, Diana, and some things it's better you don't know. And don't try to bully me about it. Tell me what you told him."

Inwardly I sighed. "Exactly what I told you. But I think you should talk to Ben. He was at the club where Jenny was the night she died."

"Did you say anything to Parson about Ben?"

"No."

"Good. Tell Heath. If it needs taking care of, he'll do it."

"I'm sure he will." I looked across the restaurant through the service opening into the kitchen. Heath was talking intently to an older man in a chef's hat.

"Robert, Parson knew Colin. He had something on him. What was it?"

"I don't know. I wouldn't worry about it. Colin's dead."

"That's not the point."

"Tell Heath to bring you to the Formosa Café. Jake Jackson, Beth Woods, and I will be there around three o'clock. If you're late we'll wait."

"You're replacing me with another actress, aren't you?"

"Jake Jackson wants to meet with you. That's all."

"Just be honest with me. Save me the trip."

"Sometimes we have to feed the beast, Diana. You know how the game is played." He hung up.

I did know how the game was played. I also knew if you had to feed the beast, in this case Jake Jackson, there had to be prey and that was me. I was surrounded by bastards.

I Googled a Camarillo cab company on my iPhone. Ordering a car to pick me up, I gave them the address. Then I leaned back in the booth and waited.

Heath returned and sat across from me. Rubbing his hands together he said, "I ordered us chicken tostadas, they aren't bad here. Or don't you like men ordering for you?"

"No, it sounds good."

His eyes narrowed. "I thought you'd be more upset."

"You mean about my iPhone? I didn't expect less from you."

"That was a well-placed jab to my chin."

"Who were you talking to in the kitchen?"

"The chef. He's a client."

"He can afford someone who has a fleet of expensive cars?"

"He's a good man who's in a little trouble. I'm just helping him out."

The waitress brought our meal, two glasses of white wine, and the check, which she left on the table underneath two red and white peppermint hard candies.

"Wine?" I smiled my soft pliable you-can-do-anything-you-want-to-with-me smile.

Heath started to respond, then stopped, wary. "Tastes like water with a bite. But I thought maybe you could use it after what we put you through. Cheers."

"Cheers."

We clinked glasses and drank. I ate my tostada. It's not easy to eat with clenched teeth.

"What did Zaitlin want?" He lustily shoved food into his mouth.

"How did you know it was him?

"Saw his name on your phone."

"You don't miss a thing, do you? I told him about Ben. He said you would handle it."

"Let's hope there's nothing to handle. I like Ben." He broke off a hunk of tostada shell, dipped it into the salsa, and stuffed it into his mouth.

"So I take it you were in the military?"

He nodded, chewing. "Army CIU."

"What's that?" I glanced out the large plate-glass window. No cab yet.

"Criminal Investigation Unit."

"And who did you investigate?" Feigning interest. "The enemy?"

"The bad guys. Ours."

I was genuinely surprised. "You mean *American* soldiers?"

"There are always a few bad apples looking to scam, to earn a buck on the side."

"How?"

"One guy was selling arms our men had confiscated from the Taliban back to the Taliban. CIU wasn't too popular among the rank and file, even though they might agree with what we were doing. They always felt we were there to spy on them while they were getting their asses blown off by IEDs. And they were right."

"They must've been confused about which side you were on."

His head jerked back slightly. I had hit a nerve.

Finally, the cab arrived. I gave my lips a ladylike dab with the napkin and put it down. Then I grabbed my purse and slid out of the booth, glaring down at Heath. Raising his head toward me, he stopped chewing, balancing in midair a neat pile of chicken, lettuce, avocado, and sour cream on his fork.

"You're right," I said in a low controlled voice. "I don't like men who order for me. I don't like men who lie to me. And you may have the biggest security firm in the world and help out a few people who can't afford you, but to me you're just another Hollywood player. A fixer getting paid the big bucks to clean up other people's shit. The army trained you well."

I felt his eyes burning into my back as I stalked out of the restaurant.

౿

Feeling miserable, I slouched in the corner of the taxi's back seat as the driver careered onto the freeway, honking his horn, tailgating, and mumbling to himself in a language I couldn't make out. I thought I'd feel vindicated walking out on Heath, but I didn't. Even though I had every right to. And now I was heading to my meeting with Zaitlin and Jackson, where I was probably going to have the proverbial rug jerked out from under me. Worse, I knew what was going to happen. Christ, how pathetic is that? But I had to play the game because if I didn't, there might not be the possibility of the next movie, the next role. Possibility and hope is what actors lived on.

Once we got onto Laurel Canyon, the cabbie was lost. I had to give him directions all the way into West Hollywood.

I took out my compact and checked my face in the mirror. Ignoring my sad tired eyes, I put on lipstick and lightly patted a little powder onto my shiny forehead and chin.

"You're an actress," the driver said in his thick accent.

Purposely avoiding his reflection in the rearview mirror, I brushed my hair.

"An actress," he persisted.

"Yes." I snapped.

"How much farther to this Formosa place," he complained.

"We're almost there. See the awning?"

"I don't know how to get anywhere in this town. I despise it." He pulled up in front of the café and hit the brakes.

"Wait here," I said. "I won't be long."

"I should've asked for more money. I'm always getting cheated."

"Welcome to Hollywood."

CHAPTER EIGHTEEN

The Formosa Café smelled of egg rolls and ghosts. Over the years the mahogany wood bar had been smoothed to a shadowy glint by the famous hands and elbows of Hollywood's heaviest drinkers. The Chinese décor, created with a set-designer's flamboyance, was bathed in a soft pinkish-red light that made all its patrons look younger. At least I had that to be thankful for.

At this time of day the place was almost empty except for a lone man at the bar and a couple huddled in a small both drinking their way through an affair. In a larger booth were Zaitlin, Beth Woods, and Jake Jackson, watching me walk toward them.

Jake, who was on the end, jumped up. "God, you look great, Diana."

The compliment of death, I thought. "Thank you," I said.

I slid in next to Zaitlin. Across the table from us was Beth. The spiked ends of her short henna-red hair looked as dull and blunted as useless knives. She took a long nervous draw from the straw in her Mai Tai. Jake sat back down next to her. The remains of pot-stickers, ribs, and rumaki lay cold in their dishes. Dipping sauce splattered the tablecloth. Zaitlin and Jake were nursing hot tea from small cups.

"We've been interviewing actresses for Jenny's part." Jake's voice was glazed with a Southern drawl.

I nodded and smiled.

"Would you like something to drink?" Zaitlin asked, attempting to ease the situation.

"No."

A faded Boston Red Sox cap was pulled low over Jackson's shaggy blond hair, shading his slightly crossed blue eyes. Somehow young girls and the camera loved him. He was the new Paul Newman, the new Robert Redford, the new Matt Damon, the new Owen Wilson, the new Ryan Gosling. He was new, new. Making me feel old, old.

"Jake has another commitment," Beth said, finally looking at me. "We have a short period of time to finish shooting his scenes."

"Where's Heath?" Zaitlin asked looking around.

"The last time I saw him he was in Camarillo, eating a chicken tostado and watching out a restaurant window as I got into a taxi. That reminds me, the driver's waiting for you to pay him." I could still feel Heath's eyes burning into my back.

Zaitlin gaped at me. "You took a cab all the way from Camarillo? How much is that going to cost!"

"I don't know. Traffic was a bitch."

"Goddamnit, Diana." He leaned into me, struggling to get his wallet out of his back pocket. I could see he had shaved unevenly and what hair he had left was beginning to sprout on his usually smooth cranium.

He pulled a wad of money from his wallet and handed it to Beth. "Pay the cab."

"I'm going to need him to take me back to Malibu," I said.

He pushed more bills at her. "Tell him to wait."

Jake stood up again to let her out.

"I'll drive you home," she told me.

"It's out of your way," I said.

"No, no. I'm glad to do it." She hurried toward the entrance.

"Don't let her order another Mai Tai," Jake said as he sat back down. "I can't stand women who drink too much. They get mouthy." Jake's crumpled shirt hung out of his jeans. Except for his expensive Patek Philippe watch, you'd never know he was worth millions. He slouched down in the booth, moody under his cap.

"What else can't you stand, Jake?" I asked.

"Diana . . ." Zaitlin warned under his breath.

Jake adjusted the bill of his cap like a baseball pitcher right before he throws at his opponent's head. "This wasn't an easy decision for us." His cupid lips drooped in sympathy.

"We haven't cast anyone yet. First we have to cast Jenny's role," Zaitlin explained into his tea.

"You were brilliant in the part, Diana," Jake said, "but it was the urn. Everything would've been cool if it weren't for you and the urn on the news. I mean, I just can't get my head around the image. And I don't think the public can either. Every time you appear on the screen they're going to think . . . *urn*."

"You mean you couldn't' get *your* image around the image."

He lifted his new, new chin. "There's no reason to make this personal."

"You're an actor. You know exactly how personal it is. Or have you forgotten so quickly?"

I knew it was coming. But there is no way to prepare for the moment when the floor drops out from under you and you're freefalling through your own career, unable to grab hold of any-thing to stop the inevitable—rock bottom.

"Jake didn't have to be here," Zaitlin said. "He wanted to tell you himself because he respects you as an actor and as a human being."

Ignoring that piece of crap, I asked him, "Did you contact Sam?" Sam Haskell was my agent.

"Yes," Zaitlin said. "But he wanted me to tell you."

A coward for an agent. Why am I not surprised? "I guess my own agent doesn't respect me as much as Jake does."

Jake was taking his sunglasses from his shirt pocket and slipping them on.

Beth returned, taking in our glum group. "I see they told you."

"Yes."

"I was against it, Diana. I think you're wonderful in the role."

"Where's my change?" Zaitlin asked.

"There isn't any, and stop treating me like your gofer."

"See what I mean about the drinking?" Jake got to his feet once more. "Well, I'm glad we got this all cleared up. I know we'll work together again, Diana." Then he said to Zaitlin and Beth, "Catch you later." And the new, new was gone, gone.

Zaitlin patted my hand. "I'm sorry. But one door closes, another opens. That's how I look at this business. That's how you have to look at it too."

"Did you fight for me?"

"He did," Beth said, still standing.

Now Zaitlin edged around the booth. It was only then that I noticed how tired he looked. He pulled himself to his feet as if he were an old man. He spotted the check on the table. "You'd think the little prick would pick up the tab, wouldn't you?" He grabbed it and went to the bar to pay.

Beth sat down and sucked up some more Mai Tai.

"Are you going to be able to drive me?" I asked.

She pushed the drink away. "Yes." With the focused intensity of a woman who sees life through the frame of a camera, she watched Zaitlin pay, put his wallet back into his pants pocket, and trod heavily out of the restaurant. "He doesn't look good, does he?"

"No, he doesn't. Neither do you. It seems Jenny's murder has taken a toll on all of us, one way or another."

"Do you have time for me to have a cup of coffee?"

"I'll have one, too."

She got the waiter's attention and ordered. I broke into tears.

"Oh, Diana, I'm so sorry." She reached across the table and held my hand.

I shook my head. "I've been crying a lot lately."

"You're a good actress. I think you're better than your mother was at your age. You won't have any trouble getting work."

"What if other people are like Jake and can't get their head around the image of me holding my mother's ashes? If I tried hard enough, I could blame her for all this and not Jake Jackson."

"He's full of shit, and you know it. He'll be gone when he's thirty."

"Not soon enough."

Our coffee arrived. The waiter gave me an extra napkin and whispered, "For your tears." Which made me cry even more because I was sure he assumed I was crying over a man and not my career.

"I may not have another job after this one either," Beth said. "You know the gender politics in this business. How hard it is for a woman on the other side of the camera." Beth reached for her Mai Tai and took another long suck.

I blew my nose and wiped my face. "Oscar Wilde said that when people talk about the weather he always thought they meant something else."

Beth let out a throaty laugh. "Are you saying I'm not really talking about how difficult it is for women in Hollywood?" She paused, then admitted, "You're right. Jenny's death has taken a toll on me."

"How?" I asked.

"I screwed up. Something good happens, and I find a way to destroy it. I hit on her, Diana."

"It happens."

"I degraded myself. I groveled." She downed the last of her Mai Tai, not bothering with the straw.

I took a sip of my coffee and once again reminded myself never to order coffee in a Chinese restaurant. "Why are you telling me this?"

"Because you were one of the last people to speak to her."

"If you're worried she said something to me, she didn't."

"But if the police find out."

"From what you told me there's nothing to find out. Making a fool of yourself is not against the law. Yet."

"But rejection can be a motive." She took the tiny paper umbrella from her empty glass and twirled it in her fingers. "I guess seeing what Jake did to you has freaked me out. Let's go before I order another drink."

∽

Even tipsy, Beth Woods drove better than the cab driver.

"Forget what I said back at the Formosa. Okay?" She smoothly shifted the gears of her dark blue 911 Porsche as we headed west on Santa Monica Boulevard. The traffic was bumper to bumper. In the daylight her skin looked puffy. Her brows too dark, too arched, for her pale worried face.

"But why would you think Jenny had told me about the two of you?"

"I thought she might try to use me in some way so Zaitlin wouldn't fire her."

"In what way?"

"Forget I brought it up, Diana. I talk too much when I drink."

"Zaitlin had no intention of firing her."

"Why not?"

"I just learned her father was backing the film. Did you know that?"

"Yes, but I didn't think he had that much control. I mean, he's only one source of the money. There are other backers, including the studio."

"One pulls out and they don't get somebody else, the movie stops dead. You know that." Being a director, Beth dealt with the finances of what it would cost to make the movie the way she wanted to shoot it. And then she compromised. "At Ben's party you told me that Jenny was evil."

"Maybe I thought she was evil because she made me feel like shit."

"Have you talked to the police yet?"

"No. But they'll get around to me."

"Do you have an alibi?"

"What lonely woman has an alibi for . . . when was she killed? Twelve or one or two in the morning?"

"Why are you so lonely?"

"Why are you?"

We grinned wryly at one another, then laughed. Female humor. My iPhone rang. I took it out of my purse and looked at the caller ID. It was Celia.

"Hi," I answered in a guarded voice.

"I'm sorry, Diana, I was so mean to you and. . . . Oh, God, my entire life is falling apart. Can you meet me at the Bel Air house?"

"Why?"

"The pool man found a dead body there."

"Oh, God." My permanent chill woke up.

"They want me to see if I can identify it. I didn't know who to turn to. I can't involve Robert. He's so distraught over this Jenny Parson thing. I don't have anybody. I'm just now realizing how empty my life really is. I have no right to ask, but I need your support. I'm almost at the house now. I have to go." She disconnected.

"What is it?" Beth asked.

"An emergency." I looked out the window. We were passing the old Troubadour, where many famous folk singers got their start. Now scraggly young men stood outside the club, guitars slung over their backs, hoping something from the past would rub off and give them a future.

I didn't want to help Celia. I wanted to go home and nurse my own wounds. Hold my own hand. I sighed. "Can you take me to Bel Air instead?"

"Where in Bel Air?"

"On Stone Canyon. I'll show you."

She didn't ask me what the emergency was; in fact she didn't talk at all after I gave her the name of the street. And I didn't believe her sudden muteness was due to her Mai Tai wearing off.

CHAPTER NINETEEN

was back on Stone Canyon Road again. The gates to Bella Casa were opened and the street was filled with black-and-whites, fire trucks, and ambulances. The men and women who manned the emergency vehicles were preparing to leave.

Beth stopped the car near the curb. "My God, what's going on?"

"They found a body."

She stared at me. "What's it have to do with you?" she asked.

"Nothing. I'm here to help a friend."

She peered at the ivy-covered wall and the two entrance gates now with yellow crime-scene tape draped across them as if it were familiar to her.

"Do you know this place?"

"No. Who's your friend?"

"Celia Dario. The house is empty and for sale. She has the listing."

"Zaitlin's mistress?"

"Small world, isn't?"

"No. Just a cruel one."

"Thanks, Beth." I got out of her car.

She waved, threw the Porsche into drive, made a U-turn, and sped off.

I strode officiously up to the patrolman who guarded one of the gates. "I'm Diana Poole, I'm here to see Celia Dario." Then taking a big chance, hoping she was on this case, I added, "Detective Spangler knows me."

He mumbled something into a walkie-talkie, then said, "You can go in."

He released the yellow tape as if he were an usher letting me into the reserved section at a screening. I started up the drive. Patrol officers leaned against their cruisers. The ME vans waited with their back doors hanging open. No one bothered me.

There was too much activity by the front door so I veered off onto a brick path that led behind the house. Heading to the indoor swimming pool, I stopped dead. A few feet away a uniformed officer stood with his back to me, legs apart, staring out at the dusky unruly garden. It took a few moments for me to realize he was taking a piss on a Bird of Paradise plant. Taking advantage of his reverie, I dashed to the swimming pool door and went inside.

I hurried around the pool. Opening the louvered doors, I stepped into the gallery and followed it into the dining room. In the middle of the room was an antique crystal chandelier that had once hung over a long table where I used to eat alone. I ducked under it and paused, listening to voices coming from the kitchen.

"You looking for another dead body?"

I whirled around. "Hello, Detective."

Detective Dusty Spangler sat on a folding chair next to a built-in marble-top buffet. Wearing her gray slacks, navy blue jacket, and a pink button-down shirt, she didn't bother to look up from the forms she was filling out. "Homicide always comes down to more paper-work." Scribbling her name at the end of the page with a flourish, she got to her feet, put the forms on the buffet, then reached into her jacket pocket and took out a Snickers bar. "Want one?"

"No, thanks."

"You look like you could use something to eat. But then every-body looks that way to me." She patted her belly. "Take it. I have another."

I unwrapped the Snickers while she found the other one in her jacket pocket and did the same. We stood eating the candy, assessing each other. She was right, I did need it.

Finally I asked, "Why do you make me feel guilty?"

She popped the last bite into her mouth. Still chewing, she answered, "Maybe because you used my name to sneak into a murder scene."

"I came to see my friend Celia."

"She's in the living room."

"Thanks." I started to go there.

"One sec."

Reluctantly, I turned around.

"I saw you on TV this morning, leaving your house. You were get-ting into a big Mercedes-Benz limo." She raised her blond, defiantly un-plucked eyebrows. "*Parson's* big Mercedes-Benz limo."

"He wanted to know about his daughter's death."

"Where was he? On his yacht? My partner and I just got back from visiting him at his house in Montecito."

I nodded.

"Come with me," Spangler said in her flat Kansas voice.

She walked me through the familiar kitchen. The place I would sneak down to in the middle of the night with one of my mother's sleeping pills, which I had stolen from her, growing sticky in my hand. I'd make hot chocolate laced with Irish whiskey, then down the pill with the delicious drink. I couldn't sleep then either. Now uniformed officers, beefy arms folded across their chests, leaned against the tile counters, talking shop while appraising me.

Spangler opened the back door and we were in the side yard. Lights had been set up to fight the growing darkness. A cold California dampness was settling in.

"Excuse us here." She guided me around the forensic technicians in their protective clothing. "Step where I step," she ordered.

We stopped near a collapsed outdoor umbrella leaning against a stucco wall overgrown with ivy. Slumped against the same wall was a man's body, his long legs extended in front of him on the grass. He was clad in black jeans and a navy blue T-shirt. The hood of his gray-sweat zip-up covered most of his sandy-colored hair. "You know him?"

The candy bar welled up into my throat. I swallowed it back down. "No, I don't."

He was young with the kind of good looks a kid could rely on to just get by. But now his skin was as gray as his hoodie, a dark stain spread across his chest, and his amber eyes stared blankly down his splayed legs to his boots.

"He's Zackary Logan. Dead about three hours. Shot in the chest. Name ring a bell?"

"I said I didn't know him."

"I'm asking if you've heard of his name." She moved closer, her belly pushed at me, forcing me to take a step back. "Maybe you even mentioned the name to Parson?"

"No and no." But I thought of the kid in Jenny's garage caught on the security camera with his hood pulled down over his face. "You think Parson had something to do with this? But he's in Santa Barbara. When did he have the time?"

"He only needs to make a phone call." She took a brown leather notepad from her jacket pocket. It had the same embossed insignia on the cover as the one Heath had read his notes from on the yacht. She noticed me staring at it.

"A gift."

"What's the CIU stand for?" I asked, even though I already knew.

"Criminal Investigation Unit for the Army. Couldn't wait to get out of it. The rank and file hate you. Feel you're spying on them. But when I got home, the experience put me on the fast track to become a detective."

"Were you in Iraq?"

"Afghanistan."

"Then you must know Leo Heath."

She actually blushed, and it made her look ten years younger. "Runs a security firm. Good guy. He gave me this."

So she was his source, I thought, as she looked over her notes.

"You know a P. J. Binder?" she asked.

"No."

"Pool man. He discovered the body. He says he knew your mother."

"A lot of people think they knew her."

"He cleaned the pool when the two of you lived here. He remembers her."

"I was fifteen, sixteen then. Are you saying he still cleans the pool at this house?"

"For about forty years. Celia Stone says the current owners rely on him, as did the past ones, and many of the neighbors in the area. Highly recommended."

"The 'mislaid man,'" I said, remembering.

"What?"

"That's what my mother called him. He's a Vietnam vet."

"Trust him?"

"I never met him. He'd come around four in the morning to clean the pool. She'd go talk with him. That's all I really know."

"Four in the morning. That's early."

"I guess he couldn't sleep."

"Why did she call him the mislaid man?"

"I never asked her. I wasn't that interested in what she did back then. May I see Celia now?"

She appraised me as if I were an exotic bird. "Novices usually can't handle viewing dead bodies. You did very well. In fact, you even kept your Snickers down."

"Did you give me the candy bar as some kind of test?"

"No. You looked hurt and hungry. You can go see your friend now. Wait a minute." She turned to a female cop. "Take her to the living room. She can see Celia Dario." She smiled at me. "Don't want you wandering off contaminating any evidence."

ॐ

The policewoman returned me to the dining room and watched as I opened the double doors onto the living room. Her profile to me, Celia sat on an old purple velvet sofa that ran parallel to the empty fireplace. There was no other furniture. A five-tiered, wrought-iron chandelier hung from the dark wood-beamed ceiling, shedding a patch of dim filigreed light over the sitting area and leaving the rest of the vast room in shadows. I closed the doors behind me.

"Celia." My voice echoed off the thick white stucco walls. My heels tapped on the walnut wood planks.

"Oh, Diana you came." She rose, extending her arms toward me. We hugged, then sat down on the sofa, each at one end. An awkward coolness settled between us. Wearing jeans and a sweater, she looked shaken. Her bruise had lightened, yellowing her cheek.

"I'm outta the movie," I finally said.

"What? Oh, God, I'm sorry. Robert wanted to keep you."

"I know he did. Where'd this couch come from? Looks like early-brothel."

"It was the only piece of furniture the owners left. I guess they thought it warmed the room."

We smiled, but it was obligatory.

"The police showed me the body," she continued. "Why would they think I'd know who he is . . . was?"

"It's what they do. How did he get in?"

"I don't know. Why would he be killed here?" She clasped her hands tightly.

Not having any answers, I pulled my gray leather jacket more closely around me and stared into the soot-blackened fireplace. Acanthuses were carved in relief on the limestone surrounding. My mother and I and the man who I had given myself to by the pool had once roasted marshmallows in it. Mother was desperate to create the fantasy of a holiday family. A Norman Rockwell sleaze-bag was a stand-in for my father. A man we had both screwed. "Look!" she had exclaimed. She held her firm white marshmallow, speared on a long-handled fork, over the flames, watching it shrivel and sag. "It's like seeing a beautiful face age in seconds." She watched the sleaze-bag pop his gooey blob into his mouth and added darkly, "And then they eat you up." And I knew she'd been talking about herself.

Celia reached over and took my hand. "I'm sorry I got so angry at you."

"You need to tell me why," I said.

The double doors opened and Spangler strode in.

"Later," Celia whispered.

"I'm pooped. Do you mind if I sit?" Spangler gestured to the small space on the cushions between Celia and me, and squeezed her wide rear end into it. Now all three of us sat jammed thigh-to-thigh and shoulder-to-shoulder.

Grinning, I said to her, "You're very theatrical in your own way."

"Am I?" She was pleased. "Maybe it's because I work the West L.A. Division. It kinda rubs off." She glanced sideways at Celia. "I just have a few more questions. You said the house has been empty for almost two years. Why is that?"

"The market. Houses like this that need work are not big sellers right now. And the owners won't come down in price."

"Does anybody ever use the house?"

"As I said, the owners live in Italy. Genoa."

"That's where the salami comes from. Do they have a son?"

"They have no children. They're an elderly couple."

"You never saw signs that the house might have been used for parties? Kids find a way of getting in and using empty homes for all kinds of things."

"There's a gardener, a pool man, and a cleaning crew that comes in when we need them. They've never said anything. I've told all this to your partner."

"The kid has keys on him but none of them fit any of the doors to this place. So somebody had to let him in."

"Or the person who killed him could've taken the key," I said.

"That was next on my list. Now why would the murderer do that?"

"I don't know but the kid, the body, looked more like a man to me," I said.

"You're right, Zackary Logan was twenty-eight according to his driver's license." She swiveled her head back to Celia. "How'd you get the bruise?"

Celia touched her cheek. "It has nothing to do with . . ."

"Then you won't mind telling me."

"I fell. I was a little tipsy. I was wearing very high heels."

"I tried a pair of those on, and I couldn't even stand up in them let alone fall down. Where did you take your tumble?"

"At home. I hit the edge of the coffee table."

"Had to hurt." She extricated herself from between us and stood, pulling her blazer down and adjusting her thick blond stub of a ponytail.

"It happened two days ago," I said, hoping to make it clear to Spangler that Celia's bruises had nothing to do with the dead man in the side yard.

Glancing up at the chandelier, she said, "I can tell even in this light that they're not fresh." She thought for a moment. "Jenny Parson was murdered two days ago. Thank you, ladies, you can go now."

CHAPTER TWENTY

t was dark when Celia drove me down Sunset Boulevard to the ocean. Her hands moved nervously on the steering wheel. "Why did Spangler make that comment about my bruises and when Jenny Parson died? She's an idiot. And what's with the Country Bumpkin in Hollywood routine?"

"I think she knows exactly what she's doing," I said.

"Do you remember when we were sixteen and driving down Sunset in your mother's Mercedes convertible, music blaring, sun in our hair, picking out mansions that each of us would live in when we were successful, madly in love, and married?"

"Gwyn was with us then."

"Sitting in the back seat."

I thought of Gwyn's chameleon-like eyes appraising me in the rearview mirror. It was the same jealous expression she'd had when her son, Ben, had kissed me at his birthday party.

"You chose a tiny clapboard house with a brick walk lined with pansies. Gwyn and I thought you were nuts."

"I chose it because a movie star would never live there."

"I picked that big Spanish house with the rolling lawn because it was grand and had great curb appeal. Everyone could see it from Sunset."

"Gwyn picked the old gracious white house with the conservatory."

"The one that the son of a wealthy Arab bought and put up naked statues all around the property which pissed off the Beverly Hills elite!"

We laughed, a weak imitation of the gusto we'd had back then.

Before I married Colin I had searched for that little clapboard house but it was long gone; an ersatz mansion stood in its place. Celia's beautiful sprawling 1920s Spanish house was still there with its rolling lawn and the same palm trees dipping toward the red tile roof. Gwyn's old gracious white house with the conservatory had burned down. The son of the wealthy Arab had fled the country.

"Heath said he didn't hit you." I stared straight ahead.

"We had such hope back then, driving down Sunset, didn't we, Diana?" she asked plaintively as if I hadn't said a word.

"We had youth."

"I had hope." An oncoming car spread a bleaching light across her bruised face.

"Did you hear me, Celia? Leo Heath says he didn't hit you. Is he lying?" I persisted.

A sob escaped her lips. She swerved off onto a side street and stopped, tires bumping into the curb. Her head drooped forward against the steering wheel and she wept.

I waited, looking out the window at a dark residential street dotted with the yellow glow of porch lights.

"Ben," Celia finally gasped. "It was Ben Zaitlin."

I closed my eyes, wanting everything to stop.

"That's why I couldn't tell you," she said.

I opened my eyes.

Celia had straightened up and was wiping her face with her sweater sleeve. "I'm so tired of crying."

"So am I."

She shook her long dark hair and breathed deeply. "I was afraid if I didn't give you a name, you'd call 911 or the police or make me go to the emergency room. I know you, Diana, you don't stop." She gripped the wheel so tightly that her knuckles looked as if they would pop through the taut skin of her hands. "I knew Heath, or whoever he said he was, wasn't interested in buying the house. I thought you and I would never see him again. And you have to admit he looked like the kind of guy that might batter a woman. I needed you to believe me. I was desperate." She turned toward me, her face twisted with grief and damage. "I'm sorry I lied to you, but . . . I couldn't tell you. I was afraid Robert would find out. And God knows what Gwyn would do. And you're probably not going to believe me, but I wanted to protect Ben, too."

Again I remembered Ben telling me that he had discovered his father had a mistress; and asking me if I had gone to bed with his father and then his defiant kiss. I'd never once considered the anger that drove him to ask that question or to kiss me.

"It's all changed," she continued. "My relationship with Robert. I can feel it. Everything I've built my life on. And now there's a man shot at Bella Casa. Say something, for God's sake, Diana."

"I don't know what to say."

"Ben made me feel ashamed. Do you remember when I screamed at you that I deserved to be hit?"

"Yes."

"I meant it. I mean, I deserved it from Ben's point of view. From how he felt I had it coming."

"Celia."

"No. Let's stop all the bullshit, Diana. I'm taking his father away from his mother as far as he's concerned. He's young. He discovered his family is a lie. You think kids are more sophisticated today, but they're not. He didn't know how to accept it." She let out a jagged sigh. "And why should he? So I could live the kind of selfish life I wanted?"

"Tell me how it happened."

"He called and asked to meet me. He was at that place called The Den. It was around eleven-thirty at night."

"The night Jenny was murdered."

"Yes. He asked if I was alone. I'd just gotten home from having dinner with Robert. I didn't tell Ben that. He said he had to talk to me. No, he said he *needed* to talk to me. He begged, Diana. He wanted to come to my place, but I said no. He gave me the name and address of a bar. He said no one would see us there. And he was right. It was a vacant lot. When I drove up, he was leaning against his car waiting for me."

"Why didn't you drive away?"

"He's Robert's son, and he wanted to talk. That was very important to me. Can't you understand?"

"I think so."

"He apologized for the location, said he couldn't think of any place where we wouldn't be recognized. Then he got into the passenger seat of my car. And the rest is as I described it to you earlier."

"You mean he just started hitting you without saying anything?"

She shook her head. "He said 'I don't know what to say to you.' Then he reached over as if he was going to rest his hand on my shoulder. Instead, he was on me, kissing me, and suddenly he was hitting me harder and harder, screaming 'bitch' at me. Then he stopped and just stared at me as if he'd never seen anything so ugly." Her voice broke. She took a deep breath and continued. "Finally he jumped out of the car and drove away in his. I hadn't expected him to . . . I don't know what I expected. I really believed we'd have some cathartic meeting where we could talk and that I might even become his friend." She let her head flop back against the headrest and closed her eyes. We sat for a long time in the dark.

Then she asked, "What are you going to do about what I've told you, Diana?"

A deep sorrow, not for the dead but for the living, engulfed me. "Nothing. It's all been done."

CHAPTER TWENTY-ONE

I t was about eight o'clock when Celia dropped me off. The paparazzi had disappeared, thank God. Drained, I unlocked my front door and walked into the dark living room. The TV in the kitchen was still repeating the news over and over like an idiot savant. Reaching for the lamp switch by the sofa, I felt cold damp air and the ocean sounded louder. The sliding glass door was open—but I hadn't left it that way.

I jerked my hand back from the light switch, leaving the room unlit. Not moving, I listened in the darkness. After a few moments I heard a drawer slam shut in my bedroom. Shaking, I crept across the room and grabbed one of Colin's Oscars. The sound of heavy scuffling footsteps came down the hallway.

Ducking out through the open sliding-glass door onto the deck, I pressed back against the side of the house and held the award upside down, ready to swing the heavy base at the intruder. I was breathing hard, as if I'd been running.

Peeking through glass into the living room, I watched the shadowy figure of a large man emerge from the bedroom. I ducked back out of sight, trying to decide what to do. I could go to Ryan's for help, but he'd probably be drunk and useless. I still had my purse on my shoulder. As I fumbled inside for my cell phone, the light in the living room went on, illuminating the deck. I froze until I realized the intruder couldn't see me. Carefully leaning toward the open door, I peered in.

Ryan Johns was bent over my side table, rifling through the drawer. What the hell was he doing? He straightened up, running a freckled hand over his face. He turned and eyed the bookcase next to the fireplace. Rushing to it, he began pulling out books, opening the plastic cases of CDs and DVDs.

I slipped into the room as quiet as one of my ghosts on the mantel. "What are you looking for, Ryan?"

At the sound of my voice, he almost leapt out of his Uggs. "Jesus, Diana, you scared the shit out of me."

"What are you doing in my house? No! Not just in my house, but searching through it like a burglar?" I dropped my purse on the floor.

He nervously wiped his hands on his gray faded T-shirt, which said: PEACE ME. "You should let me buy you a security alarm that works. I mean, anybody could break in."

"Ryan!"

"Looking for a disc."

All my sadness, fear, rejection, and anger burst to the surface in one perfect rage. "You want my CDs? Here!" I strode over to the shelves. With the Oscar still in one hand, I began picking up the square plastic cases with the other and hurling them at him.

"I can explain. Ouch! That hurt!" He weaved and ducked from the onslaught. Grabbing one of the sofa cushions, he held it up in front of him. "Stop it, Diana. Stop it!"

Running out of discs, I took my heels off and threw them at him one by one.

When the barrage finished, he peered over the edge of the cushion at me. "Are you finished?"

"Yes," I gasped.

He dropped the cushion he'd been using as a shield onto the sofa. Instantly, I threw the Oscar. He screamed as it sailed past, barely missing his head, and bounced off the wall behind him, leaving a dent. It landed hard on the floor. "You could've killed me and look what you did to Colin's Oscar." He picked it up and blew the dry-wall dust off its little gold pate.

"I've had it, Ryan! I don't think I can take any more. Tell me what you're doing here, or I'm calling the police!"

"Oh, God, Diana, don't do that. You know me. I'm an honest man. I wouldn't have broken into your house unless . . . unless . . ." He fell onto the sofa, the Oscar still in his hands. "I'm in trouble."

"Go on." I slammed the sliding glass door closed and locked it.

His mouth went slack. "I'm a dead man if I don't find it. A dead man."

"Find what?" I grabbed the Oscar from him and returned it to the mantel.

"Would you believe me if I said I don't want you involved in any of this? Can we just leave it at that?"

"You don't want me involved, yet you're in my house searching for something. That makes me think I'm already involved."

He stared guiltily down at his knobby knees. "I didn't know Jenny was Parson's daughter when I. . . ." He drooped back against the sofa, letting his legs splay out.

"When you what?" I sat down next to him.

"I thought she was a hooker. I was drunk. It was dark. I was taken somewhere, and she was there. Waiting for me, like I was told she would be. Naked, beautiful."

"You paid to have sex with Jenny Parson?" My mind was reeling.

"I tried to pay up front. But she said afterwards was fine." He sat up, suddenly righteous. "That should've been a dead giveaway. You always pay up front."

"What did you do?"

"What do you mean, what did I do? I thought she was a hooker! When it was over and I was fumbling for my pants and my wallet, she told me to put my money away. Then she got up and seemed to literally disappear into the darkness of this vast room. I heard a man's voice. I thought she was talking with the guy who had brought me there. Then she returned still naked with a nifty Canon camera and showed me the video of the two us *in flagrante delicto*. I can't believe how clear she and I looked in the dimly lit room. It's a great little camera with HD . . ."

"Ryan!"

"Sorry. She told me who she was and that she would show the video to her father if I didn't pay her three hundred thousand dollars."

"Jenny Parson was blackmailing you? And you owed her father money, too? I can't believe this."

"*You* can't believe it."

"Parson had me taken to his yacht in Santa Barbara this morning."

He shifted uneasily. "What did he want with you?"

"I discovered Jenny's body, remember?"

"He didn't say anything about her and me, did he?"

"No. He just said he wasn't worried about you paying him back. Why do you owe him money?"

"Diana, that's not the problem right now."

"You said Jenny threatened you with showing her father the video. Do you think she knew about the money you were supposed to pay him?"

"I don't know. I don't know anything. Except if I don't find that CD and destroy it before it goes viral and Parson sees it, he'll have me killed."

"Wait a minute. Why would you think I have it?"

"Last night you said you talked to her alone in her trailer. People trust you. They talk to you. I thought she might've given it to you for safekeeping without telling you what it was. I had no place else to look. I can't get into her condo or her car. The police put those off limits."

"Why would you assume she made just one disc? And even if she did, the memory card could still be in her camera. You should be looking for both." I got up and went into the kitchen and turned the light on and the TV off. Then I opened the freezer and took out a low-cal fettuccini Alfredo dinner and put it in the microwave.

Hands clasped on top of his head, Ryan stood in the doorway. "How can you eat at a time like this?"

"I'm hungry." I was also trying to think. To put pieces together. But there were so many that I didn't know where to begin.

"I need a drink."

I gestured to the cupboard that held the hard stuff, then opened the refrigerator, grabbed a bottle of white wine, and poured myself a large glass. Ryan filled a water glass with whiskey. The microwave beeped and I grabbed my food with a potholder and dumped it on a plate. It looked like puke. Then I sat down at the kitchen table and began to eat.

Drink in hand, Ryan sat opposite me. "What is that?" Disgusted, he peered at my plate.

"Swill."

"Diana, you need to get a life." He took a long gulp.

"I need to get a life? Life is crashing down on me. The latest is I'm off the movie." I shoved a forkful of fettuccini into my mouth and chewed, glaring at him.

"That's fucked. Was it Jake Jackson?"

I swallowed and ignored the question. "You have a perfect motive for killing Jenny."

He straightened as if jolted by a shot of electricity. "What?"

"You didn't think of that?"

"No. No. I didn't. Oh, God, I'm *fucked*. If this gets out, Parson will have me killed. That is, if the police don't arrest me first. You're right, I'm the perfect suspect." He slopped more booze into his mouth.

"Where were you the night she was murdered?"

"I don't know when she was killed."

"Night before last, around twelve-thirty in the morning, or at least that was when she drove into her condo garage."

"I was home. Asleep on my deck. I have the sunburn to prove it." He displayed the peeling skin on his arms. "*You* left me out there."

I thought about staggering down the beach to Celia's house. I did see Ryan asleep. "I saw you, but I'm not sure of the exact time."

"What are you saying? You don't think I killed her, do you?"

Instead of answering, I washed down another mouthful with my wine.

"Do you think I'd tell you what I did with Jenny, if I were her murderer?" he demanded, indignantly. "Give me credit for being a little smarter than that. I write movies about these things, for God's sake."

"I don't know who to believe anymore." I stared down at my almost-empty plate. I wanted to lick it. "Parson told me he knew Colin. Why would he know him?"

Ryan dropped his head so his forehead touched the rim of his glass. "A lot of us writers and actors would go up to Santa Barbara and hang out with Parson." He raised his head and looked at me. "It was sort of like hanging out with someone like Hugo Chavez when he was alive. You know, mixing it up with the bad guys that can't really hurt you. Or so I thought."

"How could he hurt Colin?"

"I don't think he could. Colin went once while you were away on location. You can't trust Parson. He could just be saying that he had something on him to gain control over you."

"I'm going to ask you again. Why do you owe him money?"

"That's my business," he said with a strength I didn't know he had.

"You'd protect Colin, wouldn't you?"

He glanced away from me. "He had everything: two Oscars and you."

"Oh, Ryan." I put my hand on his. "Are you protecting him now?"

"I have no need to."

Unsure, I got up and put my plate in the sink and poured myself more wine.

"Do you know if they found a camera in Jenny's condo?" Ryan asked.

"I didn't see one, but that doesn't mean there wasn't one. Spangler wouldn't tell me if they did find it."

"Spangler?"

"The homicide detective on the case. Has anyone from the police contacted you?"

"No."

"Maybe the camera wasn't hers. Maybe someone else has it." I leaned back against the sink and took a sip. "Jenny didn't need money. Why would she blackmail you?"

"How do I know? I'm just an innocent bystander. If they find that camera, I'm going to be implicated. I could even be arrested. Thank God we live in a community that doesn't look down on things like this." He actually looked earnest.

Ryan didn't exactly have a fully working moral compass. Did any of us?

"You may not be the only desperate person they recorded." I wondered whether Beth Woods had been taped also.

"You're right. There could be others." He brightened. "Others that had a reason to kill her besides me."

"Who took you to meet Jenny?" I asked

"I'm not sure. He didn't give me his name."

"Where were you taken?"

"A house."

"You can remember the camera that was used but not who drove you or where you had sex?"

"Let me think. There was a sofa in this big empty living room. She was lying on it. Spooky but exciting."

I tensed. "A purple velvet sofa?"

"I wasn't looking at the fabric. I was looking to get laid."

"Was the house in Bel Air?"

"Could be. I was drunk. I wasn't paying attention to where I was being taken or who was taking me. This guy just kept talking about how hot she was and how ready she was for me."

"Did the house have an indoor swimming pool?"

"Yeah! I remember he had to unlock a side door, and then we walked around the pool and into the house." He frowned. "How did you know?"

"Lucky guess." The fettuccini felt like a block of cement in my stomach.

"Have you been there? Are you being blackmailed too?"

"I lived there with my mother for a while when I was a teenager."

"I don't understand."

"How did you get home from Bel Air?"

"The same guy. And the only thing he said to me was, 'Jenny means it.' And then he dropped me off at my car."

"How were you supposed to get her the money?"

"He'd contact me."

"Did he?"

He nodded. "Two weeks ago. He phoned. He told me on a certain day at a certain time to put the cash in an envelope, then put it in my mailbox and leave the house."

"And did you?"

"Yes. And when I came back the cash was gone."

"And what did you get for that in return?"

"Their silence."

"Oh, Christ, Ryan."

Desperate, he asked, "What do you think?"

"I think you're a dead man."

"Oh, God." He rocked back and forth on his chair like a child. "Oh, God." Then he abruptly stopped and glared at me. "You're extraordinarily calm about all this."

"I've just seen two dead bodies. I've lost my part in Zaitlin's movie. And I'm angry." I paused. "Do you know a Zackary Logan?"

He shook his head. "Who is he?"

"About your height, thinner, hair the color of sand, twenty-eight years old. Handsome in that kind of bland actor's perfect-headshot way."

"Sounds like a lot of guys in Hollywood."

"They found his body at the Bel Air house where you had sex with Jenny. Could he have been the one who drove you there? Who took your cash?"

He blanched. "I *am* a dead man." Tears rolled down his red cheeks. "Dead Man Crying." He got to his feet. "I have to go home. I have to think."

"You need to talk to Detective Spangler."

"I need to work this out in my head first. I need time."

He stumbled out of the kitchen. I followed him outside to the deck.

He turned to me and pleaded. "You won't tell anybody, will you? Promise?"

"I promise," I said, remembering how my oath to Celia had worked out.

After he left, I went into the bathroom and threw up the swill, the wine, and the Snickers bar. Then I sat on the floor, leaned against the shower door, pulled my legs up to my chest, and rested my head against my knees.

I thought about Celia trying to find love on her own terms. But it never happens that way. There's always a Ben to remind you that other people have terms, too. I thought of Ryan's insatiable urges leading him to Jenny Parson, Bella Casa, and blackmail. And what about Beth Woods? Did Jenny have a video of her groveling? Jenny, who told me she couldn't play-act or pretend. Yet in the ugliest way she was play-acting, and she could have been murdered for it. Using the rim of the toilet bowl, I pushed myself up and stood in front of the mirror. I looked like hell.

I took a shower, brushed my teeth, crawled into bed, and turned on the TV—Bette Davis was blowing smoke. I popped a sleeping pill.

Waiting for it to work its magic, I stared at the ceiling and wondered why Jenny would use Bella Casa for her blackmail scheme. Keep the answer simple, Diana, like acting. Don't overthink it. Don't overact it. Maybe she used the house because it was empty and she had a key to it.

When mother and I lived there, we had a master key that unlocked the main door and other exterior entrances except for the swimming pool door. We had a separate key for the pool man. That way he didn't have access to the interior of the house. That is, if the connecting door that led into the gallery was kept locked.

Ryan had told me he was let in through the pool area, not the front door. That meant Jenny didn't have the master key. She had access to the house only through the indoor pool. So who would have that key? Celia and the pool man. Selling keys to homes of celebs or the wealthy in order to have a duplicate made was hardly unheard of. But Celia had everything to lose and nothing to gain by doing that. But what about P. J. Binder, my mother's "mislaid man"? The one who found the body.

I grabbed my iPhone and Googled his name. I found the address of P. J. Binder's pool-supply company.

Then I called Ryan. "I want to take control of my life; do you?"

"Huh?"

"If so, come over here around ten tomorrow morning."

"Will this help my . . . situation?"

"Only if you're not the murderer." I ended the call and waited for the dark soft blanket of sleep to wrap around me.

CHAPTER TWENTY-TWO

There are two kinds of pool men in Southern California: the free spirits and the dark spirits. Both drive pickups with scoopers, long-handled nets, and plastic bottles of chlorine rattling around in the back. The free spirits work just long enough so they can afford to surf, windsail, hang-glide, or just hang out for the rest of their lives. The darker souls are the haunted ones, like the vets who have returned from Iraq or Afghanistan. They clean your pool before the sun comes up and then disappear.

P. J. Binder was in the second category.

There were only a few paparazzi waiting for me when Ryan and I drove away in my Jag the next morning. I would soon be off their radar completely.

About an hour later I pulled into a space in front of a one-story building with *P. J. Binder Pool Cleaning & Supplies* painted in large blue wavy letters on its façade.

As Ryan and I got out of the car, the hot valley air slammed against me. We were in an industrial section near Pacoima. There were some other stores: a metal shop, a fencing company, and an auto-parts dealer. But mostly the buildings were boarded up, the empty lots were littered with trash, and rusted grocery carts lay on their sides here and there.

Ryan squinted at a new red BMW convertible in a parking slot that had Binder's name on it. "Expensive car."

I glanced across the street. Waiting by the curb were two paparazzi. Straddling his motorcycle, one wore a white helmet that shone in the sun like a giant Q ball. His darkened visor was flipped down. The other's helmet was black as a giant 8 ball, and his visor was also down. Cameras were slung across their bodies on straps.

"The fame suckers must've followed us from my house. Just keep walking," I told Ryan, turning my face away from them.

He immediately turned his back, dropped his Bermuda shorts, and bent over, wiggling his big, round, pale bottom at them.

"Jesus Christ, the last thing I need is to be seen standing next to your fat ass. Grow up!" I ran for the pool-supplies entrance.

He loped after me. "I sometimes wonder what's in it for me to grow up."

"How about not being arrested for murder, or not having Parson order one of his goons to beat you to a pulp for screwing his daughter! Now zip it."

"I won't say a word."

"I meant your fly." I threw open the door.

Inside we approached a blond-colored faux-wood counter. A woman in her mid-twenties sat behind it, tweeting, texting, or sexting. Peering down, her bleached white hair cascaded over part of her face as she expertly touched the tiny keys with long nails painted cement-gray.

"With you in a sec," she said, not bothering to look up.

The wall behind her held sagging shelves displaying dusty gallon-size bottles of cleaners and numerous gadgets to keep pools purified. Three rattan chairs with high-fanned backs lined another wall. A ceiling fan slowly turned, blades wobbling, feebly trying to stir the stale air.

The young woman hit SEND and smiled up at us, flipping her hair back from eyes heavily lined in black pencil. "What can I do for you?" Her lipstick was the same color as her nails.

"I'd like to speak with Mr. Binder." I took off my sunglasses.

"*Daaad . . . dyyyyy!*" she yelled at the top of her lungs.

Ryan lurched back from the counter.

She cocked an eyebrow at him. "Hung over?"

"Jesus, don't you have an intercom system?" he complained.

"What do you think this is, Home Depot?"

The door next to the chairs opened and a man in his late sixties with a thick gray beard, and shoulder-length hair to match, stepped from his office.

"You want me?" His voice sounded like two rocks rubbing together.

"Mr. Binder?" I asked.

"Yep." His belly, the size of a small bag of sand, filled his faded blue work shirt.

"We're here about the house in Bel Air with the indoor swimming pool." He looked like a man you needed to be direct with.

"Know nothing about it." He started to go back into his office.

"I think you cleaned that pool a long time ago. You knew my mother, the actress Nora . . ."

He turned slowly and faced me again. "Nora?" His weathered face softened as he studied me. "You must be her daughter Diana."

I nodded.

"Come on in."

We followed him into a small room decorated with a large metal desk, an American flag on a stand in one corner, and a rifle hung on the wall behind his desk.

"Take a seat," he gestured,

We sat on two folding chairs.

"Sorry to hear about your mother." He settled into a worn leather chair that had one arm missing and a jean jacket hung on the back. "She was damn good to me." He grinned, baring yellow teeth.

Not another one who had an affair with her, I thought. Since I had never seen him, I tried to imagine him younger but there was no shadow of youth in his worn face.

"So what can I do for you?"

"I know you discovered the corpse at the Bel Air house. Could you tell us what you told the police?"

"I saw you on TV. You discovered that girl's body."

"Jenny Parson."

"And now you want to know what I told the police about another dead body."

"That's right."

"You in trouble?"

"Yes!" Ryan blurted desperately.

"I was asking her," he said, eyeing Ryan suspiciously.

"Let's just say my life has become very complicated since I found Jenny Parson, and I'd like to un-complicate it."

"Dealing with one corpse isn't enough for you?"

"You might be able to shed some light on the death of Jenny Parson."

"You think the two are connected?"

"They could be."

He shook his head. "Sorry, but I can't help you."

"You said my mother was good to you. How?"

His eyes shined with memories. He *was* having an affair with her.

"Your mother talked about her career, about work, as if it could save a person. Make them whole. She never once asked about the war." His brown eyes fell on Ryan. "That would be 'Nam."

"I assumed by the rifle." Ryan crossed his bare legs importantly. "M-21, right?"

Binder warily took in his curly red hair, Bermuda shorts, Hawaiian shirt, and Uggs. "Right. Sniper rifle."

"Accurate up to 750 yards. Light armor piercing and equipped with a Leatherwood 3x-9x adjustable ranging telescope." Ryan sounded like a college student listing what he had memorized for a test.

"You shoot?"

"No. Only write about them."

"You write about guns, but don't shoot?"

Ryan nodded. "I write screenplays."

"Do you now?" Binder tapped an impatient, blunt finger on a pile of invoices.

"Guns are props in my world," Ryan continued blithely. "Sometimes I can even turn one into a metaphor. I just can't use the word metaphor in front of the producers because it scares them. You know, it doesn't matter what you do, just don't scare the horses." He laughed as if Binder shared his inside knowledge of the quirks of the men who got movies made.

Binder squinted. "Well, this gun is loaded with a round of reality in case some asshole comes in here and tries to metaphorically rob me."

Ryan moved uneasily in his chair.

"I remember she called you the 'mislaid man.'" I hoped to get him back to Nora and maybe helping us. "She didn't mean it in an unkind way."

"I never took it to be mean-spirited. She was my angel." Reflecting, he stroked his beard. "She'd come down and talk to me while I was cleaning. Seems she couldn't sleep either." He began to restack the already neat pile of invoices, then cleared his throat. "It took me a while to realize that this beautiful woman, this movie star, was talking me back into the world."

"She never told me."

"You look a lot like her. Are you as good of a woman as she was?"

"I try to be." I suddenly felt this man could see right through me to the lie I had just spoken.

He leaned back in his chair, resting his hands on his belly. "So you're probably wondering how the dead kid got onto the estate."

"Yes."

"And my connection is I have a key to the indoor swimming pool and I know the gate code."

"Exactly," Ryan said. "And I might add that's a very expensive car you drive."

I leaned toward Binder. "We're not saying you've done anything illegal . . ."

But Binder was fixed on Ryan. "You know, son, I'm sometimes at a party or one of my AA meetings and I find myself counting the number of people in the room. It's almost habitual with me. Every time I do, it turns out I've killed more people in war than are in that room. So you in your Eskimo shoes means nothing to me."

Backtracking, Ryan said "BMW is a great car."

Binder ignored the comment. "And now, you, who mean nothing to me, is saying I sold some snot-nosed kid a key so he could make a copy of it, and then I could what? Buy my own building? Buy my Beamer? That's a pretty magical key."

"I apologize for Ryan. He was out of line. In fact he's always out of line." Ryan snorted; I continued. "What I'm wondering is whether there's a chance one of the men who work for you sold it for a little pocket cash. You do hire other pool cleaners, don't you?"

"I do, but I screen them thoroughly. Most of them are vets like me. That's all I've got to say."

"It's important to me, Mr. Binder."

"I'm afraid you're wasting your time and mine."

"My mother helped you in your time of need." I'd always prided myself on being independent from her, and now I was relying on her, using her.

He pursed his lips, thinking. When he spoke his voice was firm. "I clean that pool myself, not one of my guys. Except I get there now around three o'clock in the afternoon, not before dawn, like I used to. I need my sleep. Age has caught up with me, even tired out some of my demons."

"Isn't that a lot of years to be cleaning the same pool?" I asked.

"I have a few houses where I've stayed on for close to forty years. The owners have changed but I always get recommended to the new ones." He adjusted his gaze to glare at Ryan. "And the reason for that is they trust me."

"Did you know the victim?" I asked. "His name is Zackary Logan."

"Never saw him before. Told the police the same. Why would anybody want a key, anyway?"

"Access to an empty house. They could throw parties, deal drugs, or loot the place." I decided not to mention that they could also video people having sex and then blackmail them.

"I told you that I'm the only one with the key, and I never saw any evidence of such goings-on."

"Do you ever go inside the house?"

"Of course not. So I can't help you there. Except I did find a condom once."

Ryan sat up. "When? And where exactly was it?"

"In the container for the garden waste about a month ago. I remember because I was wondering it if it should be put in the trash or the recycle. That just shows you how these environmental little bastards can get into your head."

"Didn't you think it was odd to find a condom at a place that'd been empty a while?" I said.

"No. Someone could've tossed it over the wall, and the gardener threw it away with his clippings."

"Did you tell the police about it?" Ryan gnawed nervously on his thumb as if were a drumstick.

"Didn't think it was important." Binder grinned maliciously at him. "You want me to tell 'em?"

I interrupted. "Did Celia Dario hire you?"

"The real estate woman? No, the owners hired me."

Deciding I wasn't going to get any more information from him, I stood and extended my hand. "It was nice to finally meet you." We shook hands.

"Same here. Too bad you brought the asshole with you."

"I'm not always like this, I'm under stress." Ryan stood up just as the door opened behind us.

We turned, watching the young woman with bleached white hair and cement-colored lips saunter in with a plate piled with vegetables and rice. She set it in front of Binder.

"What's this crap?" he demanded.

"Your lunch, Daddy. If you don't eat it Mommy's going to be very upset with you." She wagged a finger at him, then kissed him lustily on the mouth and swayed out of the room.

Noticing our surprised expressions, he said, "I know I'm too old for her. When she told me she was a vegan I thought she said virgin." He chuckled to himself. "What do I have to lose except eating meat?"

We walked out past the receptionist's desk and through the door into the blistering sun. Across the street, the paparazzi were waiting.

"Ignore them," I warned Ryan as we got into my car. I put down my window. "That was a bust. We didn't learn anything that we don't already know."

Buckling himself in, Ryan said "They didn't take the money shot."

"What?" I started the engine and pulled out of the driveway past the two fame suckers.

Ryan looked back at them. "They should've taken pictures of me, famous screenwriter, mooning them, and you, sexy actress, discoverer of dead bodies. They didn't."

"You're right." I rounded the corner onto the main drag, heading back to the freeway.

Ryan asked, "Do you think that condom was mine?"

"Did you use one?" I looked in the rearview mirror. No paparazzi.

"I can't remember."

"God, Ryan."

"DNA. My DNA is probably all over that sofa. The police are going to find it."

"They have no reason to check the sofa for your DNA. And even I know they have to match it to something to be sure it's yours."

"Binder has to be lying," Ryan decided. "He's got a young girl-friend and a red Beamer. That's called overhead. He's got to be selling keys and codes."

"I don't think he's lying."

"Why?"

"I just don't think he'd take money for a key, especially that key."

"Why not?"

"My mother." I could feel my emotions coming undone.

"You mean because she may have gone to bed with him?"

"Because she may *not* have, Ryan." I snapped. "She may have done just what he said—helped him."

I realized I wanted to think of her as caring for the "mislaid man." I wanted to find a way to love her. I looked into the rearview mirror again. The guy wearing the white helmet was leaning low over his handlebars speeding close behind us.

"What's the word for a single paparazzi?" I asked.

"Paparazzo. The term comes from a character's name in the movie *La Dolce Vita*. Paparazzo was a photographer who took pic-tures of stars by hiding in bushes and stalking them. He was based on a real person Fellini knew. Why?"

"Look behind us."

He craned around to peer out the back window. "There *is* only one."

"You're right, Ryan. They should have taken the money shot." I gripped the steering wheel more tightly. I checked the rearview mirror again. The guy on the bike was right on my tail.

CHAPTER TWENTY-THREE

P ressing down on the accelerator, the old Jag surged forward. I swerved into the other lane.

Ryan clung to his seat belt. "So if they're not fame suckers, then they're . . . ?"

"Parson's men?"

"Oh, shit, Diana. I am a dead man."

I made a sharp turn onto a narrow neighborhood street. The biker did the same. Small bungalows fronted by patches of brown grass lined the uneven sidewalks. Plastic tricycles stood in a few of the yards like lawn ornaments. I slowed down; so did he.

"Where is the other guy?" Beads of sweat dotted Ryan's forehead.

"Maybe he wanted to find out from P. J. Binder what we talked about. He might still be back there."

The street emptied out onto a busy four-lane avenue. I sped up again, racing past old one-story stucco buildings housing barbershops, bleak bars, and bail bondsmen fighting for space with McDonald's, Taco Bell and Burger King. I ran a yellow light and glanced in the rearview mirror. The biker was so close that he looked like he was connected to my bumper. Moving in and out of the traffic, I cut in front of a bus and swung a right, tires screeching, then quickly made a sharp left.

"Not into an alley!" Ryan stiffened his hands pressing against the dashboard. "They always dead-end into brick walls."

The biker was still there in my mirror.

"Look out for the garbage cans," Ryan gasped as we careered by iron-gated back doors.

"Oh God," I blurted, slamming on the brakes.

"Fuck, a brick wall! I *told* you. I told you." Ryan braced himself against his seat.

It rose up in front of us like a big YOU'RE DEAD sign. I pressed the brake pedal to the floor. Rubber burned. The wall loomed closer. The Jag made a grinding noise as it veered and skidded to a jolting halt, its hood inches from the bricks. We pitched forward and then backward.

Adrenalin pumping, my eyes darted to the rearview mirror again. I watched the bike tilt sideways, sliding down on the pavement as it flew toward us.

"He's going to smash into us," I warned. There was a loud thump as the bike hit us and the Jag lurched again, bumping the wall.

"Perfect. We've killed one of Parson's men." Ryan craned around, looking out the back window. "Unless he *was* paparazzi and then we could be sued."

"I don't care anymore." I flung open the car door and got out.

His white helmet on and visor down, the man had been thrown against a pile of garbage bags. Grabbing at his leg, he writhed in pain. His bike lay half under the car.

"Who are you?" I stared down at him. Ryan came up behind me, peering over my shoulder.

"You fucking bitch. You broke my leg." He struggled into a sitting position, leaning against the rust and piss-stained wall.

Extending below the knitted cuff of his blue windbreaker, I could see two words tattooed vertically down to his wrist: With You. The thug at the yacht had had a tattoo that read: One Night With You.

"Tell Parson to leave me alone," I ordered.

He lifted his face guard so I could see his cold eyes. "I should kill you right now."

"Diana, let's not irritate him," Ryan whispered in my ear.

"What does Parson want from me?" I demanded.

"What he always wants now. Information about his daughter," he said through clenched teeth.

"Where's your partner?"

"He left."

"He's talking to P. J. Binder, isn't he?"

"Fuck off." The guy squirmed and moaned, his right hand reaching behind him toward his lower back.

Ryan bolted from behind me and stomped his foot down hard on the man's arm. The biker groaned and swore. Ryan and I stared at each other, both of us startled by his bold action. Then I moved quickly and reached under the man and grabbed the gun from his waistband.

"Glock. 47." Ryan said, still pinning the man's arm to the asphalt.

"Move the bike, Ryan." I pointed the Glock at the biker as Ryan loped toward the motorcycle.

"I thought you guys were pros," I said. "But you're not even as good as Ryan and me." I glanced quickly at Ryan. Grunting, he had the bike righted and was wrestling it toward the side of the alley. I looked back at Parson's lackey.

His emotionless eyes were riveted on me. "You're dead," he said in a flat voice.

I knew he meant it, but I kept my voice and the gun steady, continuing to talk as if no threat hung in the air between us. "Rule number one in acting. If you're playing a photographer, pretend to use your camera. You should've taken the money shot."

Turning on my heels, I got into the car and slammed the door. I stared at the thug's gun in my trembling hand. The grip felt a little big and I wondered if they came in different sizes, like tennis racket handles. Ryan slipped in next to me. I put the weapon in the glove compartment and started the engine.

"You're going to keep it?" Ryan wiped sweat off his face with a crumpled paper cocktail napkin he'd found in his shirt pocket.

"Yes." I threw the car in reverse.

"Can't you turn the heat off?"

"No."

As I backed the Jag slowly down the alley past the thug our eyes met for a chilling moment. And I knew he was watching me all the way, letting me know he would be seeing me again. Finding an opening in the traffic, I swerved backwards onto the street and put the car into DRIVE.

"Do you believe what I did?" Ryan beamed.

"You saved us." I smiled gratefully.

"I did, didn't I? Shouldn't we be going the other way?" He shifted in his seat.

"I'm going back to Binder's place. We may have unintentionally gotten him involved in this whole thing."

"This is crazy, Diana. Turn around." His bravery had disappeared as quickly as it had appeared. "We're artists," he pleaded. "We create situations like this, we don't live them. That's for. . . ." He waved a hand in the air. "Other people."

"Get used to it, Ryan. We're other people now."

CHAPTER TWENTY-FOUR

sped into the pool-supplies lot and slammed on the brakes. The red Beamer was still parked in its place, but there was no sign of a motorcycle.

"The others guy's not here. Let's go," Ryan said.

"If you didn't want to be seen, you wouldn't park your bike in front, would you?"

"Yes, I would." He tried to look sincere.

I retrieved the gun from the glove compartment.

"Oh, God, Diana, don't take the gun."

"Come on."

Squinting in the sun, I gestured to a narrow path that ran beside the pool supply store. "Check it out."

"For what?"

"The bike."

Constantly peering over his shoulder as if an assassin waited on every roof, Ryan hurried to the path, then rushed back to me. "What if I told you there was no motorcycle hidden down there?"

"Writers are terrible actors. What happened to your new-found bravery?"

"An aberration," he said as we headed for the entrance. "We could get killed! I mean with real bullets, real knives, real bombs, real fists, real pain. Keep that thing pointed toward the ground!" With his fingertips he pushed the muzzle down. "I need a drink."

I peered through the dusty front window; nothing looked disturbed. Slowly, I edged the shop door open. Inside, the whirring of the overhead fan was the only sound. The young woman with gray nail polish and lipstick was nowhere in sight, but Binder's office door was ajar.

Pulse pounding, I raised the gun and used my foot to open the door wider. Ryan pressed close. I could feel the tension in his body. Or was it in mine? I slid inside the room. A few feet away from me lay a black helmet and a gun. The biker, sitting up against the back wall of the office as if he had been blown there by a strong gust of wind, had a hole in his chest the size of a grapefruit. A bloody trail on the wall showed where he had slid down.

"Oh, shit," Ryan murmured, turning ashen. "We're not in Kansas anymore, Toto."

"We never were, Dorothy."

Opposite the corpse was Binder's desk. The chair had been spun away to face the wall. On the floor lay Binder's invoices and white chunks of drywall blown loose by the power of a gun. I moved closer and saw Binder sitting on the floor behind the desk, holding a blood-soaked shoulder. He stared up at me unspeaking, eyes dazed.

I dropped to my knees beside him. "Thank God you're alive." I shouted over my shoulder, "Call 911, Ryan!"

"I already called 'em," Binder managed through his pain.

Ryan grabbed the jean jacket from the floor and crouched beside Binder, pressing it against his wound. He was brave again.

"Where's your girlfriend?" I asked Binder.

"Pearl? She ran. The bastard wanted to know what I told you."

"What did you say to him?"

"Nothing. He talked to Pearl like he knew her. Wouldn't let her leave my office. Kept grabbing at her."

"Like he knew her in what way?" Ryan asked.

"A way I didn't like," he snapped. "The little shit had the swagger of a man who was carrying."

"Do you think he intended to kill you?" I asked.

"I wasn't going to wait to find out. As he pulled Pearl to him, I swung around to snatch my rifle. When I spun back his gun was already out. He shot high, I shot better." He grinned, then winced. "Mommy ran like a dog loose on a freeway. See if you can find her." He leaned his head against the wall and closed his eyes. "I don't want to lose her."

"Stay with him," I told Ryan, getting to my feet. Moving back into the anteroom, I wondered how one of Parson's men, now dead, had known Pearl. The air stirred with the overhead fan. "Pearl!" I called out.

Soft whimpering sounded from behind the receptionist's counter. Walking to it, I peered behind. The young woman was on her knees, hands over her ears, rocking back and forth. Her black eyeliner had smudged and streaked her face. I crouched next to her, easing one of her hands from an ear.

"It was so loud. It was so loud. Is Daddy dead?"

"No. Help is coming," I told her.

"I have to go see him."

I held on to her hand. "How did you know the dead man in Binder's office?"

Her eyes looked away from mine. "I didn't."

"He thought you did. The police are going to be here any minute. Do you want to tell me or them?"

"You won't tell Daddy?" she asked in a low, desperate voice.

"No." I shook my head for emphasis.

"He was a client from way back."

Way back? She had to be all of twenty-five, I thought. "What kind of client?"

"What do you think? But I stopped hooking when I met Daddy. Until. . . ." She fell silent, her lips pressing together.

I thought about a young woman living with an old man who had a key that somebody wanted. "Tell me about the key, Pearl."

She blinked at me.

"Did you have a copy made?"

"You won't tell the police, will you?" She clutched at my shoulder. "I never thought I would miss it. But I did."

"Miss what?"

"The game. It was a lot better at the Bel Air house. The money was good, and some of the men were celebs. We weren't hurting anybody. The men got what they wanted, and I made a little extra cash."

"Did the dead man in Binder's office go to the Bel Air house for sex, too?"

"No. That was a long time ago."

"Who asked you to get the key?"

"Zack."

"Zackary Logan?"

She nodded. "He used to be my pimp. We sort of started out together in our teens. He was looking for a posh kinda place. I told him about the house where Daddy cleaned the pool. I knew it was empty."

"Did you know Jenny Parson?"

"The actress who died?" She shook her head. "But Zack knew her."

"Was she one of his girls?

She bit her lower lip. "Zack bragged about her. I didn't believe him. Pimps always talk big. But I never saw her at the house. I was always alone when I went there."

"Alone except for a celeb and the man with the video camera?"

"No. He never taped me."

"Are you sure?"

"Yes. No. I don't know. Then one day he says I won't be needed anymore."

"Did he say why?"

"He was changing his business plan. Like he really had one. Then he told me to keep my mouth shut or he'd tell Daddy what I'd done there." Her chin quivered.

"Did Zack mention any other names?" In the far distance I could hear sirens.

"Sometimes he'd get calls where he seemed to be taking orders from someone. It sounded like he was talking to a woman. Sometimes he seemed scared."

"He was murdered yesterday."

She recoiled from me. "I didn't have anything to do with that!"

I heard a shuffling sound and glanced over Pearl's shoulder. Leaning on Ryan for support, Binder stood in his office doorway, stooped, holding the bloody jacket against his shoulder.

"You won't tell Daddy, will you?" she continued, unaware of his presence. "I don't want to lose him." She dropped her head and began to cry.

He had said the same thing about her. Staring back at Binder, I thought about the hell Pearl had unintentionally created by going back to her old life and selling a key. And the pain I had just caused Binder because he had heard most of our conversation. The hurt that showed on his blanched face wasn't just physical.

"You two better go before the cops arrive," Binder ordered.

At the sound of his voice, Pearl froze.

"There's no reason for you to be involved," Binder continued. "Or for Pearl. We know nothing about a key. We know nothing about the Bel Air house, you both understand me?"

"Yes." Holding the Glock, I got to my feet.

"I'll tell 'em it was an attempted burglary. Get up, Mommy. Daddy's going to take care of you."

Pearl climbed unsteadily to her feet. Holding out her arms, she went to him.

The rescue sirens grew louder as Ryan and I ran for the Jag.

CHAPTER TWENTY-FIVE

Returning to Malibu, we stopped at our local bar, Kiki's, on Pacific Coast Highway. It was within walking distance to our homes. As I slowed to find a place to park, Ryan leaped out of the Jag, slamming the door behind him, and loped into the lounge.

I found a spot but stayed in the car resting my head against the seat, mulling over what I had I learned. Pearl had sold the key to Zackary Logan who was pimping. She met the clients at Bella Casa, which she had told Logan about. But she wasn't sure if he was videoing her. Pearl also said he'd talked to a woman on the phone, a woman he seemed to fear. Jenny Parson? Then Zackary had let Pearl go, told her he was "changing his business plan." Was Jenny the one who had changed it into a game of blackmail?

I gave up trying to figure it out and checked the messages on my cell. My agent's hyper-energetic voice told me he had set up a reading with Pedro Romero, the director I'd met at Ben's birthday party, for his new movie. Hope shot through my veins. I may have lost my part in Zaitlin's film, almost gotten a nice man killed, found two corpses, but miraculously I was an actress again. And all because of a chance. A possibility to try. I got out of the car and went into the bar.

Removing my sunglasses, I let my eyes adjust to the tranquil darkness. Kiki was a collector of antique surfboards and old hot-air balloons, which he rented out to the movies. It was a small lounge with his boards and fertility-god masks covering the walls. He also was the proud owner of the first bungee jump rope ever used. How he knew its pedigree I could never figure out. It was framed in teak wood behind glass and hung on the wall over the center booth. It looked like a cross between a noose and a decaying cobra. Kiki's was the kind of place where stars, working actors, the locals, and surfers could mingle without getting in each other's way. Tourists were frowned upon. And Kiki could spot one a mile away. But since Kiki's purposely looked like a filthy dive bar, they rarely found their way in.

Ryan was hunched in the black fake-leather center booth. The coiled noose/cobra hung above him like an albatross. An empty Martini glass stood elegantly on a cocktail napkin as he nursed a second. I slid in next to him. A martini with three olives waited for me.

"Thanks." I took a sip. "And thanks for the three olives."

Kiki was sitting at the end of the bar. He raised his ubiquitous cup of coffee to me. I waved back. In his late fifties, he was a small wiry man with skin so tan and shriveled it looked like beef jerky. Tattoos covered most of his body. His ink art consisted of quotes and writings such as: "One day at a time." "Don't tread on me." "God is good, so is Heavy Metal." He called his tattoos notes to myself.

"My agent left a message that Pedro Romero wants me to read for him."

Ryan raised his glass. "That's fantastic. His new movie is about death. You'll be perfect."

I laughed, then we clinked and I drank again.

"If you think about it, Binder saved our asses. We'd have the police and the media all over us right now," Ryan said.

"He did it for Pearl."

"He did, didn't he? Why can't we make movies about love anymore?"

"Have you ever been in love?" The minute the words came out of my mouth I regretted them.

"Yes." He avoided my gaze. I didn't ask him who the woman was, I already knew. Then he said in a forced light heartiness, "Let's run away together, Diana. I have a ton of money. We could hide out where Parson could never. . . ."

"If you have a ton of money, why do you still owe Parson?"

"A debt like the one I have never ends. There's no PAID IN FULL stamp for it."

I changed the subject. "Pearl said she sold the key to Zackary Logan and gave him the idea for using the Bel Air house."

"Do you think Binder knew that?"

"I don't know."

"At least there's no way anybody can connect us to the pool-supply store. Binder will make sure of that."

"There's a man, Leo Heath, he owns a security firm."

"I've heard of him. He helps people out."

"You mean he's a fixer."

"You can look at it that way"

"He's searching for Jenny's killer for Zaitlin. And sharing information with Parson."

"What?"

"Didn't I tell you?"

"No. You mean Heath is looking into this besides the police?" He downed his drink, then raised the empty glass so the bartender could see he needed another refill.

I caught the bartender glance over at Kiki, who gave him a nod, and only then did he begin to fix Ryan another. So Kiki was keeping count on Ryan's number of drinks.

"Did you tell him about me?" he asked.

"No. But Heath isn't stupid, nor is Detective Spangler. Someone will eventually put the so-called robbery at Binder's store and his cleaning the pool at Bella Casa together."

"The Valley's not Spangler's bailiwick, is it?"

"West L.A."

"Then she may never see the report on the shooting. And Parson isn't going to make trouble over losing one of his men. Not with the police anyway. What do we have to worry about?"

"It's not the dead man I'm worried about. It's the one we left in the alley. He knows where we live. And so does Parson. Maybe we should go to the police," I said in a low voice.

Ryan looked stricken. "We've discussed this. You promised not to tell them."

"We almost got Binder killed and Parson's thug doesn't strike me as the kind guy who likes a woman getting the better of him."

"He was hurt. Probably a broken leg. How much damage can he do?"

"He can talk to Parson. I got us in over our heads, Ryan. This isn't what I had in mind when I said we should take control of our lives. The police could protect us."

"Protect us? By arresting me? And you have a reading with Pedro Romero. Going to the police could destroy your chances for a part in his movie. Think of what you've just been through with Jake Jackson."

"There's also Leo Heath. He doesn't have a bailiwick. He can roam anywhere. And he has contacts inside the force. What if he discovers we were the reason for the shooting at Binder's?"

"I heard he never goes public with any information he has. That's why people trust him. We may still be safe."

I chewed an olive, then said, "He may not go public, but he can tell Parson. I don't know if I can go on living like this."

"You have to. For God's sake, Diana, you have an incredible opportunity with a famous director. Go for it. Colin would have wanted you to."

"Christ, your sense of reality is so screwed. I don't think Colin would want me to 'go for it' if it was going to get me killed." Studying Ryan's tense profile, I took a long sip. I put my glass down. "Tell me what Parson had on him."

"Get off this, Diana. I told you, he has nothing."

"Then tell me why you still have to pay Parson off. I have ghosts."

"You told me to leave the dead alone."

"I told you not to compete with them. Actually, Heath told me to leave them alone."

"Take his advice. You're being self-destructive."

The bartender arrived at the table and set down the martini and took away Ryan's two empties. I watched Ryan shake his olives dry over his drink, then toss them on the table. And I knew if I was ever going to get the truth from him, it was now.

"How is my wanting to know what Parson had on my husband self-destructive?" I decided to force the issue even further. Reaching into my purse, I pulled my cell out and set it on the table. "Ryan, tell me the truth or I'm calling Spangler."

"My owing Parson money doesn't matter in any of this." He downed half his martini.

"Getting drunk isn't going to save you." I picked up the phone.

"Wait." He grabbed my arm and shook his head accusingly at me. "Women. You're all the same. You never keep your word."

The candle in the hurricane lamp flickered.

He let go of me and rubbed his face, then he leaned close and whispered, "Remember, you asked for this, Diana. Parson has pictures of Colin."

I could feel my gut turning hollow. "With another woman?"

He nodded.

"Who?"

He blinked his reddish-golden lashes, waiting for me to understand.

"Do I know her?"

He continued to wait for me to get it, to see the obvious.

"Jesus. My mother." I felt limp.

"He met her on Parson's boat. It was just a one-night kind of thing. You were off on location. But Parson's guy, Luis, was secretly taking pictures."

"She won," I said. "All the Berts and the Barts I went to bed with and she won."

"You made me tell you."

I clutched the stem of my glass until it broke in half. The martini spilled.

"Are you all right?" Ryan took my hand and checked it as Kiki hurried over with a bar towel.

"Cheap glasses. I'll bring you a fresh drink, Diana."

"I don't want any more."

Kiki scooped up the bowl and stem of the glass and dabbed at the spill, then hurried away

"No blood, you didn't cut yourself." Ryan let go of my hand. "Diana, Colin and your mother were drunk. It just happened, that's all." He gulped down the rest of his martini. "Parson showed him the pictures and Colin began to pay. He didn't want you to know. He understood that was the one thing you would never forgive him for."

"But it didn't stop him, did it? Did my mother help him pay?"

"According to Colin she wouldn't, in fact she told him not to."

I studied his rebellious red hair, his Hawaiian shirt with the hula dancers printed on it, beckoning me to paradise. "And you helped Colin with the money. And when he died you took over his debt."

"He loved you, Diana."

I gripped his hand. "Oh, Ryan."

I leaned back in the booth and wondered if there was anything in my life that didn't somehow in one way or another belong to my mother. I thought of Colin's memorial service at the Writers Guild. Mother had handled that. I was too distraught. Or had I just let her? "Not because somebody has to care, but because," she'd said, "the man deserves it for trying to be true to himself in a town where nobody knows who the fuck they are. We're all walking into mirrors."

"Do you think Colin was a man who was true to himself?"

"More than most of us."

"My mother thought he was."

"He loved you, Diana, not her. You know that."

"Why didn't he just tell me?"

"Why do you think? Because he knew he'd been in the wrong and he also knew you couldn't handle it. 'The awful emptiness of the truth' is what I think he said. You would've left him. And that would've killed him."

"He was right. I would have." Tears rolled down my cheeks.

"Don't do that, only drunks cry in Kiki's." He handed me a cocktail napkin.

"The blackmail, not being able to pay, not being able to tell me, maybe that caused his heart attack."

"You don't know that." He held his empty glass up toward the bar.

I watched Kiki give another okay and wondered what his cut-off number was for Ryan. Or did it just make Kiki feel important. "You can stop paying Parson," I said.

"He'll find a way to use the pictures."

"What can he do to me now? Take Colin away from me? Ruin my career? Make me hate my mother? The most horrible possibility has been accomplished. Colin's dead. And she won."

"Diana, when are you going to let her go?"

"Colin wasn't true to himself. And he wasn't true to me. But you were."

"I did it for both of you."

"I'm going home. Do you want a ride?"

"No, I'll walk."

"Don't drink too much." I leaned over, put arms around his shoulders, and kissed his cheek. "Thank you, Ryan."

He shrugged in my embrace. The martinis had dimmed his intelligent eyes.

Gathering my purse and phone, I slid out of the booth and stood looking down at him. "Tell Parson to call me when he wants his next payment. That is if he, or his lackey, don't kill us first."

It's always depressing to leave a bar and walk out into the daylight, but this time it fit my emotional state perfectly.

CHAPTER TWENTY-SIX

The tether that held me to Colin had snapped completely and I sat in my car not knowing what to do with myself. I couldn't go home. What would I do? Stare at Colin's Oscars and my mother's urn? Christ. How could she? And I'd been trying to find a way to love her. I decided to go grocery shopping. I drove further up the coast to Ralph's Market in the Malibu Colony Plaza.

Filling my cart with Lean Cuisine, a lot of wine, and the antidote coffee, I thought of Beth Woods telling me that lonely women don't have alibis for the early morning hours. And Celia realizing her life, which she had so carefully structured, gave her no support. And I'd been clinging to eight years of my past for support.

A blond actress I knew from various readings where we'd been up for the same roles pushed her cart toward me. I stood riveted by the freezer cases. Seeing me, she immediately ducked down another aisle. Had she seen me with the urn on TV? Or didn't she want me to see her doing something as humdrum as shopping for dish soap? I caught my reflection in the glass of the freezer door. An un-tethered, abandoned, frightened, forty-year-old child in the clothing of a confident actress. Okay, so it wasn't the urn or her own concerns that made her turn away. It was the expression on my face.

On the way to the cashier I tossed a California Wrap, a kind of healthful gourmet burrito, into my cart.

Now with a bag of frozen swill wedged onto the passenger seat of my car, I was forced to go home or it would defrost.

In the kitchen, I put the food away and poured myself a very large glass of white wine. Taking a few gulps, I opened Colin's office door. I gazed at the computer, the mementoes, the books, and the empty chair that was turned toward me, always waiting for me.

"You bastard!" I threw the wine at the chair and watched the chardonnay run in rivulets down its tufted-leather back and eventually drip off the edges of the seat. "Why her? Why?"

I slammed the door.

Standing on my deck watching the sun make a fiery red dramatic exit, I ate the California wrap. Swallowing it back with my tears, I thought of my mother, Colin, and me sitting out here one summer afternoon drinking Margaritas and chatting about which famous star was better at shooting a gun. Colin had said it was James Cagney. I went for Clint Eastwood. My mother had chosen Bette Davis.

"She killed men while wearing a mink coat and holding a handbag," she said. "And Davis was always walking downstairs toward her male victim, arm straight out, gun unwavering." She'd extended her arm, her hand, imitating a gun, and said in a deadly voice, "Bang. Bang. Bang."

Colin laughed. "No, it's got to be Cagney. When he shot a gun, it was as if he were dancing."

Then I said, "Bette Davis's mother wanted everything her daughter earned. If Bette got a new mink, her mother had to have one too." I looked off across the ocean. "I wonder if that also included her daughter's husbands and lovers."

Turning somber, Nora stared down at her gold-sandaled feet, her blond hair falling across her face. "I need another drink." And even though her glass was full, she went into the kitchen.

I'd closed my eyes against the sun, assuming she'd interpreted my comment about Davis and her mother as Diana not wasting any chance to attack her. So sure of the one person I loved, it had never occurred to me that I'd spoken a truth. Or had I intuited in some deep primal place the truth all along: that my own mother had known what Colin's naked body had smelled and tasted like.

"Diana?" The sound of my name jolted me back to the present. I recoiled back into the shadows of my house.

"It's Heath!" The voice called out louder.

One of the last men I wanted to see. Wiping my tears away, I stepped forward and peered down. Looking up at me, Heath stood on the beach, the wind blowing his dark brown hair, and his graying temples almost silver in the dimming light. "I rang your doorbell. You didn't answer." He wore an expensive suit jacket, jeans, a white shirt open at the neck, and lug-sole shoes too heavy for the sand. He was a man who belonged on cement.

"I can't hear it when I'm out here on the deck," I shouted back.

"We need to talk."

"I'm busy."

"The pool man at the Bel Air house got shot."

My muscles tightened. "What does that have to do with me?"

"I know you were there."

"I'll give you ten minutes."

Inside the house, I sat down on the sofa. Legs apart, Heath stood in front of the fireplace, my ghosts on the mantel lined up behind him. He moved toward me, placing a wrapped piece of candy on the table.

"What's this?"

"Your mint from the Red Pepper Restaurant in Camarillo. Two of them came with the check. I ate mine. That's yours. It reminds me that you and I should be more truthful with each other."

"Really? You go first." I leaned back and crossed my arms.

He returned to his spot before the fireplace. "In Santa Barbara I held on to your cell phone because I knew if you had it you'd do just what you did . . . call a cab so you wouldn't have to drive back with me."

"Why was it so important I drive back with you?"

He ran a finger down the ridge of his battered nose. "To see that you got home safely."

"And?"

"And I needed information."

"Who told you I was at Binder's?"

"I can't tell you. But I know Parson's men were following you. Your turn. What happened at the pool-supply store?"

"I haven't lied to you. I haven't abducted you. I haven't threatened you."

"Parson is a man out of control." Urgency filled his dark-chocolate eyes. "His daughter has been murdered. One of his men got killed and another is very pissed off. And you don't want Rubio pissed at you, Diana."

"Is Rubio the guy with the tattoo?"

"Yes."

"Too late," I said.

"Christ."

"I may have broken his leg. Unintentionally."

"You really don't know the people you're dealing with, do you?" His voice rose with anger. "You can criticize me for what I did in the military while you run home and sit here smug and secure in your little make-believe Hollywood bubble . . ."

"The same bubble you get paid to keep intact for a lot of ugly people."

"I need you to tell me what you found out at Binder's and why one of Parson's men ended up dead. And I need it to be the truth."

I thought of Pearl, who had stolen a key so she could go back to hooking. An old man who loved her. Ryan, who'd had sex with Jenny Parson not knowing who she really was, and who had protected me and Colin by paying Parson off all these years. "I can't."

He let out an exasperated sigh. "Are you trying to save your friend Ryan Johns?"

I sucked in my breath. "Why do you ask?"

He rubbed the back of his neck. "A DVD was mailed anonymously to my office this afternoon. It was Ryan Johns and Jenny Parson having sex."

"Did you give it to Parson?"

"No. I locked it in my safe. Nobody has seen it but me. But that doesn't mean whoever sent it didn't send a copy to Parson. I recognized the purple velvet sofa. It's the same one that's in Bella Casa. Talk to me."

I needed time to think. I needed to talk to Ryan before I even thought of turning him over to Heath.

"Your ten minutes are up."

As I started toward the front door to let him out, he stepped in front of me, blocking my way. "Guilty or innocent of Jenny's murder, Ryan Johns is in real danger. And he's probably not the only one."

"I can't say any more."

The sound of a sharp pop, like an exploding arc light on the set, filled the room. As I looked toward the deck, where I thought the noise had come from, Heath grabbed my shoulders. There was another quick pop and my feet were no longer under me. He was pushing me down. I landed on my back on the floor with him on top. My breath slammed out of me. And then there was nothing, only an eerie silence.

"What happened?" I gasped.

"Somebody just tried to shoot you. I guess Ryan isn't the only one in danger."

My permanent chill sliced through me. "Maybe he was aiming for you."

A hint of a grim smile. "Keep down." Quickly getting to his feet, he stayed low, took a gun from a holster on his belt, and crept toward the deck door.

I rolled onto my stomach and then up on my hands and knees and stared at two jagged bullet holes in the pane of my sliding door. Fissures radiated from the holes like giant, icy spider legs. I felt as fractured as the glass.

Heath glanced over his shoulder at me. "Stay here."

Holding his gun in one hand, he reached out with the other and carefully slid the door to the side. As he did, the glass broke into shards and clattered onto the floor. The damp ocean air billowed in as he ducked out onto the balcony and crouched behind the wicker chair. We both froze in our positions, waiting. Then the roar of a motorcycle, its tires squealing, came from the walkway between my house and Ryan's. I jumped to my feet and ran out on the deck. Heath was already bounding down the stairs. I was right behind him.

With Heath in front of me, we sprinted up the path to the front of my house. The biker had disappeared into the traffic, but not before I glimpsed the back of his bomber jacket and his white helmet.

"I guess Rubio didn't break his leg." I was out of breath.

Heath whirled around, facing me. "You finally ready to talk?" Headlights from the highway spread across our faces.

"Take me to Kiki's bar," I said. "Ryan's there."

CHAPTER TWENTY-SEVEN

t was seven o'clock and the bar was two deep. Over the din of conversation the Beach Boys sang in high-pitched voices about surf, cars, and girls. Instead of Ryan in the center booth there was a young long-haired celeb with great cleavage and the aging record producer Bobby Sanders. Heath followed me over to see Kiki, who was still on his stool at the end of the bar, coffee cup in front of him and a swizzle stick hanging from the corner of his mouth. His nappy peroxided hair covered his head like a badly knitted cap.

"Did Ryan leave?" I asked.

"He's in the back room, sleeping it off."

I sighed with relief. "I've come to take him home."

"I'm glad you care about him. He's a good guy. Come on." Kiki slid off the stool. His legs were bowed as if he'd once been a cowboy instead of a surfer. He pulled himself up to his full height of five foot two, and we followed him through the bar and past the restrooms.

Kiki opened a door to a storage area filled with cocktail-napkin boxes, extra hurricane candleholders, and other necessities for the bar. In the middle of this was a narrow cot covered with a Bird of Paradise print quilt. Next to it was a table with a hula-dancer lamp. The cot was empty.

"Where is he?" I asked.

"He must've left, but I didn't see him go," Kiki observed.

"He could be walking home." But on the way to the bar I'd scanned the highway for a weaving Ryan.

I hurried to the men's room and peered in. Tom Smits, an agent who wouldn't take me on as a client when I returned to acting, stood at a urinal.

Glancing sideways, he gaped at me. "Diana!"

"Have you seen Ryan Johns?"

"No." I took a moment to assess his penis, shook my head, then I stepped out, closing the door. "He's not in there."

Kiki's black-button eyes were wide. "What's going on?"

"You keep your exit door open during business hours?" Heath asked tersely.

"Always," he responded. "You a cop?"

Shaking his head, Heath shoved the door open, and the three of us stepped out into an alley that backed onto a wind-eroded mountain which threatened to slide down on the bar every rainy season. The only illumination came from a rusty lantern hanging from the eaves. Taking a small flashlight from his pocket, Heath shined its intense beam to the alley's left, then to the right.

"What's that?" I saw a dark lump in the middle of the cracked asphalt.

Heath moved toward it, leaned over, and snatched up something that looked like a boot. I sucked in my breath. He retraced his steps, his face harsh in the single overhead light.

"Recognize it?" He handed me an Ugg.

"Yes, it's Ryan's."

Heath turned to Kiki. "Anybody in here earlier who wasn't a regular?"

"We always get a few, but usually they leave after one drink. We don't make 'em feel too comfortable. I gotta protect my clientele. People like Diana need a place they can be themselves and not see it on TV the next day."

"So was there anybody unusual at the bar?" Heath persisted.

"A guy with a shaved head. A Bruce Willis wannabe. But he looked more like an ex-con to me."

"Did he have a blue bomber jacket on?" I asked.

"T-shirt. And he had notes to himself."

"What's he talking about?" Heath asked me.

"Tattoos," I explained, then to Kiki: "Did his ink art say 'One Night With You?'"

"Didn't get close to enough to read it. But it ran down the length of his right arm."

"What time was he in here?" Heath pressed.

"An hour ago, maybe longer. He talked on his cell a lot. I think I should put up a sign: no cell phones allowed. But then everyone would stop coming."

"Where was Ryan when the guy came in and sat at the bar?" Heath asked.

"He was in his booth. And then Mick, bartender, and I had to help Ryan to the back room. Now that I think about it, the guy must've followed us because he came in as we were putting Ryan on the cot and then he asked me where the men's room was. I told him to turn around and he'd fall into it."

"So he knew Ryan was in the back room," I said.

He nodded. "Ryan was passed out by then. When I got back to my place at the bar, this guy was already on his stool talking on his cell again. Then about a half hour later he leaves."

I looked at Heath. "You think he was calling Parson?"

"Telling him where his boys could find Ryan."

"Does that mean Parson got a DVD sent to him, too?"

"Hey, what's going on here?" Kiki asked.

Ignoring him, Heath aimed his light at a dumpster.

I hadn't noticed it there, hidden in the dark shadows of the rocky hillside. Now it loomed up in the glow like a giant coffin. Clutching Ryan's boot, I stepped back and leaned hard against the doorjamb.

"You want to help me look in here?" He gestured to Kiki.

"You kidding? For what?"

"Ryan," I whispered.

"Shit." Like an aged cricket, Kiki hopped up on the side rungs while Heath pulled himself up and over the rim.

I turned away, peering back inside the club. My legs felt weak. If Ryan was in the dumpster, I didn't want to see his body.

Paul Meany, a character actor, came out of the men's room, his hand automatically checking his fly.

"Diana," he acknowledged. Years ago he and I had had a bumbling sexual encounter while he was having an affair with my mother.

"Paul."

"Sorry to hear about your mother. She was a true pro."

"A pro."

"You look great. Are you seeing anyone?"

"Yes."

He stared at the Ugg I was holding, seemed to decide it wasn't worth asking about. "Well, see you later." He headed back toward the bar.

I forced myself to look back at the dumpster.

Soon Kiki's head popped up over the edge like a perverted jack-in-the-box. "He's not in here." His white teeth flashed.

I let out a deep breath and lessened my grip on Ryan's boot.

The two men scrambled out of the bin and brushed themselves off.

"I gotta get back to the bar," Kiki told me. "Anything I can do to help you, just let me know, Diana. They don't call me the major-domo of Malibu for nothing."

"There is something, Kiki. Could you find someone to go to my house and board up the sliding door on my deck? The glass broke."

"No problem. And don't worry about Ryan. He always turns up."

I wasn't worried. I was terrified.

"I'll tell you what I know," I said to Heath, hoping it wasn't too late.

CHAPTER TWENTY-EIGHT

Still clutching Ryan's boot, I sat in Heath's car, which was now an Escalade instead of a Mercedes.

"Talk to me, Diana." He turned in his seat, facing me.

I described everything that'd happened at Binder's; from our first arrival at his office to our return and finding Binder wounded and that his girlfriend, Pearl, had sold the Bella Casa key to Zackary Logan. I also told him what happened after I left him yesterday; the meeting at the Formosa, Beth Woods driving me to Bella Casa, and the discovery of Zackary Logan's body. I didn't tell him about Colin, or Celia and Ben's encounter.

"Sorry about the movie," he said when I finished.

"Thank you."

He drummed his fingers on the steering wheel, then, making a decision, he started the car.

"Would they take Ryan to Santa Barbara?" I asked.

"No, it's too far away. They'll want to question him quickly." He threw the car in reverse. "Parson has a penthouse in a building he owns. He uses it when he's in town. I'll start there."

"*We'll* start there. Where's his penthouse?"

He glanced sharply at me. "9000 Sunset."

"Parson owns that? It's filled with production offices and business managers. My agent's in that building."

"Parson loves Hollywood and its real estate." Backing up, he swung the Escalade around, pointing toward Pacific Coast Highway, waiting for an opening in the line of rushing cars. "Why would Jenny prostitute herself if she didn't need to?"

"I don't think she thought of herself as a prostitute, like Pearl did. She had to be the brains behind the blackmailing scheme. Maybe she wanted to be like her father."

There was a gap in the traffic, and he made a quick left, speeding toward Santa Monica.

"Do you think Parson ordered Rubio to shoot me?" I asked.

"No, I think you pissed him off when you slammed on your brakes and he didn't stop fast enough and banged into your car. That didn't make him look very good." He grinned malevolently. "Image is just as important for hit men as it is for movie stars."

"Great. Another insecure narcissist in Hollywood."

"Except Rubio doesn't knife people in the back. He shoots them."

Shivering, I looked out my side window. The reflection of my gaunt face stared back at me. "Will Parson let Ryan live?"

"They'll want information from him before they seriously hurt him. Everybody thinks it's the pain that makes you talk. But that's not entirely true. It's the anticipation of it, especially if you're a novice."

"Novice?"

"I'm assuming Ryan has never been trained on how to handle torture."

I glanced at Heath and wondered if he had. "So they'll hurt him."

"Yes."

"But he doesn't know anything." I tried not to imagine the horror Ryan might be experiencing.

Suddenly Ryan's house loomed up in the Escalade's headlights, and I knew I couldn't bear living next door if he wasn't there. Slowing, Heath spun the steering wheel and swerved sharply, tires screeching, into my driveway. The Escalade came to an abrupt stop behind my Jag.

"What are you doing?" I demanded.

"I'm dropping you off." Staring straight ahead, his voice was even and without emotion. "You need to be here for Kiki's guy when he comes to board up the broken door."

"I need to *what*? I need to find Ryan! I owe him."

"Diana, I don't know why you owe him, and if I did it wouldn't matter."

"What if Rubio comes back and tries to shoot me again?"

"He won't. He'll be with Parson now."

"How can you be so sure?" I snapped, furious.

"I know these guys. They're like dogs, they need the alpha male." He turned on me, his voice rising angrily. "I don't want you involved."

"I'm already involved, and you're just wasting time."

His face hardened and his lips spread thin. I knew the expression well. I had seen it earlier in Zaitlin's office at Ben's party, and later in the limo going up to Santa Barbara. It was the look that said "I don't know you."

"Get out of the car, Diana." He leaned across me, his shoulder brushing against my breasts, and threw open the door. "Now!"

"Why do I keep walking into the propeller where you're concerned?" I grabbed Ryan's boot, got out, and slammed the door.

As he drove away, I ran down the path and up onto my deck. Stepping over the jagged pieces of glass, I stood in my living room. The cold ocean air rushed through my house as if it didn't exist. As if I didn't exist.

I left Ryan's Ugg on the coffee table and found a warm jacket in the hall closet and put it on. Then I grabbed my purse, making sure my cell phone was in it, and ran into the kitchen. Opening the booze cupboard, I uncorked the brandy, tipped the bottle, and tossed back two slugs.

As it burned through me, I wondered why Heath had given me the address of Parson's penthouse if he'd really wanted me to stay here and take care of the old homestead. He knew me well enough to know that I wasn't going to back off. Was he just hoping I would? Or was he using me in some way?

It didn't matter what he was up to. I needed to find Ryan, and the address was the only lead I had.

I went back into the living room and grabbed the Ugg. Praying that Ryan would still need it, I hurried out to the Jag, jumped in, and opened the glove compartment.

The Glock was still there.

CHAPTER TWENTY-NINE

Taking the curves too fast, I sped east on Sunset, trying to plan what I was going to do when I got to Parson's building. How was I even going to get in? He had his bodyguards. I had a Glock. Somehow it didn't seem to even things out.

Someone once said there are only two seasons in Los Angeles—day and night. In a way it's true. There are no seasonal transitions here, we live in Technicolor, and then we fade to black. And for some reason it makes our nighttime feel more dangerous, more final. I wondered what kind of darkness Ryan was experiencing. I thought of the night blowing through my house. Had I left the TV on? Or was there only the sound of the wind?

I raced through the sedate darkness of Beverly Hills into the garish lights of the Sunset Strip and slowed down. The black glass high-rise at 9000 Sunset rose above the smaller buildings, restaurants, and clubs. It reminded me of the ebony glass tower that Lew Wasserman had built on the Universal Studios lot in my mother's time. A dark reflection of cold power.

I turned down a side street and found a place to park. Opening the glove compartment, I reached for the Glock—then stopped. If I got into the building, Parson's bodyguards would search me and take it away. The gun would make them more suspicious, more watchful. Grabbing the Glock, I wedged it under my seat, thinking it would be easier to reach if I had to escape back to the car. Of course, in the meantime someone could steal the gun because I couldn't lock the damn doors.

I left it and ran up the side street to Sunset.

Peering through the thick glass entrance door, I could see a security guard sitting at a desk that matched the black marbled floors and black marbled walls. The lobby looked like a place of interment. A lone light lit up a laptop, but the guard wasn't interested in it: his head had lolled down until his chin rested on his chest. His uniform was the kind that rented security guards wore. He wasn't dressed like one of Parson's men.

I pounded on the door. His head jerked up, he looked in my direction and waved me away with a dismissive hand. As he settled back into his comfort zone, I used both fists, banging harder. When he didn't react, I stomped my feet and shouted at the top of my voice, "Let me in! Let me in!"

People on the sidewalk hurried past me as if I were a crazy woman and they didn't want any part of me. "When acting the role of a mad woman, always keep a soupçon of reality to your performance," Mother had told me. "Otherwise you're just another ham."

I was all ham now. Pounding, screaming, stomping, and shaking my head so my hair flew wildly. My only fear was that he'd call the police, but if Parson was there I doubted they'd want the cops around.

Still indicating I should get lost, the guard climbed begrudgingly to his feet. From an alcove near the desk a man in a black suit appeared. My hands were beginning to hurt. The two men conversed, then both walked toward me. As they neared, I recognized Gerald, Parson's chauffeur. He knew me immediately and stopped, unsure.

"Open the door," I demanded. I was out of breath but easing back into being Diana Poole. "I have important information for Parson."

The guard looked at the chauffeur, waiting for instructions. Gerald seemed confused. He was a driver, a man used to taking orders not giving them.

"Parson will want to hear what I have to say," I yelled.

He didn't move.

Finally I used the one word I knew would force him into action. "It's about Jenny. His daughter!" I shouted.

Confused, he looked over his shoulder at a phone on the desk, then back at me. Finally he nodded to the guard, who took a bunch of keys from his belt, found the right one, and unlocked the door. But Gerald pushed in front of him, blocking my entrance.

"What about his daughter?" he asked.

"It's personal."

"Tell me. I'll pass it on."

"Really? You think that's what Parson would want?"

"He's not here."

I doubted that, since he was Parson's chauffeur. "Where is he?"

"Not here."

"What's Parson going to say to you when he finds out you wouldn't let me in, but instead asked me to give personal information about his daughter in front of this rent-a-cop?"

Glowering at me over the driver's shoulder, the security guard shifted his weight to let me know how big he was.

I continued my rant. "Parson knows I'm the one who cared about her so much that I went looking for her and found her dead body. Do you think I'd be pounding on this door if it wasn't an emergency?"

Gerald was paralyzed with indecision.

I should have brought the damn Glock so I could shoot him. "How do you think I knew about his penthouse if Parson didn't give me the address?"

He blinked his dull penny-shaped eyes

"All right," I said. "I won't be responsible for what Parson does to you when he finds out how you treated me. And I'm sure you know how he handles people who disobey his orders." I adjusted my purse on my shoulder, flipped my hair back and, taking a big chance, turned and walked away.

"Wait!" The word sounded as if it had fallen from his mouth like a rock. "Let her in."

He stepped back as the security guard opened the door all the way. I was in the lobby.

Now all I had to do was act my way up to the penthouse.

CHAPTER THIRTY

Parson's driver was wearing an earbud. After checking my purse and patting me down, he talked rapidly into his lapel mike. "I got Diana Poole here. She wants to see Parson about his daughter." He paused, listening. "I told her he wasn't here. I'm not going to take responsibility for this. *You* deal with her. She's fucking crazy." He angrily jerked the bud out of his ear, letting it dangle on its plastic wire. He nodded to the security guard. "Let her go on up."

The guard led me deeper into the lobby to a single glossy black elevator. He pressed the button beside it. In seconds the doors slid open. I stepped inside. He leaned in, slid a small key into a slot, hit the button marked "PH"—there were no other floor numbers—and stepped back out. The doors closed with a whisper, encasing me in what felt like a chic coffin. Fighting off creeping claustrophobia, I wondered what I could offer Parson to get Ryan back.

The elevator opened onto a long brightly lit hallway lined with closed office doors. At the end of it a man sat in a leather club chair, his feet resting on a small table alongside his vente-sized Starbucks. His huge thighs pressed against the sides of the chair, and his broad chest bulged under his dark jacket. He peered up from the magazine he was thumbing through and watched as I walked toward him. He wore an earbud like the chauffeur's.

"Turn around and go back. Mr. Parson's not here," he ordered.

"Then where is he?" Clenching my jaw, I kept walking toward him.

He didn't answer. Instead, he sighed heavily, heaved his feet up off the table, and stood. Rolling the magazine up, he pounded it against the palm of his hand. *Slap. Slap.* He looked like a man who was going to swat an irritating fly—and I was the fly.

Acting is all about focusing. If you lose focus, you lose believability with your audience. I had an audience of one, and I needed him to think I was a woman he had to deal with.

Now the table was between us. Never taking my eyes off him, I spoke in a firm voice, "Tell Parson that Diana Poole is here and I have important information about his daughter's death."

Slap. Slap. "Mr. Parson's not here. Give me your phone number. Someone will call you."

"You're going to write my number down with that?" I gestured at the magazine.

The *slap, slap* stopped, and his eyes narrowed menacingly.

I glared back, my heart throbbing. "Parson told me to get in touch as soon as I learned anything new about his daughter's death. He's going to be pissed as hell if you don't let me see him."

"That still doesn't make him here."

As the *slap, slap* resumed, a door to my right flew open. A gaunt woman in her forties with a mass of uncombed auburn hair reached out.

She gripped my arm. "In here."

Surprised, the guard frowned and blurted at the woman, "That door's supposed to be locked from the outside."

Before he'd finished talking, she yanked on my arm and I let her pull me inside. She slammed the door behind us, threw the bolt, and locked it with a key.

The guard pounded on the door. "Open up! Open up, dammit!"

"We don't have much time." Hands twitching, she was terribly thin but had Jenny's sharp, intense animal-like eyes. "I stole the key from that bastard out there, Bruno. They'll have to find another one."

"Mrs. Parson?" I asked.

"Yes. And you're Diana Poole. I used to go to the movies and eat popcorn. That was when I was like other people. Sit down."

She pointed to a long black leather sofa. Behind it, primitive Peruvian statues were displayed in a perfect line on a steel console table. Looking at them, I felt the weight of even more ghosts. Only ancient ones. We sat on the sofa in a sleekly decorated living room with a 180-degree view of the city lights. Our reflections, two desperate women, were superimposed over this panorama.

Bruno had stopped his pounding. The silence felt more dangerous than the constant banging.

Her eyes nervously shifted to the door, then back to me. "I'm being treated like a prisoner. Nobody tells me anything. I was listening at the door. You said you had information about my daughter. What is it?" Her face had been lifted but no burden had been eased. "The only thing I know is that she was murdered and left in the garbage." She shuddered and tears rolled down her sunken face. "Why? Who would do something so awful to Jenny?"

"Is your husband here?"

"No."

"But his driver . . ."

"Sometimes he uses Luis instead of Gerald as his chauffeur."

I thought of the young manservant—Luis—who solicitously watched over Parson on the yacht. Then I said, "I know why Jenny was murdered. I'll tell you, but first I need you to help me. My friend Ryan Johns is missing. Your husband has him. Can you tell me where he is?"

Her body stiffened as she eyed me cynically. "There's always a deal involved."

"I'm trying to save my friend."

She stared at the stony distorted creatures on the table behind us, probably worth millions. "We collect from the dead." Her gaze shifted back to me. "Are you collecting from the dead, too?"

"I told you, I just want to help Ryan."

"I locked myself in here to keep them all away so I could . . ." her voice faltered.

"You said yourself we don't have much time," I prompted.

"I'll tell you where he is, but first you tell me why Jenny was murdered."

I decided I had no other choice. "How strong are you?"

"A dead daughter has given me strength I never knew I had." She held up the stolen key to prove it.

I explained how I had discovered Jenny's body. When I described the sex taping and the blackmail, her face went rigid and her lips drew into a sad bitter line. I didn't tell her about Ryan and Jenny.

She stood and walked to the wall of glass and stared out at the shadowy hills above Sunset Boulevard. Clinging to their steep lots, the houses glimmered with lights.

I rose to my feet. "Mrs. Parson, the guards will be back any moment. Please, I have to find your husband. He'll know about Ryan."

"I watched Jenny change. She stopped loving me."

Her back was to me, and her bony shoulder blades pushed at her white T-shirt. Her tight jeans seemed to be holding what was left of her skin and bones together.

"Now and then," she continued, "her sweet façade would slip, and in its place would be that heartless look of her father's. She admired him, wanted to be like him. I wish his mask had slipped before I married him. He knew he would've lost me if I'd seen who he truly was." She peered back at me. "He's the consummate actor. He makes the rest of you look like amateurs."

The sound of fists banging on the door started up again. This time two male voices demanded to be let in. A key rattled in the lock. But the bolt held.

"Where is Parson?" I prodded.

She stared at the front door as if she didn't know what it was. Now there was the loud thumping of men throwing their bodies against it. The door shuddered. It wouldn't hold for long.

I grabbed her shoulders, trying to force her attention back to me. "Tell me where he's gone!"

"The Rock," she spoke distractedly, as if she had something more important on her mind.

There was the noise of a huge thud against the door.

As it wobbled on its hinges, I said urgently, "I need the address."

"He never took me to The Rock. He took Jenny. When she came back, she wanted to be an actress. Anything he wanted, Jenny wanted."

I shook her hard. "Give me a location!"

"I don't know where it is!" she screamed at me, then took a deep breath, and collected herself. "I do know he goes there for solace . . . or to kill someone. That's probably why Luis drove him. Luis is an expert at killing."

My heart sank. I released her.

The front door buckled and crashed open.

Mrs. Parson quickly tapped the glass wall. It slid open, revealing a narrow balcony and harsh city noises rising up from the street. At the same time, Gerald, Bruno, and the rent-a-cop from the lobby rushed into the room.

"Stop!" I yelled at them. "Leave her alone!"

I whirled back to Mrs. Parson. She was on the balcony facing us, pushing herself up onto the metal railing and sitting precariously with her back to the night.

"What are you doing?" I worked to keep my voice calm. I was about four feet from her but afraid to get any closer.

"What I intended to do all along. Why else would I lock myself in here?" Her hands were a bloodless white from gripping the rail.

"Get down, Mrs. Parson," Bruno said, breathing hard.

Bruno and Gerald moved next to me. The rent-a-cop lingered in the background, nervously pulling at his lip.

"If I die, my husband will kill both of you." Her voice was high-pitched but strong. The truth of her statement froze them in their tracks. She smiled triumphantly as the wind pulled at her hair. "Tell Diana Poole where The Rock is."

"You know we don't know where it is." Bruno spoke in a pleading voice.

"You always lie to me."

"Swear to God, we don't know." Sweat poured from under the chauffeur's chin. "That's why he had Luis drive him. Only him and Rubio know, and they're with Mr. Parson."

"Tell her!" She released her hold on the rail and raised her hands into the air, her thin body swaying back and forth dangerously.

"The Rock, Mrs. Parson, that's all we know." Bruno inched forward again.

"Please get down," I said to her. "This is no way to . . ."

She cut me off. "You don't understand. This is the only control I have left." She grinned at the two guards. "You two bastards are dead."

She leaned back, her legs extending out in front of her, and for a brief moment she looked as if she were resting against a pile of dark pillows.

"No!" I lunged for her.

Bruno rushed after me.

But before we could reach her, she tumbled backward, falling into the night.

CHAPTER THIRTY-ONE

On the balcony, Bruno swung away from the railing and was instantly in front of me, his massive body blocking my way back into the penthouse. His sweaty eyes held mine.

Still reeling from Mrs. Parson's death, I knew if I made one wrong move Bruno would murder me.

Through the open glass wall I could see Gerald in the living room pacing in a small circle, dragging his hands through his dyed hair. "Jesus fucking Christ, Parson's going to kill us!"

Next to him, the rent-a-cop stood, stricken.

Gerald stopped pacing. He had an idea. "We have to shoot her. We can't let her go," he said to Bruno.

"Shut up, you useless piece of shit." Bruno's arm shot out and he clamped a hand on my wrist. My back was only inches from the railing—he could easily toss me over to join Mrs. Parson. But the pain from his death-grip caused my mind to click into gear.

I talked quickly: "Your only chance to get out of this alive is if Parson never finds out I was here." Bruno tightened his squeeze on my wrist. Pain ripped up my arm, but I had his attention. "And you don't want Parson to know that his wife stole the key from you, Bruno. Think about it, if she was locked in properly and jumped off the balcony on her own, you're not to blame."

Unnervingly composed, Bruno assessed me.

"I didn't do anything. I didn't do *anything*!" The rent-a-cop began to cry. "I'm not part of any of this. I get minimum wage."

Gerald jammed his fist into his face. "Shut the fuck up." The man staggered backwards, holding his jaw.

"You don't have much time," I told Bruno. "There are people down there on the street. They've probably already called 911. It'll look bad if you don't call, too."

Bruno said over his shoulder to Gerald, "Do it. Just say a woman's jumped and give the address. Then hang up. I'll call Mr. Parson myself."

He pulled me back into the living room and glared at the rent-a-cop. "Get back down to the desk. When the cops arrive, show them up here. And if you want to go on with your useless life, make sure you don't know shit."

As the man fled, Gerald talked to 911. Bruno dragged me across the living room and out the front door into the brightly lit hallway just as the elevator doors closed.

"You have to let me go, Bruno. It's the only way." I struggled against his grasp.

Pulling me across the hall, he opened an office door. But it wasn't an office. He shoved me into another, smaller elevator. I stumbled, and he lunged after me, grabbing my throat and pushing me with his body against the wall. Fingers digging into my flesh, he leaned his full weight on me, shoving one of his legs between mine so I couldn't knee him. I struggled to breathe.

"Remember one thing." His damp cheek rested heavily against mine, and I felt his hot sweat seeping into my skin. "If Parson finds out you were here or if he thinks you had anything to do with his wife's death, he'll kill you too. Do we understand each other?"

I tried to nod but couldn't. I blinked. Tears formed.

"Push the basement button. The elevator will take you down to Parson's private garage. There's an exit door that'll take you to the street at the rear of the building." With one last shake of my throat, he released me, backed his massive frame out the elevator, and watched me suck for air and fumble for the basement button. I finally hit it.

Plummeting downward, I tried to swallow, I tried to take deep breaths, I tried not to think of Parson's wife falling to her death—the only power she'd had over her husband and her guards.

The elevator came to an abrupt halt, and the doors slid open. Chest tight, I peered out, looking for more men who might be hiding, waiting for me. But there was no place to hide in this windowless, fluorescence-lit room that looked big enough to hold just one limo. There was a steel corrugated garage door. Across from it was the exit. I ran for it, still not knowing where I was heading or how I could find Ryan.

CHAPTER THIRTY-TWO

Sitting in my car on the side street, I heard the sirens from Sunset Boulevard winding down to a whine as the emergency vehicles reached Mrs. Parson's body. The black sky was aglow with the red swirl of their lights mingling with the starker blue lights of the LAPD patrol cars.

God, I didn't even know her first name.

I leaned my head against the steering wheel, frantically trying to gather my thoughts. The Rock was the only clue I had to find Ryan. I took my cell phone from my purse, hit the Google icon, and tapped in "The Rock Los Angeles." I got a wrestler named The Rock, the Hard Rock Café, the city of Eagle Rock, The Rock coffee house and a gem store. I thought of Jenny going to The Rock and, when she returned, according to her mother, she wanted to be an actress. These were hardly the places, or person, for that kind of epiphany. I clicked off.

Come on, Diana, you're a smart woman. Okay, this is all about Parson. Jenny wasn't inspired; she had the part of a lifetime for a beginning actor, and she blew it. She didn't want to be an actress; what she really wanted was to please her father—and he wasn't a professional actor, he was a criminal. She knew she was her father's daughter.

So why did Parson want her to have a career in the movies? Because *he* loved them. He had grown up watching movies. He loved hanging out with movie people, he wanted to control their lives.

I grabbed the wheel tightly. On his yacht Parson told me he used to sneak into a movie house when he was a child. And he would eat the candy dropped on the floor by the customers in order to survive. And if he didn't get kicked out, he'd sleep there. A movie theater was his home, his salvation. But how many years ago was that? Fifty or more? Could the theater still exist?

It might, if Parson had bought it. What had his wife said? "A place to find solace—or kill someone."

Fear for Ryan ran through me, then self-doubt. Was I really any closer to finding him? He could be dead or dying while I sat here putting together Parson's past as if it were a character study for a role I was going to play. Shaking off my uncertainty, I concentrated again.

Old movie houses didn't have names like The Rock. That had to be Parson's personal name for it. I remembered spending a hot boring summer in a small Nebraska town where mother was filming a period movie titled *Gaily, Gaily*. It turned out to be a flop. I whiled away my afternoons in an air-conditioned theater grandly called the Alexandria. The locals called it The Alex. So the Rock could be short for what? The Roscamoor? Rockefeller? Roc . . . Roxy? *The Roxy.*

Excitement stirred in me. I vaguely remembered hearing about old movie theaters called The Roxy years ago. Maybe Parson used the term *The Rock* as a kind of alias for *The Roxy*.

I grabbed my cell again. Parson said he had grown up in Boyle Heights. I Googled the information. And there it was: The Roxy on Figueroa Street, as far away from the wealthy Westside as it could possibly be.

Reaching under my seat, I felt for the gun. It was still there. I quickly started the ignition. The police would have Sunset blocked, so I swung a U-turn. Heading south, I turned left on Wilshire Boulevard and sped east, running lights and swerving in and out of traffic like every other L.A. driver. The ever-going heater warmed me.

Twenty-five minutes later I turned onto Figueroa Street. I slowed, searching for an address to get my bearings. Feeling like a lost tourist in a small Mexican town, I saw store signs in Spanish and shops painted blue, pink, and chartreuse. The windows were barred. There was a sad feeling of a fiesta that had gone on too long. Then I saw it—a shadowy spire atop a dark marquee empty of movie titles or show times. But the theater's name was still intact: The Roxy.

I swerved to the curb and parked. Reaching under the seat, I pulled out the Glock and slipped it into my jacket pocket, then I took my iPhone and put it into the other pocket. After hiding my purse under the seat, I got out of the car and hurried toward the box office, which looked as if it had been designed to resemble Cinderella's regal carriage before the ball was over. Now the windows were boarded up with graffiti-covered plywood, and what remained of its baroque trim had been smashed and broken. The tarnished brass entrance doors were blanketed by security grates. I tugged at them, but they were locked.

Hearing footsteps I whirled around, jamming my hand into my pocket and gripping my gun. A woman herded two small children along the sidewalk. Waiting until they were gone, I wondered what had happened to all the fathers. The wise old men. The mentors.

Everybody was young now. And no one wanted to be a father. Except one man who could be taking his revenge out on Ryan right now.

I rushed around to the corner of the building, searching for another entrance. Instead, I stared into a long dark tunnel that was an alley. Taking out my iPhone, I clicked on its flashlight. In the light of its weak beam, I edged along the theater's wall. Slowly my eyes adjusted to the darkness, and I became aware of how clean the alley was: no trash, no bins, no addicts, no homeless, and no limo. I tried to dismiss the niggling idea that this ruin of a building was just what it appeared to be—another old movie house as dead as all the stars that had once strode across its screen.

Soon, my light came to rest on a chain wrapped around the handles of steel double doors. The chain was padlocked, and the doors led to the service entrance. I pounded on the steel. There was no response.

I called Ryan's cell number, then pressed my ear against the crack where the doors joined, hoping I could hear his ring tone—"Satisfaction." But I heard only my own jagged breathing.

As I stepped away I glimpsed a shadowy movement out of the corner of my eye. Heart knocking in my chest, I slowly turned to face it. The black silhouette of a man walked from the mouth of the alley toward me. Hanging from his right hand was something that looked like a long pipe or tire iron. Instinctively I backed away, and Ryan's words came back to me. "Alleys always dead-end." I hit a wall.

I took the gun from my pocket. Mouth dry, I held up my cell and yelled, "I've called 911. The police will be here any minute. And I have a gun pointed at you!"

"Turn your phone off. You're just wasting the battery." Heath came into view. "And where in hell did you get the Glock?"

I let out my breath. "It's Rubio's. I took it when he crashed his bike into my car."

"Jesus, Diana, no wonder he wanted to kill you. Give it to me."

"So you can have two Glocks? Not a chance in hell." I slid it back into my pocket.

He grinned, shaking his head. "I carry a Colt 911. Semi automatic." He reached into his jacket pocket with his free hand and came out with his flashlight. "Hold this and shine it on the chain."

I held the light for him. "What are you doing here?"

"Staking out the theater."

"I didn't see your car."

"You weren't supposed to." He took the iron bar and slammed it repeatedly at the padlock and chain. The sharp loud banging shattered the stillness.

"Aren't you making a lot of noise?"

"Parson sped off in his limo just before you arrived. You think I'd be doing this if he were here? Let's hope he didn't take Ryan with him."

I knew why Parson had left. He got the call from Bruno about his wife.

Heath's jaw muscles tightened each time he swung at the lock and chain, and I wondered how he knew about this place and that Ryan was probably inside.

"You purposely sent me on a wild goose chase to the 9000 building, didn't you?" I said.

"Something like that. I knew you wouldn't do as I asked and stay put," he spoke in rhythm to his swinging the crow bar. "Stay safe, stay out of the way."

"You thought I wouldn't get into the building and I'd just give up and go home."

"We all need hope, Diana." Now he jammed the crowbar between the door and chain. Sweat had beaded on his forehead.

"I got into the penthouse." I heard myself say. I hadn't intended to tell him.

He stopped what he was doing and looked at me. "You got past Bruno, the gatekeeper?"

I nodded. "With the help of Mrs. Parson." My voice quivered.

"What happened?"

"She killed herself. She leaped off the balcony in front of Bruno, Gerald, and me. Bruno called Parson and told him. That's why he left in such a hurry."

"And you're alive to tell me about this?"

"Bruno and I have a deal. I don't tell anyone I was there, and he won't kill me. I thought it was a pretty good compromise at the time. Are you going to tell Parson I was in the penthouse?"

"You still don't trust me, do you?"

"I just put my life in your hands, Heath."

"So you did." He frowned. "Why?"

I didn't have an answer. "We're wasting time."

"Remind me never to underestimate you again." He put one foot against the door for leverage, then pulled the iron pipe toward his body. The muscles in his face strained with the effort. The chain snapped.

Holding the pipe down close to his leg, he shoved the doors open and we stepped into more darkness.

I shined his flashlight around. We were in a long, narrow high-ceilinged space. The floor was cement. Without grandeur the backside of a movie screen towered in what looked like an enormous painted black box. All the magic was on the other side. The constricted space had been turned into an office. There was an antique desk and an impressively carved chair in one corner. A beckoning sofa and coffee table nestled on an expensive Indian rug.

A creaking of a floorboard sounded from above. Arcing the light toward it, I started to call out to Ryan but Heath put his finger against his lips, stopping me. Then he quietly laid the crowbar on the floor and reached inside his jacket and came out with his Colt.

I wondered why he was being so careful, especially since he'd seen Parson leave. Unless that noise hadn't come from Ryan but someone else. A man Parson left behind. With my free hand I pulled the Glock out of my pocket and waved the flashlight around with the other. The beam caught a spiral staircase in a dark corner. I steadied the light and nodded to Heath. He took the lead as we carefully circled our way up.

Reaching a landing, we paused. We were in a small hall, more like an anteroom, facing a single closed door. A light shone beneath it. I quickly cut the flashlight and slid it into my pocket. Now with just the thread of light from the threshold, Heath motioned for me to stand to the side of the door. As I did, he held his gun with two hands straight in front of him, balanced himself, then swiftly kicked the door wide open and rushed into the room. Adrenalin flowing, I was close behind, telling myself "this is real, this is real."

CHAPTER THIRTY-THREE

eath and I had entered a richly appointed bedroom. A small crystal lamp on the marble-top nightstand illuminated an expensive Aubusson area rug partially covering the rough floor planks. A stiff wooden chair had been pulled up to the rumpled gold damask-covered bed as if someone had been sitting there, talking to whoever had been lying on it. Except for the chair, the room had Parson's taste written all over it—expensive and overwrought.

Across from the bed was a bolted door. "Ryan?" I called out.

Hearing a low moan, I rushed toward the door. Heath grabbed for my shoulder, but I jerked away, pulled open the bolt, and hurried inside. Lamplight from the bedroom seeped into the chamber, revealing a six-by-six-foot space with cement walls and floor. A cell. A common garden hose snaked from a spigot to a drain in the center of the floor. To the right was the only piece of furniture, a wooden table. Ryan was lying on the floor next to it, wearing an Ugg on his left foot. The other foot was bare. His face was lost in shadow.

Pocketing my gun, I knelt beside him. "Ryan, it's me, Diana."

Suddenly a harsh glare from an overhead blub filled the room. Heath had found the light switch. I repressed a gasp. Ryan flinched, then peered up at me with one clear blue eye. The other was a swollen slit surrounded by bloody gashes.

I took his hand. "Can you talk?"

His distended lips parted. "Uh-huh." The sound was small, painful.

The floor felt damp on my knees. Heath crouched on Ryan's other side and stared warily back into the bedroom.

Then he picked up the hose. "So this is where Parson tortures his victims. Makes the cleanup easy." Disgusted, he threw it behind him, and said to Ryan, "Can you move your legs and arms?"

Nodding, Ryan gestured at the small bloody-black wounds seared into his legs.

"Cigarette burns," Heath said.

"I'm calling 911." I reached into my purse.

"No," Heath said.

"But he needs to go to an emergency room."

"They'll ask too many questions about how he got his wounds. The police could get involved. Ryan's the perfect set-up guy for Jenny's murder."

Ryan's hand touched mine. "He's right."

"We'll put Ryan into your car, and I'll follow you back to his house so I can make sure it's secure. You should call a private doctor. You must know one of those feel-good guys. Hollywood's full of them. He can book Ryan into the celeb wing of a hospital where the docs can take care of him and security is trained to keep the patients under wraps." Heath peered down at Ryan. "We're going to sit you up, okay?"

Ryan grunted. It was good enough for a yes.

Heath and I lifted him into a sitting position and leaned him against the wall.

"Are you dizzy?" I asked.

"No. Couldn't take it." Tears oozed from his eyes. "Couldn't . . ."

"There aren't many of us who could, Ryan."

"She's right." Heath moved to the table and looked through the items on top. "Wallet, cell phone, change, keys, and a comb. The possessions a man carries in his pockets can look pretty dreary." He checked the driver's license. "They're Ryan's." He rubbed the back of his neck as he gazed down. "This is a cement floor, something's not right." Heath tapped his foot. Then he swept Ryan's belongings into his pockets and asked him, "You weren't in the other room, were you?"

"No," Ryan winced. "Parson got a phone call. They left in a hurry."

Mrs. Parson's suicide saved Ryan, I thought, as Heath walked back into the bedroom. I got to my feet and stood in the doorway.

With his foot, Heath pressed the old floorboards, making them creak. "We heard this sound downstairs. Ryan couldn't have made it—he's on a cement slab and was locked in. So who else was walking around, and where are they?" Dark with concern, his eyes met mine as his hand slipped inside his jacket and again pulled out his Colt. Then he ran his hand along the top of the wooden chair. "Looks like this chair goes with the table Ryan's things were on." He lifted his chin, peering up at the ceiling. "Shit . . ."

Above his head was an open crawl space. Before Heath or I could move, a man plunged down, sending both Heath and himself crashing to the floor. I froze as Heath's gun flew from his hand, skittering under the nightstand, while a second gun vanished under the bed. His sleeve had slid up, showing a too-familiar tattoo—it was Rubio.

I pulled the Glock from my pocket. Rubio started crawling across the floor, going for his gun. Heath got to his knees, Rubio turned, swinging a fist at him. The blow glanced off Heath's jaw. Grabbing each other, they rolled. I tried to keep my aim on Rubio, but the pair had become a unit, their bodies rolling and tossing together while their legs thrashed and their fists pounded. This was not a choreographed fight by stunt men. It was raw, ugly, and awkward. The Glock shook in my hands. What were the odds of shooting Heath if I fired at Rubio, I wondered desperately. About 100 percent, I decided.

Hell, I was standing there like a B-movie actress, gasping, eyes wide. I aimed the gun at the ceiling and fired. Ceiling plaster fell like chunks of dirty snow.

"Back off, asshole!" I shouted with all the butch authority of a female superhero.

The noise from the gun had been deafening in the small room. Rubio momentarily shifted his eyes toward me, and Heath head-butted him. Dazed, Rubio fell backwards. Heath clambered up to his feet. Weaving, he leaned over the downed man, grabbed his shirt collar, jerked him up, and smashed his fist into his face again and again. Blood poured from Rubio's nose and mouth. I didn't move. I didn't try to stop Heath.

Breathing hard, Heath finally let the motionless man fall back onto the floor, then straightened up. Working his jaw, he looked around the room, his eyes darting like a man who had lost something very important.

"Your gun's there," I pointed under the nightstand.

Snatching up the weapon, he holstered it. Then he tucked in his shirttail and adjusted his jacket. Finally put together again, he looked at me. "Back off, asshole?"

I smiled. "It was all I could think of at the moment."

"You all right?" A black-and-blue mark was forming on his chin. Another bruised person in my life.

"I'm waiting for the prop man to take the gun out of my hand."

Knuckles raw, Heath's hand covered mine as he slipped the gun from my grip and slid it into my pocket. "Let's get Ryan the hell out of here before Parson's men come back."

"Is Rubio alive?"

"Yeah, we'll leave him where they put Ryan." He cocked his head and frowned at me. "You look surprised. You think I was going to kill him?"

I didn't answer. I honestly didn't know, and it left me feeling uneasy with him and with myself. Rubio had tried to murder me, and he had tortured Ryan. When Heath was pounding him bloody, I wanted Rubio dead and out of my life. I thought of the wind blowing through the shattered glass of my living room and wondered if I'd ever be the woman I once was, or thought I was, before I tried to help Jenny. But I already knew the answer.

Heath strode past me into the cell. "We're gonna get you on your feet, Ryan."

I helped Heath lift Ryan into a standing position. Then we got him into the bedroom and sat him on the edge of the bed. I settled beside him and watched Heath pick up Rubio by his feet and drag him across the floor.

As he got him into the cell, Ryan said to me, "I need to tell you."

"Are you in pain?" I asked.

He licked at the caked blood on his lips. "Parson wanted a name."

"You mean someone he could get more information from about his daughter's death?"

Hanging his head, he nodded.

"Whose name did you give him?" Heath asked sharply over his shoulder as he closed the cell door and bolted it on Rubio.

"She was selling the Bel Air house. All I could think of."

"Celia?" I felt my entire body tighten. "You gave him Celia's name?"

"I couldn't take the pain." He looked up.

I put my arm around him.

"It was the smell of my own flesh," Ryan mumbled.

"I'm calling her." I took out my iPhone.

"Tell her to get the hell out of wherever she is and don't tell anyone where she's going. Even you. It's safer for her that way." Heath stared at me. "Safer for you, too."

The phone rang only once.

"Yes?" Celia answered quickly, as if she were expecting a call.

"It's Diana."

"I've been meaning to call you . . ."

"Don't talk, Celia. Listen. You're in danger. You have to leave your house, office, wherever you are. Go to a hotel and don't tell anybody where you're staying. Even me. Just go. *Now*."

I could hear her sharp intake of breath. "Is it Parson?"

"Yes. I can't talk now. I'll call you on your cell as soon as I can and explain it."

The phone went dead in my hand.

"She's leaving," I told them.

Ryan sighed heavily, relieved.

Puzzled, Heath said, "Did she ask you exactly why she had to go?"

"No. In fact she asked me if she was in danger from Parson. A man she'd told me she didn't know."

CHAPTER THIRTY-FOUR

Forty-five minutes later, we arrived at Ryan's house. From the car I had called the number of a doctor Ryan knew; I'd hoped he was more that the feel-good kind. His place was dark, no lights showing, which was the way it should be. Ryan gave Heath his house keys, and Heath walked through, checking it. Then we helped Ryan into his room and onto his bed.

In the kitchen I found a baggie containing a stale bagel and dumped it out, replacing it with ice from the freezer, which was filled with vodka bottles. Then I wrapped a hand towel around my makeshift ice bag.

By the time I got back to Ryan's bedroom, he was stretched out, his head on his pillow, his hands clasped over his stomach. Heath had put the other Ugg on his bare foot. Now in the doorway, he leaned on the jamb and watched.

I pressed the ice gently to Ryan's bruised eye.

"Ouch!" Ryan groaned. "That hurts."

"Keep it there. Or you're going to end up looking like the Elephant Man."

He grabbed my wrist. "I want to get out of show business. What's in Idaho?"

"Potatoes."

He sighed heavily. "I wanted to die, Diana."

I stroked his arm. "I'm glad you didn't."

"They kept hitting me and burning me." He raised his forefinger toward the ceiling. "Turn my train on."

I clicked a switch built into his nightstand. A replica of a "1930s" Santa Fe Super Chief with Pullman cars started chugging along a railed shelf erected high around the walls. Tiny silhouetted passengers showed in the windows. We watched the train roll around the room, disappearing into tunneled mountains, then reappearing. It tooted and flashed its lights at the railroad crossings. Even Heath moved into the room and stared at it intently. Watching seemed to calm both men. Is that all it took?

Ryan's house was decorated in early puberty. A sparkly purple drum set sat in the corner of his bedroom. Drumsticks had been scattered on the floor like old bones. A prized Martin guitar and a shiny alto sax leaned against a chair. On the wall across from his bed was a Sony screen as big as Picasso's *Guernica*, while remote controls, play stations, and X boxes were stacked on shelves.

He closed his eyes. I moved the ice pack to the corner of his bruised lips.

Grimacing, he said, "Parson has a copy of the video of Jenny and me."

"How did he get it?" Heath moved closer, to the end of the bed.

"I don't think he knew who sent it. He wanted me to tell him who'd mailed it."

"And who was running the blackmail operation?" Heath asked.

"I thought it might be the dead guy, Zackary Logan."

"But that wasn't good enough?"

"They wanted the name of a live person." He slowly opened his good eye; the other remained a slit. "It wasn't Rubio who scared me. It was the little one. He looked like he was going to perform a tango any moment."

"Luis?" Heath asked.

The train tooted. "You know him?"

"Oh, yes." Heath nodded.

"He kept smoking like Bette Davis, then he'd lean over me and press the cigarette into my leg and hold it there. He enjoyed it."

"Is your doctor reliable? Is he going to show up?" I asked.

He rubbed the tips of his forefinger and thumb together indicating cash. That didn't make me feel confident.

"While Rubio beat me," he continued, "and the other one burned me, Parson sat on his bed, howling like an animal, demanding I tell him who did this to his little girl."

"Did he mean who killed her? Or who videoed her having sex with you?" Heath asked.

"I don't know."

"They could be one and the same," I said.

"Or not," Heath countered.

The doorbell chimed.

"My doctor." Ryan said. "I told you."

"Remember," I warned. "If he asks what happened, you tell him you got beat up. That's all you know."

"I love it when she mothers me," Ryan said to Heath, who repressed a smile.

I hurried downstairs and looked through the peephole. It was the doctor, all right. I opened the door and stepped back. A seedy cliché wearing an Armani suit, Italian loafers, and sporting a Rolex strolled in. Even his medical bag had a Gucci racing strip down the middle of it.

"You're kidding," I said.

"I beg your pardon?" He peered over gold-wire glasses at me.

"Nothing. Ryan's been badly beaten. You can't just throw pills at him. He's up here." I started up the stairs.

"Drunk?" He followed me.

"Not now."

In the bedroom he peered down at Ryan. "You've had some going over." He set his bag on the floor and leaned over him. "His right eye will have to be looked at."

His sterile-looking hands felt Ryan's abdomen and ribs. The Rolex gleamed. The train's guardrail went up.

"Pain?" the doctor asked.

"Ribs." Ryan groaned.

"He could have a punctured lung." He studied Ryan's legs. "Your attackers burned you?"

"Yes," I answered for Ryan.

Now he peered at me as if I were another wound he had to fix. "Odd thing for them to do."

"Ryan's a lucky man." Heath shifted his weight.

The doctor's shady eyes turned skeptical. "Extremely lucky."

"This is luck?" Ryan burbled.

"I only ask to know whether I may be implicating myself in something . . . that could be a . . . problem."

"You aren't," I assured him. "Ryan's a drunk. You're not responsible for what he can or can't remember." Hearing my words aloud, I knew I'd just demeaned my friend and the beating he had taken. But at the same time, I had to make sure he was taken care of.

"Well, I can't treat him here. He must be hospitalized."

"But under your care and no publicity," Heath said.

The doctor looked over his glasses at Heath. "Who are you?"

"I'm none of your business." Heath casually pulled open his jacket, showing him the holstered Colt on his belt.

He nodded submissively. "Under my care and no publicity. It's what I get paid the big bucks for. I'll call a private ambulance service I've used successfully in the past." Taking out his cell, he dialed and issued orders. When he'd finished, he smiled obsequiously at me. "Sorry about your mother. I attended to her often, especially in her later years. If you ever need anything else. . . ." He reached into his jacket pocket and handed me a pristine white engraved card.

How could one person be so clean and sleazy at the same time? This was the first man I had met lately whom I was completely sure my mother had not gone to bed with.

"I'll be taking him to St. John's in Santa Monica. He'll be in the VIP wing, if I can get him in." He punched in another number.

"That's not good enough," I said. "Make *sure* you get him in the VIP wing. It's what you get paid the big bucks for."

Another obsequious smirk. "Touché." He made arrangements for Ryan in the VIP wing and then disconnected.

"Would you two mind waiting downstairs?" Ryan asked the doctor and Heath.

"Of course not." The doctor picked up his bag and slipped out of the room.

Heath went with him.

After they had both gone, Ryan beckoned me with a finger, and I leaned close. "He's not right for you, Diana."

"What are you talking about?"

"You're from the world of the arts." He winced in pain. "You're creative. He's a fixer. That's what you called him, remember?"

"You said he was a good guy."

"But not for you."

I stroked his face. "Don't worry. I like men who have a way with words."

"Yeah. But how many words?"

Heath's voice cut through the room. "The ambulance is here."

Making a face at Ryan, I reached over and turned off the train.

Heath and I watched the ambulance leave with Ryan, and the doctor followed in his white Bentley. Then we locked the house and went down to the beach.

Not talking, we stood feeling the cold wind on our faces. The houses overlooking the ocean were dark. My neighbors were away or sleeping; secure their multi-alarm systems would keep them safe. I looked toward my house. In the dim moonlight I could see that Kiki, the majordomo of Malibu, had found someone to board up the shattered glass doors. And now my house, my home, my tiny oasis appeared as abandoned and as dilapidated as Parson's movie theater.

A bone-deep sorrow flooded me, and I didn't want to go home. I wanted to run away, putting as much distance as I could between myself and the dead and the wounded in my life.

"You must be tired," Heath said.

"Yes. Also hyper."

"You're running on adrenalin. I could use a drink. You wouldn't want to offer me one, would you?"

"What do you really want?" I confronted him, clasping my arms around myself against the cold.

"You want an honest answer, or one of my very believable lies?" The wind blew his hair back from his high forehead and he hunched his shoulders.

"Honesty would be refreshing."

He thought a moment, then said "I want to fuck your brains out."

I could feel his dark eyes moving over me, and my body responding as if his hands were on my flesh.

"I don't have any brains left."

"Then another part of your anatomy. . . ."

I laughed.

"That was nice."

"What?"

"Your laughter. I'm not a total cretin. We could have dinner before we . . ."

I turned away and started walking toward my house.

"Is that a 'yes,' a 'no,' or a 'maybe' to any of the above?" he yelled after me.

"I'll fix you a drink and dinner. Then we'll see," I shouted back.

I still didn't know what to make of him, but I did know Heath could help me run away from my ghosts. At least for one night.

CHAPTER THIRTY-FIVE

My house smelled of damp raw wood. The TV chattered from the kitchen—Kiki's guys must've left it on for me. My boarded-up living room looked dark even with the lamps turned on. Heath peered at the only objects that shined with any life—Colin's Oscars and the nameplate on my mother's urn.

"Would you like to hold one of Colin's Oscars? Most people do."

"No." He turned his bruised chin toward me. Dark stubble shadowed his jaw line. "I want to hold what's real and present." He took my hand and I felt a wonderful surge of passion rush through me. Was that all it took? Hands touching? How Jane Austen of me. It had been a long time since I felt this kind of desire.

I pulled away. He followed me into the kitchen.

I opened the cupboard near the sink. "Booze and red wine." I spoke over the TV noise.

He picked up the remote and clicked it off. "If you're leaving the TV on so a prowler will think you're home, it won't fool him."

"I leave it on because I'm alone. The white wine is in the fridge."

He leaned against the wall. "You don't strike me as a woman who'd be afraid to be alone."

"I'm not afraid. But the silence wears on me." I pushed my hair back from my face.

He nodded, and by his expression I knew he understood. Then he rubbed his hands together and announced "I'm hungry. Are you?"

"Starving."

He opened my freezer. This was a man who could make himself at home. He took out one the many frozen meals I'd just bought. "Lean Cuisine? Isn't that an oxymoron?" He tossed the frozen box back into the freezer and opened the fridge. "You got eggs." He took out the carton and peered in. "Four eggs. It's a start."

Smiling, I thought of how talkative men become when they're trying to seduce you. Even the strong silent ones.

"I want you to know that I'm not usually attracted to very beautiful women," he announced.

"Then you're in the wrong town."

"They're too insecure, they take too much care. I have the feeling you don't need a lot of confidence-building."

"I'm not usually attracted to men who are fixers."

"Dismissing the fixer part, did you just say that you were attracted to me?"

"You can pour me a glass of red wine while I take a shower."

In my bathroom, I took off my shirt and jeans. My clothes were streaked with Ryan's blood. I held them a moment, then tossed them at the hamper and stepped into the shower. Letting the hot water run over my body, I felt like a different woman. Different from the insecure beauty Colin had loved. I ran the soap down my breasts and stomach. I was washing myself for Heath.

Dried off, I opened the bathroom door to let the steam out, and the smell of eggs cooking and toast browning wafted in. My heart lurched. It had been a long time since someone had cooked for me. It's always the little things.

Naked except for Colin's silk paisley robe, I stood in the kitchen. Heath faced the stove, his broad back toward me. He'd taken off his holster and jacket, placed them on a chair, and rolled up his shirtsleeves. His forearms were strong, and the watch on his wrist looked functional and purposeful.

"It's been a long time since someone cooked for me," I said. "Thank you."

He turned, fork in hand, then slowly put it down and in one fierce movement his arms were around me, his body pressing into mine, pushing me against the wall. His mouth hard on my lips. I was ripping at his shirt while he untied my sash and the robe fell to the floor. A shedding of another life. I pulled him onto the kitchen table. Silverware clattered to the floor. He sucked at my breast. My back arched and my legs wrapped around his waist. And while the eggs and toast burned we devoured each other, ending up on the living room floor.

I peered up at the two Oscars and the urn on the mantel. Then closed my eyes against them, feeling the weight of this man.

Now we sat at the kitchen table eating Lean Cuisine, having dumped the burnt food in the garbage disposal. Heath's shirt hung open, his chest bare. I had torn the buttons off it. My robe wrapped loosely around me.

"This stuff is awful." He shoveled in the plastic food as if it were his last meal.

Sipping wine, I stared at the scar just above his heart, which my tongue had discovered earlier. "Were you shot?"

"Sniper."

"I thought they usually aimed at the head."

"I moved. But the heart's a pretty good target." He peered over the rim of his wine glass and wiggled his eyebrows at me as if we were making a joke.

"Why did you sign up?"

"Because terrorists flew planes into the Twin Towers and the Pentagon."

"For the love of country."

"You could say that."

"You still have that feeling?"

"Yes."

"I can't figure you out."

He placed his hand on mine. "I can't figure you out either. Do we have to?"

"Yes."

"Did you have Colin figured out?"

"No."

"What about Celia?"

"Back to reality." I withdrew my hand from his. "You are a relentlessly good interrogator."

"Habit, sorry."

"What about her? Why don't *you* tell me what you think?" I pushed my finished plate aside.

"Maybe Ryan accidentally picked the right name to give to Parson. Celia has 24/7 access to the Bel Air house. And when you called her to tell her she was in danger, the only question she asked was whether it was Parson. A man she told you she didn't know. Also the night Jenny Parson was murdered, Celia was struck in the face and then lied about who did it. Why lie? It makes me think she still hasn't told you the truth about how she got bruised."

"She says she was in her car being attacked by Ben Zaitlin around the time Jenny died."

He put his wine glass down. "Ben?"

I explained how Ben wanted to meet with Celia, the woman his father loved instead of his mother. And how he began to hit her.

"And this happened while Jenny Parson was in her underground garage being murdered?"

"Yes."

"Doesn't sound like Ben. Working for Zaitlin, I've gotten to know the kid a little bit. He's not violent. He's an insecure rich kid who doesn't know his real father. Except that he raped Ben's mother. He doesn't know how he ended up in the life he's living."

"So what are you saying? Celia made up the story about Ben?"

"First she said it was me and now she says it was him."

"But she was protecting him when she lied about you. She needed a name to give me and thought we'd never see you again."

"I'm glad we did." Taking his plate, he stood. "Are you finished?"

"Yes. Her bruises were real."

"I'm not saying they weren't." He rinsed the dishes and put them in the dishwasher. "Has she called you?"

I went into the living room and took my cell out of my purse. With the dishtowel thrown over his shoulder, Heath watched from the doorway. He seemed as comfortable doing the dishes as he did aiming his Colt.

"No message," I said. "Are you saying she was involved in Jenny's murder?"

"Maybe it wasn't her choice to be involved."

"What do you mean?"

"I'm not sure."

"I can't see her shooting Zackary Logan."

"I didn't say she did."

"Ben would confirm her story. I mean, they're each other's alibi. And what about Beth Woods?" My voice sounded defensive and high-pitched. "She told me she had been rejected by Jenny. Or Zaitlin? She was ruining his movie. Or me? I don't have an alibi for that night. Or all the others who may have been blackmailed by Jenny?"

"I didn't realize how close you and Celia are."

"We've been friends since we were sixteen." Was it our friendship I was defending so vehemently? Or maybe I couldn't handle another betrayal? "Let's change the subject. How did you know where to find Parson's movie theater?"

"I've been following Parson for a while."

"Working for the same client that led you to the Bel Air house?"

"Yes."

"Beth Woods?"

"She isn't my client."

"Then who is it? I know you're working for Zaitlin. Why not tell me?"

"Everybody knows I work for him." He leaned his shoulder against the doorframe.

"Tell me how you knew where The Rock was." I asked.

"One night I tailed Parson there. Luis drove down the alley and parked. He and Parson went into the theater."

"Did you go in after them?"

"I didn't want them to know I had followed them. Also, I'm not suicidal."

"What were they doing in there, torturing people? Or watching old movies from the decade he was eating candy off the floor?"

"About two hours later they came out dragging a very limp man between them. They threw him into the trunk of the limo and left."

"Did you recognize the man?"

"Not from where I was."

"Did you ever hear anything about a missing man, or an unidentified body?"

"Unidentified bodies are not unusual in Los Angeles. But no, I never heard."

"Not even from your source in the LAPD?"

"Not even from my source."

"You and Detective Spangler should get different notebook covers."

He moved to me, tilted my chin up with his fingertips, and kissed me. "Time to change the subject again."

"How did you meet Zaitlin?" I asked.

He walked over to the wall opposite the boarded-up sliding glass doors and took a Swiss Army knife from his pants pocket. "I was an actor."

"Oh, God, you mean I've gone to bed with another actor?" I collapsed on the sofa dramatically.

Laughing, he reminded me, "We didn't make it to the bed. I starred in a movie called *Horror on the Run*. Don't tell me you never saw it?"

"I don't know how I could have missed it."

He began to pry loose the two bullets Rubio had left in the wall. My permanent chill awoke.

"I went to read for a small role in one of Zaitlin's movies and he asked me if I really wanted to be an actor. It was a good question. I should've asked myself that. I thought about it and said 'no.'" He dislodged one of the rounds. "I started doing a little security for him, and then 9/11 happened. When I got out of the Army he helped me start up my business by recommending me." He dug the other slug out. "You have something to cover these holes with? If the police come here to question you for any reason, it's not a good idea have bullets in your wall." He folded the knife and placed it and the rounds in his pocket.

From the side table I took a large framed photograph of Colin and me that had once hung on his office wall and handed it to Heath. Then I went into the kitchen and got a hammer out of the drawer and dug around to find a nail. When I returned Heath was studying the picture.

"You two look very happy," he said.

"I thought we were." I looked at the picture and for the first time noticed the strain around Colin's smiling eyes and mouth.

"I've seen people die. But I've never lost anyone I loved." He tucked the picture under his arm as I handed him the hammer and nail.

"Because nobody close to you has died? Or you've never loved?"

"Never been in love. Never intend to." He pounded the nail into the wall and secured the photo over the holes.

"Don't worry, Heath, I'm not going to stalk you to the ends of the earth," I said in a cold firm voice.

Puzzled, he turned from the wall. "What?" Then realizing, said, "Sorry. I'm used to setting up parameters even when I don't need to." He tossed the hammer on the sofa.

"Probably got it from your military experience."

"Maybe."

"I found out what Parson had on my husband."

"You don't have to tell me."

"I want to. Colin had sex with my mother when I was away on location. My last movie. I was giving up my career for my marriage. It's cruel and uncaring what they did, but if I think about it now, it's hardly a reason to keep paying money to hide it. Except Colin knew I would've left him. Back then I was the high-maintenance insecure beauty you were talking about in the kitchen."

"Aren't you being a little hard on yourself?"

I shrugged. "I would've left him. That way I could put the blame on my mother for destroying our marriage. Not on Colin. Not on me. But on her alone. It was the only way I could've gotten back at her. The only way I could keep her from winning, the only way I could keep the battle going with her. I didn't know it then, but I see now that my conflict with her was more important than my marriage." I moved close to him. "I'm not that high-maintenance insecure beauty anymore. So your parameters are safe with me." I put my arms around his neck. Looking up at him, I said, "I want to thank you for the mindless sex. You helped me forget my ghosts for a while." I kissed him, slipped the dishtowel from his shoulder, and stepped back.

"That felt like a good-night and good-bye kiss."

"Just good-night." I went to the front door and waited for him to get his jacket and Colt. I've never waited for a man to get his gun before, I thought, amused.

In the foyer we stared at each other, wondering if we could or should go back to the people we were before tonight, when the lies and the contradictions didn't strike so deeply.

He brushed his lips against mine, reminded me to lock the door, and was gone. I was abruptly surrounded by silence again. But if stillness can vary, be different, less oppressive, less threatening, this one was. Was that all it took? Great sex?

CHAPTER THIRTY-SIX

t was ten o'clock the next morning when I awoke. Stretching,
I heard Mother's voice. I sat up. She was on TV, seducing Jack
Nicholson on a sofa. Jack was wry, my mother was serious, her
blond hair cascading around her bare shoulders and soft cleavage.

"Enough," I said.

She didn't hear me. She was busy earning her one and only Oscar.
I turned off the TV.

Dressed in jeans, a black sweater, and suede driving shoes, I went
into the kitchen and put the coffee on. While it perked I checked
my cell to see if Celia had called. She hadn't. I left a message asking
her to call me, that it was important. Then I found the number of
St. John's Hospital and asked to speak to Ryan. He had a collapsed

lung and an ego to match. It was his depleted confidence that worried me the most. Men such as Ryan are like birthday balloons, fun, but they popped easily. Promising I would see him soon, I hung up.

Now slathering marmalade on toast and sipping coffee, I wondered why I was so adamant that Celia was innocent. It was more than she was my friend and that I didn't want to be deceived by her. Then I realized it was hearing her scream over the phone and the terror I'd felt. And the next morning seeing her bruised face. I'd forgotten to tell Heath about that. My body grew alert at the thought of him.

Smiling, I forced myself to concentrate on Celia. The only thing I didn't understand was how she knew she was in danger from Parson. If only she'd answer her phone. Why didn't she? Had Parson's men found her? I stood up. Was she hurt or in trouble?

I went into my bedroom, found her house key, put it in my pocket, and left.

The fog had come in and settled like a wet gray rag over the coast. Running down the beach, I tried to outpace the ebb and flow of the tide, hoping I would find something, anything, in her house that could tell me where she'd gone.

As I ran up onto Celia's deck, I saw that the drapes were drawn across her French doors. I tried the handle. It was locked. Using her key I unlocked it, pushed aside the curtains, and stepped in.

It took me a moment to make sense of the chaos. All her possessions had been thrown onto the floor, smashed. Drawers hung open, contents scattered. Lamps lay on their sides and sofa cushions were ripped open. Goose down had settled over the room like a blanket. Fear shot through me as I realized I might not be alone in the house.

I picked up the oldest prop in the world, a fireplace poker, and moved toward her bedroom, peering in. The linens had been ripped off the bed, nightstands tipped over, and paintings torn from the walls.

Tightening my grip on the poker, I edged sideways to the open closet door and paused, waiting for any sound or movement that might emanate from it. Not hearing any, I crept in.

Celia's closet was the size of a small boutique. Her clothes had been pulled off the hanger rods and thrown onto the floor, creating a tangled pile of clashing bold colors. The red-framed full-length mirror was shattered. Had Parson's men done all this damage? But why break the mirror? I couldn't believe his thugs cared much about their reflections. I stared at my mirrored face, fractured by the cracked glass, and wondered who did care. Who hated their own image so much that they had to ruin it?

I went into the kitchen and abruptly stopped. Ben Zaitlin, his profile to me, was standing there staring intently at the door that led to the garage as if he were in a trance.

"Ben?"

He jerked his shoulders, startled back to reality. "Diana. I was looking for Celia. She's not here." His black hair was uncombed and he was unshaven. Dark circles shadowed his creaseless eyes.

"Did you do this?" I gestured with the poker toward the living-room entrance. Then I put it down on the table but still within reach.

"What?" He blinked his long lashes and rubbed his face as if trying to wake himself up.

"The destruction of Celia's . . ."

"Perfect life?" He shrugged. "Yes. I was pissed off, I guess."

"How did you get in?"

"Stole Robert's key." He slumped against the sink counter, hands stuffed in his cargo pants pockets, head hanging. He wore a black polo shirt, and flip-flops on his strong wide feet. "I've been up all night. No sleep. The police want to see me in about an hour." He lifted his wrist to look at his watch and saw he wasn't wearing one. "Guess I left it at home." He raised his eyes to meet mine. "Do you know where Celia went?"

"No. But she had to leave."

"She didn't tell me."

"Why would she?"

"Because she's my alibi. That's why I came here, to make sure she would back me up."

"And because she wasn't here, you trashed her house?"

"I told you I was pissed off," he snapped, like a truculent teenager.

"Why do the police want to talk with you?"

"They saw me on The Den security tape talking to Jenny Parson the night she was murdered."

"I thought you didn't know Jenny."

"You could never know her. But we shared the same . . . disgust. We hated the same people. But in different ways."

My stomach tightened. "What people?

He fell silent staring at the Sub-Zero refrigerator. Pushing his hair from his forehead he finally said, "The people we were blackmailing."

"Ben." I sat down at the table, smelling the soft aroma of its polished old wood.

"Jenny felt this rush of power. I just felt a kinda revenge. But then I was sick of all their old naked bodies. Sick of their needs. Sick of her, sick of me." He tossed his head back defiantly. "Aren't you going to ask me how Ben Zaitlin, who has whatever he wants, could do such a thing? Aren't you going to say I'm disappointed in you, Ben?"

"No."

His expression softened, and he looked even younger than his twenty-one years. "No, you wouldn't, would you? You're the sanest person in this fucking town."

"Not saying much, is it?"

For a moment I thought he was going cry, but he quickly turned toward the sink, flipped the faucet on, and threw water on his face. He tore off a section of paper towel from its wrought-iron holder and dried himself. Wadding it up, he threw it into the sink.

He swung around to face me. "Those people we blackmailed were just like my parents, only concerned about what they needed at the moment. Jenny said that we were *feeding the beasts*. Some of them were even at my birthday party." He smirked like a frat boy talking about a prank. "They sucked up to me because I'm Robert's son. They'd asked me what projects he had lined up, as if I could do something for them. And they didn't know I was the one taping them, making them pay. I stayed in the shadows just like a cinematographer on a set."

"Not quite."

"Shit. It wasn't even good porn. It was pathetic. Zackary Logan was the only one true to himself. He knew who he was. A pimp. Even Jenny in her own sick way was trying to please her father or be like him. I never knew who I was . . . except that I had always been used. And I hate it!" His cheeks flushed and he looked at the garage door again.

I kept my voice calm. "You said you came here to see whether Celia would back up your alibi. Why wouldn't she?"

"She's a liar."

"You weren't with her the night Jenny was murdered? You didn't hit her?"

"Yes, I was with her." His eyes settled on mine. "And what else would the son of a rapist do but attack a woman? It's so believable, isn't it, Diana?" He pushed himself away from the counter. "I have to talk to the police." He strode past me and down the hallway to the front door, his flip-flops slapping at his feet.

I sprang up and hurried after him. Grabbing his arm, I turned him toward me. "I'll call Robert. He'll get you a lawyer."

"You do that, Diana. Call the biggest loser there is besides me." He opened the door, pulled away from my grip, and beat it down the flagstone pathway.

Running after him, I yelled his name.

His Jeep Cherokee was parked on the side of the highway. He jumped into it. Revving the engine, he swung it out into traffic and made a screeching U-turn, causing oncoming cars in both directions to brake and skid. Horns blared. I watched him speed north, away from the West L.A. police station, away from his parents, away from Celia's house, away from Hollywood.

When I couldn't see Ben anymore, I went back into the kitchen and stared at the door that had so fixated him. My hand trembling, I slowly opened it. The garage was empty, no white Lexus. I let out my breath. What did I think I would find? Celia's corpse? Closing the door, I stepped back and felt something crunch under my foot.

I bent down and picked up a crumpled photograph. Had Ben dropped it?

Sitting down at the table, I pressed it flat with my fingers. The very young faces of Celia and Gwyn looked back at me through the creased folds. Gwyn was holding a newborn. Ben. She had the righteous, enlightened look of those who see another reality. Celia had her straight-ahead-feet-on-the-ground expression. This had to have been taken when Gwyn was in Switzerland, after having given birth, and still recovering from her breakdown. For a woman who didn't keep photographs, why was Celia keeping this one?

Studying it, I tried to think back twenty years. I would have been maybe twenty, Celia and Gwyn were twenty-one, Ben's age now. How long had Celia been trekking in Europe, staying at hostels and visiting Gwyn? Five or six months?

I rubbed my forehead. Gwyn had been raped while she was hearing voices and hiding in bushes. Crazy and pregnant, her parents had swept her off to Switzerland. Three or four months later Celia decided to take a trip, to get her head together, to figure out what she wanted to do with her life if she couldn't make it as an actress. And also she wanted to visit Gwyn. Three or four months after Gwyn had left the country. A pregnant woman would begin to show around that time.

Feeling the oppression of the perfect domestic kitchen Celia had created for herself—a woman who didn't cook, who didn't want a family—I peered at the two young women again and sighed. Was I weaving a fictional story that had nothing to do with the reality of this picture? It could just be what it looks like—Celia, the friend, sharing a moment with Gwyn and her baby. Or was it a picture of Celia standing next to *her* infant son, who was now cuddled in Gwyn's arms? And that was the true picture. The one Ben had found, then crumpled in his hand and dropped on the floor. Christ.

I reached for Celia's landline and called Robert and Gwyn's home but got the machine. I tried Robert's office number and got voicemail. But no answer didn't mean they weren't home.

I slipped the picture into my pocket and left.

CHAPTER THIRTY-SEVEN

I drove up the long driveway to Gwyn and Robert's elegant "farm" house. The coastal fog never seemed to reach up here. It gathered below their hilltop like a smoky moat.

A team of gardeners were trimming and feeding the country garden. Getting out of my car, I smelled freshly mown grass wafting through the air. Bees hovered over the lavender plants. Some homes are too perfect, too beautiful. I felt the photograph in my pocket. There is no way their center can hold. I rang the bell.

Gwyn quickly opened the door. "Diana," she said surprised. "I thought you might be Heath." Strands of hair hung messily around her ragged face. Uncharacteristic for her. Behind her the Zaitlins' pasty-faced houseman, Olin, craned his neck at me.

"I've been trying to get ahold of him," she rambled on, chameleon-like eyes flicking.

"I need to talk you, Gwyn," I said.

"I can't. Maybe later."

A primal moan erupted from the area of Zaitlin's office and echoed off the limestone walls in the high-ceilinged foyer.

"Is that Robert?" I asked.

"He's been drinking," she said.

Robert was many things, but not a heavy drinker. I started to walk in but she blocked my way. The houseman's eyes widened. Another sobbing groan rebounded around the foyer.

"Go away, Diana." Gwyn was shaking with emotion now. "You started all this. Why did you have to find Jenny's body?"

I shoved her aside and ran past the houseman and into the office.

Behind his desk, Zaitlin weaved and swayed. A pistol lay on his desk beside an empty vodka bottle and a pile of scripts. A crystal-cut glass had been knocked on its side.

"Robert," I said his name softly.

He stopped pacing and swung his body toward me, mouth sagging, lips wet with saliva. Sweat covered his shaved head. He swiped at the desk; now the gun dangled from his fingers.

"I was . . . smartest guy in town."

"You still are."

"Ju..sh another asshole. Right, Gwyn?" he said to his wife who now stood inside the office door next to Olin.

I took a step closer to Zaitlin. "Give me the gun."

"Can't. Parson told me to kill myself."

"Some men were here earlier. They searched the house for a camera," Olin said. "Before they left, this man called Parson gave him the pistol."

"You know what?" Zaitlin staggered.

"What?" I asked.

"I'm . . . an asshole *and* a coward." His eyes turned toward Gwyn. "Get out of here!"

She fled. Olin held his ground.

"Why would Parson want you dead?"

"Ben." His head lolled.

I edged closer. "Then you know what he was involved in?"

"Never loved him. But . . . if I knew . . . if I knew. . . ." Knees buckling, he swayed backward.

I lunged and grabbed the gun from his hand. He collapsed into his desk chair. I knelt next to him. His eyes were closed, mouth open. A perfect expression for a producer, I couldn't help but think. Thankfully, I could hear him breathing.

"Is he all right?" Olin ventured.

Standing, I shoved the gun into his hand. "Make sure he doesn't get near this and that he doesn't choke on his own vomit. Where's Mrs. Zaitlin?"

"Living room."

Looking lost, Gwyn stood in the middle of a room designed for entertaining important people. From their gilt-framed oil paintings lining the walls, the women of another century peered out from behind parasols, up from their baths, or over the top of their books at Gwyn and me.

"Why are you trying to get hold of Heath?" I asked her. "So he can fix what Ben and Jenny have done?"

"I don't know what you're talking about."

"I'm talking about them blackmailing your friends, your business acquaintances. The people you need to keep up your important position."

She slapped me. I felt every bone in her hand. I slapped her back with equal fury. Eyes watering, breathing hard, we glared at each as our cheeks turned red. Neither of us apologized. The women from another era were not amused.

I took the photo from my pocket and handed it to her. "I think Ben dropped this after he trashed Celia's house this morning."

"He was at her place?" She traced Ben's tiny face and body with her finger. "He was so small. Where is he now?"

"The last I saw of him, he was driving north on PCH."

She grabbed her cell from a table and punched in a number. "Heath, Diana said he was driving north on Pacific Coast Highway. What time?" she asked me.

"Let me speak to him."

"It's his voicemail." She handed me the phone

"Heath, it's Diana." As I relayed what Ben had told me earlier, Gwyn slumped on the sofa, staring at the photograph again.

"What have you and Celia done?" I tossed the phone onto the sofa next to her. "Celia wasn't one to keep photographs, Gwyn. I never saw any. She didn't want a family life. Why did she keep that one?"

"I guess because that's when we were friends and we cared about each other. That was before she took my husband away from me."

"You weren't the one who was pregnant, were you? It was Celia."

She stiffened. "Are you saying I imagined my rape? Even crazy women know when they've been violated, Diana."

"Parson was here. Robert was trying to kill himself, and Ben is driving God-knows-where. Yes, it would be terrible to lie about being raped. It would be equally terrible to lie to Robert and to Ben."

With restless, jerky movements she got to her feet and went out onto the veranda. I joined her. We stood where Ben and I had talked on his birthday night. But instead of a party tent and a cake, there were gardeners sweeping the gravel paths with palm fronds.

"They sweep when Robert's working at home." She watched them. "That way he doesn't have to be bothered by the noise of the blowers." She wrapped her arms around herself so tightly she could've been wearing a straitjacket. She faced me and continued. "I got crazy. Celia got pregnant. I wanted a baby, Diana. I wanted a mooring, to keep me from blowing away. Do you know what that feeling is like?"

"Yes."

"No, you don't. You're always so together. Except for the night you found Jenny's body and wouldn't let go of your mother's ashes. But that was the exception. Even when we were young and sailing down Sunset in your mother's car, you were the one in control. Even then, I knew I was cracking into little pieces. And no matter how hard I tried to hold onto . . . something . . . I couldn't."

I remembered her jealous expression reflected in the rearview mirror as we picked out the houses we were going to live in when we grew up. Now I understood what she had envied. My self-confidence, which of course I didn't have. I was a good actress even then. I just didn't know it.

"When did you find out Celia was pregnant?" I asked.

She relaxed her arms. Turning back to the garden view, she rested her hands on the stone balustrade. "Not until she visited me at the sanitarium in Switzerland. She wanted to have an abortion. I talked her out of it. It wasn't difficult. No matter how much she rebelled against her Catholic upbringing . . . she was still Catholic. As the baby grew inside her, I grew saner. After Ben was born I paid a doctor to make the birth certificate out in my name." She paused, looking at me. "I loved Celia for what she did. She gave me a reason to try to be normal."

"Who was the father?"

"I thought you figured that out. Robert. They had a brief affair. He wanted to marry her. Not because she was pregnant, she never told him. But Celia being Celia, she didn't want marriage. So she left him and went traveling around Europe ending up in Switzerland. Looking for help from crazy me."

"And you knew Robert was Ben's father when you married him?"

"When I returned to L.A., Robert and I began to date. He was on the rebound from Celia. When he asked me to marry him, it was out of hurt and anger over her."

"Why did you accept?" I persisted.

"I was a wealthy woman who had had a mental breakdown, who supposedly got pregnant by an act of rape. I was well aware that for whoever married me, it would be for my money. Robert was more than I could have hoped for."

"And you never told him he was Ben's father?"

"No. Celia didn't want him to know."

"And you?"

"I didn't want him to look at Ben and see Celia. Ben was mine this way. What I didn't expect was Celia and Robert becoming involved again."

"Because she could be closer to Ben?"

"That's what I thought at first. But all she wanted was Robert on her own terms. No child. No marriage."

"How did Ben find out he was Robert and Celia's son?"

"I don't know. He came to the house last night and said to me, *you're not my mother.* Robert was there. I had to tell him the truth. Robert felt betrayed by Celia, by me. How could he not? All the years he'd kept his distance from Ben. The woman he really loved had never told him. And the woman he didn't love had kept him obligated."

"And his reaction to Ben?"

"Robert attempted to put his arms around him but Ben wouldn't let him. He said things like '*Now* you care?' '*Now* you want to be my father?' Then he ran out and got into his car and drove away so fast I thought he wouldn't make the sharp turns of the driveway. I thought he would kill himself."

"So you let Ben grow up thinking he was the son of a man who had taken advantage of a mentally ill woman."

"It had to be believable, Diana. Nobody doubted it."

"And it made you more of a saintly victim, a woman who had kept her baby against the worst possible odds."

"I was raped. I just didn't get pregnant."

"Did Celia tell Ben she was his mother?"

"I don't know who told him."

"Did Parson know that Ben wasn't your son?"

"No. But he knew what Ben had been doing. Robert pleaded with him not to hurt Ben. Now that he knew he was his real father, Robert asked Parson to kill him instead. But he didn't. He handed him the gun and said 'Do it yourself.'" She pushed her hair back with both hands, her lips twitching.

"You need to call the police."

"Heath will take care of it."

"But he's not calling you back. Where is he?"

"I don't know."

Why wasn't Heath returning her calls? I spoke as calmly as I could: "You have to call the police. Of course Parson doesn't want Robert, he wants Ben. He's in danger."

Her back stiffened. "If you call the police, I will deny everything I've told you."

"But why? Oh, God . . . did you kill Jenny?"

"Don't be ridiculous. I just found out last night what they were doing, when Ben told us. He wanted us to know every sordid detail."

"You don't care that he could be in danger, do you?" I walked back into the living room and picked up the cell phone from the sofa.

She was right behind me, snatching it from my hand.

"Don't you dare call the police. Don't you destroy my life, Diana."

"It's already destroyed. It was destroyed in Switzerland. It was destroyed when you married Robert and didn't tell him Ben was *his* son."

"We are still a powerful couple in this town." She looked like a desperate actress who clings to every word in her script because she was afraid to ad-lib, only to discover her script has been thrown out.

"Christ, Gwyn. I liked you better when you were nuts."

I turned on my heels and walked out of the room, out of the house, past the gardeners, and got into my car. I rooted through my purse and found Detective Dusty Spangler's card and called her. I got her voicemail. Was nobody answering their phones? I left a message saying it was urgent and disconnected.

I drove down the long driveway to Sunset Boulevard. Glancing at my gas gauge, I saw I was driving on empty. What a perfect metaphor. I pounded the steering wheel with my fist.

CHAPTER THIRTY-EIGHT

I coasted on gas fumes into the station at the corner of PCH and Sunset. With the nozzle jammed in the tank and the dollars ticking off like seconds, I thought of Robert, Gwyn, Ben. And Celia. If Celia could lie to Robert and Ben, what else could she lie about? Jenny Parson?

I watched two surfers secure their boards on the top of their dented-up Jetta. A wet Lab with sand stuck to his black nose hung his head out the back window, keeping an eye on the two young men. I called information on my cell and got the number of Platinum Security, Heath's firm. A girly female voice answered.

"This is Diana Poole. Is Leo Heath there?"

"Isn't he with you?"

"No," I said, taken aback by the question.

"Oh, well, don't worry," the girly voice continued. "He sometimes disappears after spending the night with someone he likes. I think it's because he wants to build his defenses back up again. And trust me, he always does."

I gritted my teeth and breathed in ethanol. "Look, this is an emergency. I'm calling about a case he's working on. I have very important information. Would you tell him I called?"

"Okey dokey."

"*Okey dokey*? Who the hell am I talking to?"

"Collette. I was just here picking up a few things. Bra. Panties. But I'm quite capable of leaving a message. You got his home, sweetie, not his office." She hung up.

Hell. The dog and I stared dumbly at each other. My cell rang in my hand, causing me to jump.

"Heath?" I answered.

"Where are you?" I recognized Parson's cajoling voice immediately. My permanent chill crawled up my legs.

"Where are *you*?" I asked back. Out in the open I felt exposed, a perfect target for Rubio. I quickly got back into my car.

"I'm at Celia's house." His voice lowered. "I discovered something heartbreaking."

"Her house has been trashed."

"Do you really think I would consider that heartbreaking?"

"You don't have a heart. So I have no idea."

A long pause. I heard the gas hose click off. The gallons, the dollars, the seconds, stopped. Then he spoke, "I hope you're not too far away. Heath is not feeling very well."

My stomach tightened as he continued. "And you sounded, let's say, emotional, when you spoke his name. No police." He hung up.

I got back out of the car and quickly took the nozzle out of the gas tank and replaced it. Twisting the cap back on, I wondered if

Heath was simply being used as a ploy to get me there. Maybe Bruno had told Parson I was with his wife when she jumped. Maybe he wanted to hurt me. But that would compromise Bruno. No, it was Heath. He would've returned Gwyn's calls. Leo damn Heath. The two surfers and the dog grinned at me lasciviously as they drove off.

In my car again, I turned on the ignition, threw it into gear, and, tires screeching, pulled out joining the traffic, driving right into Parson's dark world with my sunglasses on.

CHAPTER THIRTY-NINE

pulled up behind the Mercedes limousine parked in front of Celia's cottage. Ben's Jeep was in Celia's drive, and Heath's SUV was blocking her driveway entrance.

Leaving my purse and gun, I got out of my car. Running past the Mercedes, I saw Gerald in the driver's seat, ignoring me. At Celia's front door, I hesitated a moment, then tried the knob. It was unlocked. Opening it, I stepped in and walked down the hallway. Glancing into the living room, I continued to the kitchen. Peeling an apple, Parson sat at the table. He did not bother to look up. Dressed in polo shirt and slacks, Luis stood behind him. Lithe and lethal looking, his teak-colored skin glowed as warm as the table. Bruno leaned against the Sub Zero, managing to make it look small in comparison. I could almost smell the stink of his sweat when he'd pressed his body against mine in the elevator

"Luis found this in the refrigerator for me. He's always trying to get me to eat more. I think apples are better left out in the fresh air. Please sit down, Ms. Poole." Parson wore a gray cashmere windbreaker with the collar turned up and gray slacks. His skeletal face looked as if the flesh had been scooped out from under his cheekbones with a spoon. His lips drawn down toward his goatee, he cut the apple in half.

I remained standing. "Is that Ben's car in the drive? Where's Heath?"

"Right to the point."

"You're a sick bastard."

Luis moved swiftly to my side, a knife appearing in his hand.

I stopped breathing for a moment. "Where are Heath and Ben?"

"You're a ballsy woman. Just like your mother." Parson set down the two halves of the apple and pushed himself up from the table. "She told me to go fuck myself. But I'm afraid you won't be able to do that. Come along." He moved to the door that connected to the garage and opened it for me. Luis pocketed his knife.

Inside, a single ray of dusty light shone through a small window. A chair lay on its side in a faded oil stain, flip-flops resting nearby, and a shadow moved over them. I looked up. I staggered backwards. From the garage's crossbeam Ben hung by a rope, the noose tight around his neck, his face swollen, his eyes looked down at us.

I lunged for him, screaming, "No, no, no!" As I tried to lift his legs up, to take the weight off the noose, Luis and Bruno pulled me back.

"He's been dead almost an hour." Parson watched from the door.

"You did this." Tears ran down my face as I struggled to free myself from the two men.

"Let her go," Parson ordered. "No. I found Ben hanging just as you see him."

"I don't understand. I spoke to him here and then he left."

"He must've returned."

I leaned against the wall for support. I thought of Ben standing in the kitchen fixated on the door. Was he thinking of suicide when I had surprised him?

"When I arrived," Parson said, "Heath was trying to get him down. Ben may have been alive then. It's hard to say. Of course, Luis and Bruno had to stop Heath."

"Where is he?"

Parson nodded and Luis moved to a pile of tarps in the corner and flipped one up. I followed him. Heath lay on his back, bound and gagged. Blood ran down his unshaven face from the top of his head. He still wore the shirt I had ripped the buttons off of last night.

Luis slapped Heath twice. Heath groaned and opened his eyes. Seeing me, he immediately began to struggle to free himself. I put my hand on his bare chest and he stopped moving. Feeling the warmth of his skin, his heart beating wildly, I leaned close and whispered "I'll be all right. Remember, you promised not to underestimate me."

Heath closed his eyes, then opened them. Bruno moved in and struck him in the head with the butt of his gun. I grabbed for Bruno, but Luis pulled me away and shoved me back into the kitchen.

"Now, shall we talk?" Parson was already easing his long body back into the kitchen chair. Meticulously, he sliced the inner core from each apple half.

Shaking, I wiped my tears with the sleeve of my sweater. "You want me to tell you where Celia is."

"Personally, I don't think you know where she is. But I think you'll find her. You know her better than any of us. Even Zaitlin." He shook his head sadly.

"I'm not sure of that anymore."

"Yes, you must feel deeply betrayed by her. I know that feeling. Did you know my wife killed herself?"

"No." I glanced at Bruno, who was busy wiping Heath's blood from the butt of his gun with his handkerchief.

"We kept it out of the news. Suicide is a betrayal, too. First my daughter dies, now my wife. This has been the blackest period of my life."

"I wonder if Hitler felt as victimized as you do."

Luis was trying to decide if that was a slur against his boss.

"What am I supposed to do when I find Celia?" I asked.

"Get the memory card from the camera that Ben and my daughter used to film their . . . clients. We will do the rest." He neatly sliced each apple half into two more equal parts, creating quarters.

"You mean kill her. How do you know she has the camera?"

"We've searched Ben's condo. He didn't have it. We searched the Zaitlins' house. They don't have it. It's not here. We know the police don't have it."

"How do you know that?"

"Let's just say I have contacts. I think when Celia killed my daughter, she took it. Or maybe she took it when she shot Zackary Logan. You look perplexed."

"Why would she murder either one?"

"A mother's love, however late it may be. She was trying to protect her son." He stabbed his knife into one of the apple quarters, raised the piece to his mouth, and bit.

"You know?"

"Of course." He chewed.

"Protect him from what?"

"From my daughter. I'm speaking from Celia's point of view. I see it the other way round, of course. Logan was probably an act of necessity. Under duress, Zaitlin told me he had just found out that Ben was his son and Celia his real mother. He pleaded with me not to hurt Ben. He even asked me to kill *him* instead. So I gave him a gun to use on himself."

"You are an evil bastard."

242

"Is that the same as being a sick bastard?" He grinned. "Keep your cell phone on, Ms. Poole. I will be in contact with you. Any more questions?"

"No."

"Odd. I thought you might ask me when I was going to let Heath go."

"You have no intention of letting him go."

His jaw tensed. "Don't try to be more clever than me."

"I wouldn't think of it." I was just hoping to be *as* clever. "I know why you were blackmailing my husband. You should be very proud of your daughter. She was just like you. A psychopath."

He rose up out of his chair, slamming his hands down on the table. The apple pieces danced. I turned my back on him and left. They let me walk out of the house. They had to. Parson wanted Celia more than he wanted me. Until he was finished with her, that is.

I stopped and watched Gerald position his rump against the side of the limo and adjust his sunglasses, getting ready to take in some beach air and sun. I had no idea how I was going to find Celia, or how I could save Heath, or even myself. But I did know I had one small area of power left.

I approached Gerald. "Don't forget about the bargain I made with you and Bruno in the penthouse."

Straightening up, he wiped off his sunglasses. "I didn't make any deal."

"Sure you did. I don't tell Parson I got into his penthouse because the two of you screwed up and made it easy for his wife to jump, and you and Bruno will get to live."

"We can take you out any time."

"I've thought of that. So if I should die prematurely, I've made sure that what I know about that night will go viral."

"Viral?" He was confused.

Christ. "I've made sure every TV station and newspaper in town will have my story."

He blinked his penny-shaped eyes at me. "You're full of crap."

"Oh, and the same goes if Heath dies."

"He wasn't part of the deal."

"So we do have one. Excellent, Gerald." I patted his arm.

Heading toward my car, I hoped he bought my story. If nothing else, I knew he didn't feel quite so secure anymore.

I drove a few blocks, then pulled over to the side of the highway. No longer able to control my anger, my fear, or my grief, I called Celia and screamed at her voicemail. "I know Ben is your son. I know what he and Jenny Parson were doing. I know . . ." I stopped and took a deep breath. I couldn't tell her that I knew Ben was dead, hanging from a beam in her garage. Not in a voicemail. I continued in a calmer voice. "I need to talk to you. I'm in danger. I need your help. You probably need mine. If our friendship means anything to you, call me."

I threw the phone onto the passenger seat and leaned my head back, closing my eyes against the images of Ben's distended features and Heath struggling to free himself when he saw me. I felt the sun hit my face through the windshield, the heater hot on my legs, and I listened to the endless line of growling cars racing by. I was completely alone, and I had no idea how I was going to find Celia.

There is an acting term called *the star pause*. It's when the actress is left alone on stage, waiting for the next character to enter. In those few moments, she must find something real to do, something the audience can believe and not think she's just waiting for her next cue. My mother told me all great actors relished this moment. "So don't blow it, darling, by pacing, smoking, or running your hands through your hair. Any idiot can do that. Find something that reveals your character."

I ran my hands through my hair. Then I grabbed the steering wheel, stepped on the gas, and drove off. Drive, it's what L.A. people do. I didn't know where I was going until I found myself on Sunset Boulevard. It was then that I realized I was headed back to Bella Casa.

CHAPTER FORTY

Bella Casa was a house you could hide in. Years ago I had done the same thing when I wanted to get high so I could obliterate my feelings. Or to keep out of reach of Brad, Beau, or Bob, who wouldn't take no for an answer after I had said yes the first time. Celia knew the house as well as I did.

Peering in the rearview mirror, I checked to see whether Parson's men were following. There was no limo, and all the other cars behind me looked the same—unfamiliar. I turned left and went through the Bel Air arches and started up Stone Canyon Road.

The gates to Bella Casa were open. Pieces of yellow crime-scene tape still clung to them. Maybe the cops had forgotten to close them. Driving in, I didn't see a car parked in the driveway. I got out of the Jag and tried the front door. Locked. I walked around to the side of the house and tried the pool door. It opened. Somebody had been here, or still was. Wondering if Celia was a physical threat to me, I adjusted the strap of my bag on my shoulder and felt the weight of the Glock.

Moving quickly around the pool, I entered the gallery, then veered into the foyer. I stopped, waiting for any sound that might tell me another person was in the house. Not hearing anything, I crept up the tile stairs and down the long hallway past what was once my mother's bedroom. At the end of the hall I carefully opened a door that let out a loud creaking noise reminiscent of the bad sound effects in a slasher movie. I froze, listening. But I seemed to be the only one making noise.

I entered my old bedroom, which was big and square with a small, pretty crystal chandelier hanging daintily from the ceiling. In the night when I couldn't sleep, I used to observe how it scattered its prismatic stars above my bed, making me feel there was a better world, a better way of life. Somewhere.

Crossing to the closet door, I rested my hand on the wrought-iron knob, then turned it. I walked in and stood facing the back cedar-paneled wall and whispered "Celia?" No answer. I pushed twice on it, and the panel popped open, revealing a long narrow room with one window that held a view of the top of a shaggy eucalyptus tree.

My mother had explained that this was a room where people used to store trunks when they traveled by ship or train. "Think of Marlene Dietrich or Greta Garbo perched on top of a pile of Louis Vuitton suitcases. I should have been a star then instead of in the eighties when people's hair is bigger than their talent." I knew immediately it would be my safe room.

There was no sign that Celia had been hiding here. On one wall was a built-in cabinet. I opened it, reached into the deep wide shelf, and felt around with my hand. I found a wrinkled newspaper. I looked at the date on the front page of the *Los Angeles Times*. It was yesterday's date. The day I had told Celia to leave her house. What were the odds of that?

Had she wrapped the camera in the papers and hidden it here until she could come back for it? But why hide it at all? Why not take it with her? Because Parson would want the memory card. If he found her with it he'd kill her and take it. But if he found her without it, she might be able to buy some time. So had she left it here and then come back to get it. The one thing I was certain about was she wouldn't have left the security gates open.

I rubbed my forehead. I was thinking too hard. Concentrate on one thing, Diana. The gates are open. There is no car in the driveway.

I ran down the stairs, out the back door, and across the area where Zackary Logan had been found dead to the old rickety garage. I lifted up the wooden door. Inside the dank space was a bright red BMW convertible, just like the one P. J. Binder owned. The beige leather seats smelled of a too-sweet perfume. With the severity of his wound, Binder had to still be in the hospital. So Pearl was here.

Before I went back to find her, I decided to check and see if I had been followed. Skirting the drive, I hurried down to the wall that fronted the house and edged to the entrance, peering around the gate. About two blocks away was a parked blue van. I stepped back quickly. Christ. It could be a delivery van, but I doubted it.

I ran back into the house and strode through the first floor, yelling. "Pearl! I know you're in here. Pearl!"

In the foyer I heard a tapping sound, and then Pearl's muffled voice, "I'm locked in. Get me out of here."

She was inside a four-foot-high cubbyhole built into the side of the stairwell. The door latched only on the outside. It was where we had kept logs for the fireplace. I lifted the lever.

Pearl scampered out on all fours, then leaped to her feet, madly brushing at her bleached-white hair and slapping at her body. "There're spiders in there! I couldn't open the door. I thought I was going to die!" She waved her cement-gray nails for emphasis, then frantically brushed at her low-cut pink T-shirt.

"What are you doing here, Pearl?"

"What? I was looking for something."

"A camera?"

"An earring." She slapped dust from the knees of her jeans.

"Really? After all this time you expect to find an earring? Where's your purse?"

"In my car."

"How do you think I knew you were in the house? I just saw your car in the garage. There was no purse in it." I pointed to where she'd been hiding. "Get it."

"You'll lock me in there."

"I'm not going to do that. Get it!"

Trying to keep an eye on me, she bent over and pulled out her purse by the shoulder strap. As she stood up, she swung her bag at me. I ducked, but not far enough. She hit the side of my head.

Stunned, I grabbed the straps. Letting go, she ran. Clutching both of our purses, I chased her through the living room into the dining room and down the gallery. She darted into the swimming-pool room. I caught up to her as she careered around the pool's corner where the deck angled down to the water. Losing her balance, she slipped and fell to her hands and knees. Before she was completely up on her feet again, I reached her and shoved her into the water.

She thrashed around. "I can't swim!"

"You're in the shallow end. Stand up." I rummaged in her purse, pulled out the camera, and opened it. There was no memory card. "Where is it?"

Spitting water, she stood up, angrily pushing limp hair out of her eyes. "I don't know what you're talking about." She extended her hand up to me. "Help me out."

"So you can pull me in? I don't think so. There are steps in the corner."

As she sputtered and waded her way to the stairs, I checked the recent calls on her cell. I saw Celia's number.

Crawling out, she realized what I was doing. "Give me that." But it was a half-hearted demand. She was dripping and shivering, her arms wrapped around herself trying to get warm.

"Is Binder still in the hospital?" I asked.

"Valley Presbyterian."

"Does he know you're in contact with Celia?"

"Who's she?"

"There's no way you knew where this camera was hidden without someone very familiar with this house telling you. And her number's on your phone. Why don't I call Binder and tell him you've been in touch with Celia and . . ."

"No, no. Please don't!" Her smooth brow knitted in fear. "She called me at the store this morning and told me if I didn't do what she said, she'd tell Parson I was the one who made Jenny have sex with all those guys. And that he would kill me. I want my purse. I want to go. I'm all wet." She reached for it.

I let it slip out of my hand. As she bent over I shoved my hand down the front of her scoop-neck shirt between her rock-solid breasts and grabbed the card. Then I gave her a hard push back into the pool.

Waiting for her to stop splashing and swearing, I put the memory card between my soft breasts. "Where's Celia?"

"She wouldn't tell me," she spat. "I'm supposed to call her when I get the camera."

I thought a moment. "Okay, here is what's going to happen. Parson's men are parked outside the house, so I'm going take your car. I need to make sure I can get away."

"What?" she slogged through the water again. "No way!" She crawled out, shivering worse.

"You'll take my car."

"Parson's men will follow me. They'll try to kill me. Everyone wants to kill me!"

"Are you on one of the videos?"

"I thought I wasn't, but Celia said I am."

"Listen to me. You'll drive to Valley Presbyterian Hospital. Stay with Binder until you hear from me. You'll be safe there."

Her eyes narrowed. "How do I know Parson's men are even out there?"

Christ. "If I'm lying, you don't need to worry, do you?"

"What if they push me off the road?"

"They won't. They need you alive. They want you to take them to Celia."

"I can't do this. I'll lead them to P.J.!"

"The hospital has security. Anyway, you should've thought about him before you got involved in this mess." I held out her cell. "Call Celia and tell her you have the camera. Get her address. Don't screw with me, Pearl."

"I can't." She pursed her lips.

"Why?"

"Please just give me the memory card, please let me go." She stamped her feet, her teeth chattered.

"You were going to double-cross Celia?"

"I have to protect P. J. and myself."

"Call her now. I have a Glock in my purse."

"Who doesn't."

"You don't. Call her."

She snatched the cell phone away, closing her fist around it, and punched in the number. Listening, she finally spoke, "I have it." She hung up.

"You didn't get the address."

"I'm supposed to leave a message on her voicemail. She'll call me back." The phone rang. "See?" She answered it and listened. "Okay. Okay." Ending the call, she looked at me. "Celia's at the Larchmont Motel off Ventura Boulevard on Kinross. Room 10."

I grabbed Pearl's wrist with my left hand and wrenched the cell lose from her tight grip with my right hand.

"That's mine. I may need it," she said.

"I'm keeping it in case Celia calls. Remember, you'll be safe in the hospital. They want Celia. Not you. Especially if you don't have the memory card."

She blinked water from her big eyes. "You sure?"

"Yes." I was lying, but she needed some sense of security, and I needed to get out of there. "Stay with Binder. Don't leave."

"I won't." She sniffled like a child, which she was, in a way. "Does your car have a heater?"

"The best there is, trust me." I handed her my keys.

Reluctantly, she gave me hers and then hurried outside.

Hearing her rev the Jag's engine, I walked back through the gallery and into the living room and looked out the front window in time to see her pull out onto the street. I waited, hoping she would make it safely.

A few seconds later Bruno and Gerald appeared at the opening of the drive, trotting up to the house. My permanent chill shot through me. Shit. Why weren't they following the Jag? Frantic, I ran back into the foyer, up the stairs, and down the hall to my bedroom. In the closet I tapped on the panel and hid myself in the safe room. Heart thumping, trying to control my loud breathing, I took the Glock out of my purse, fumbled off the safety, and gripped it in my hand.

I could hear the sound of doors being opened and slammed shut below. The men were moving systematically through the house. There was a pause, and I figured they might be coming upstairs. Soon I heard the opening and closing of doors in Mother's bedroom. I didn't dare move or the floor would creak.

Then they were in the guest room. My bedroom was next. Sweat ran down my back. My black sweater itched my skin. I heard my bedroom door groan open. Aiming the gun at the cedar panel, I listened to the two men stride across the floor toward me. My pulse throbbed in my temples. The closet door opened, and my body involuntarily stiffened as if they could see me.

"Nobody." Bruno's voice.

"What do you think they're asking for this piece of shit? It needs a lot of work." Gerald's voice.

"What, you thinking of buying it?"

"Who says I can't?"

"You still tracking the Jag?"

"Yeah."

"Let's get going before she drives out of range of the GPS."

Finally, the sound of their heavy footsteps grew distant. I waited for anther ten minutes, thinking that Gerald had to have put some kind of device on my car so could they track it. I tried not to think of Heath. I tried not to think he could already be dead. I didn't want him to be another ghost. Then I fled the house, got into the BMW, and sped away. I looked about as inconspicuous as a blond in a red convertible.

CHAPTER FORTY-ONE

made it over Coldwater Canyon and down into the tangled spread of buildings, shops, and traffic that was Ventura Boulevard. Turning right, I went a few blocks and found Kinross, then another three blocks and I was at the Larchmont Motel. It sat in the middle of a parking lot. The asphalt had lifted, and weeds and pretty wild flowers had popped up between the cracks. Just one story, the motel looked as if a 1.0 earthquake would rattle it into a pile of sticks and chunks of stucco. The sun beat hard on its façade. In each window a liver-colored blind had been pulled against the glare. This was the kind of place for quick sex, a quick high, or a long binge.

I didn't see Celia's white Lexus as I pulled in and parked. Taking the camera out of my purse, I got out of the car, found room 10, and knocked. The door opened only inches because the chain was on. Celia peered out at me through the crack.

"I've got the camera." I showed it to her before she could slam the door in my face.

"Goddammit, Diana. Were you followed?" she asked.

"No."

Sighing heavily, she slipped the chain off, let me in, and relocked the door. A bolted-down dresser lamp was the only light in the darkened room. The air conditioner built into the back wall heaved out moldy air while rattling the picture hanging above it.

"How are you?" I asked hesitantly.

"How do I look?"

"Not too good."

Dressed in a wrinkled short black skirt and rumpled red silk blouse, her skin was sallow and dry as the brittle shade covering her only window. The bruise around her eye and across her cheek had paled to a jaundice color. She reminded me of Parson's wife, a woman who knew death was near. But Mrs. Parson welcomed it, even planned it. The shattered expression in Celia's eyes told me she feared death with all her being.

She eyed the camera with all the intensity of a drug addict waiting for her fix.

"Where's Pearl?" she asked.

"It's a long story. Let's just say two of Parson's men are following her to Valley Presbyterian Hospital, where P. J. Binder is recuperating."

"If they catch her, she'll tell them where I am."

"Then you and I should transact our business quickly."

"Give me the camera."

I let her grab it.

Sinking onto the edge of the unmade bed, she ripped it open. She looked up at me. "The memory card is gone."

"I have it."

"On you?'

"I wouldn't be that stupid." I felt it pressing into my breasts,

Jumping up, she ran to the window, pushed aside the shade, and peered out. She let it drop back and demanded "Where is it?"

"I want something for it."

"What?"

"We were friends once, remember?"

She leaned against the dresser. The dust-filmed mirror reflected the back of her hunched shoulders and her tangled dark hair. "I remember." Her voice softened. "Knowing you, you probably came here for the truth."

"Yes. And Parson wants me to bring you and the memory card to him, or he'll kill someone I know. Someone I care about."

Her violet eyes flashed, her expression hardened. "You're going to try to take me to Parson? And how in hell do you think you're going to manage that?" She reached for her handbag on the dresser.

"Don't." I slid the Glock from my bag and aimed it at her.

She stared. "I don't believe this."

"I don't either." I edged nearer to her and yanked her purse away. Feeling around inside, I pulled out a gun.

"Funny, we both keep voting for gun control." She smiled ruefully.

"I've changed my mind on that." I put her weapon inside my purse, then threw hers on the floor.

Then I sat in the only chair, still holding the Glock on her.

"Listen to me, Diana, I'm a businesswoman, and you're not." She paced, barefooted; her five-inch heels were on the floor by the nightstand, "I know how to deal with men like Parson. He'd rather have the video of his daughter screwing everybody under the sun than kill me. He's more concerned about her image. Or maybe he wants to continue her blackmailing business, who knows? I don't care." She was a boss tossing off ideas to her assistant instead of a woman with a weapon pointed at her. "The memory card is my only protection. I can make this work. It's what I do. I make people buy houses they only think they want."

"Is Ben in any of the videos?"

"Ben?" She stopped.

"You can't make it work, Celia." I leaned to one side and slid the photograph of her, Gwyn, and Ben as a baby from my jeans pocket and held it out to her.

Taking it, she ran her finger over his face just as Gwyn had done. Two mothers, and yet Ben was so unloved.

"How did you know about this?" She looked at me, eyes narrowed. "I kept it tucked in a book on my nightstand."

"I found it crumpled on your kitchen floor, where I think Ben must've dropped it. He trashed your house."

"Why?"

"Anger, probably. He was looking for some sign that you really are his mother. Gwyn confirmed my suspicions that you were."

"She would never tell anybody."

"Her world has fallen apart, just like yours. Just like mine, come to think of it."

"My world is intact as long as I can stay in control of the situation. You have to help me, Diana. You have to give it to me."

"Your world isn't intact, Celia. Ben's dead. He hanged himself in your garage." As I told her what had happened, her face crumpled. Her body sagged.

On the other side of the adjoining wall, a toilet flushed.

Celia slumped on the bed.

CHAPTER FORTY-TWO

listened to her cry and moan, and I wondered who she really was crying for. Then she sat up, wiping her hands across her eyes. "Suicide?"

"Parson said it was."

"You believe him?"

"I believe he can kill someone without laying a hand on them." I thought of Colin. "But he told me that when he arrived at your house, Leo Heath was trying to cut Ben down. He may still have been alive then. But Parson's men stopped Heath."

"Heath?"

"The one you lied about. I think that was your first lie to me, at least that I know about."

"Are you saying Ben wanted to kill himself?"

Not wanting to keep the fury out of my voice, I said "The kid grew up thinking his biological father was a rapist. That his stepfather didn't love him because he loved his mistress more. Then the mistress turned out to be his real mother. Robert didn't even know, for Christ's sake."

"Shut up!"

"And to get back at them, Ben joins Jenny in blackmailing everyone who's important to Robert and Gwyn. Yes, Celia, I think he wanted to kill himself."

She stared at me, shocked at my rage.

The TV turned on in the next room. Its low muttering mixed with the rumbling of the air conditioner.

"I want to know what kind of killer you are," I said. "Are you cold-blooded, or accidental?"

She pushed her ink black hair from her face. "Jenny was an accident."

"Start from the beginning."

"Ben found out I was his father's mistress. I don't know who told him." Her expression hardened. "Was it you?"

"He grew up, Celia. He put the pieces together all by himself. It wasn't difficult for him."

"He wanted to meet me."

"On the night of Jenny's death?"

"No, a few days before. He came to my house. He was drunk or high on something. He wanted to see where Robert slept with me, wanted to see where his family's money was going. He was shocked when I told him I wasn't taking any money from Robert. I told Ben that I loved Robert, but that I also loved my independence. And I never wanted to marry or have children." Her voice broke.

"You said that to your son."

"Ben didn't know that then. He asked if I didn't worry about his mother's feelings. I told him she had her relationship with Robert and I had mine."

The TV grew louder. I could make out two actresses speaking in Spanish.

"He told me he was working in the video business. That his father and mother would be very proud. And then he blurted out what he was really doing. He ranted about how he and Jenny were going to show up all the hypocrites like Robert, like me. Then he tried to kiss me while taking a picture of us on this small video camera. I pushed him away, and he fell on the sofa and passed out."

"You checked to see what was on the camera?"

She nodded. "I recognized Bella Casa immediately, Jenny Parson with Ryan, and Jenny taunting Beth Woods while she was having sex with her. God, it was a Who's Who of Hollywood elite. There was no security protection. No password. Anybody could've seen the videos. What were they thinking?" Furious, she jumped up and pounded the wall. "Keep it down in there!"

The volume on the TV lowered. Celia leaned against the dresser, hands clasped in front of her. Her face was ragged. "In the morning Ben was frantic when I told him that I wouldn't let him have the camera back. He became a little boy again, pleading with me, telling me that Jenny was dangerous. That he didn't want anyone to know what he was doing, that he wanted out. That she and Zackary Logan would kill him if he didn't have the camera."

"So you had Ben set up a meeting with Jenny?"

She nodded. "Ben called me from the club. He said Zackary would be driving her home. Jenny had been drinking and was threatening him. If she didn't get the camera back that night, she would tell Robert. He told me where she lived and to wait in the shadows by the garbage bins in the alley. He would be following them in his car so he could bring Zackary back to the club. When they arrived, Zackary drove Jenny into the garage and parked in her slot. Ben, who had a key, let me in through the side door next to the gates. Keeping us out of view of the security cameras, he guided me to Jenny. She made Zackary get out of her Audi and told me to get in. I slid into the driver's seat." She paused, unclasping her hands, then rubbing them over her forehead and into her hair.

"I thought I could talk her out of what she was doing," she continued. "That was my intention, anyway. But she threatened me. She said if anybody found out about their business, she'd tell them I was a full partner. That I'd let them bring the johns to Bella Casa. She was hysterical, out of control, making all kinds of wild threats, so I shook her. She screamed, and then she started hitting me. That's when my cell must've somehow got turned on."

"It was Jenny I heard screaming, not you."

"Yes. You understand, don't you Diana? I really didn't have a choice. I had to stop her. I shook her harder and harder until her neck snapped back and her head hit the passenger window. It made an awful sound, a kind of dull crack. I couldn't believe it had gone that far. . . ." She sat down on the edge of the bed and buried her head in her hands.

"Oh, Celia," I murmured.

"It was Zackary Logan who took charge." She looked up. "He got the key from her purse, and he and Ben went up to her condo and got the bags to put her in. All three of us wrapped her up and carried her out to the bin. Ben kept saying 'You didn't have to kill her.' The boys drove away in Ben's car, and I walked back to mine and went home."

"*Did* you have to kill her?"

"I didn't mean to. I was trying to protect everyone."

My long-time friend, the girl I had grown up with, had become a woman who could spend most of her adult life living a lie about her child and her lover, and then lose control and kill someone. Another lie, another person I didn't really know. The TV was loud again.

She was peering anxiously at me. "What are you thinking about?"

"Remember the night we sat on the side street and you told me how Ben had attacked you in your car in the vacant lot? You were so believable."

"The essence of what I said about him and me was true. I didn't plan to kill Jenny. I just saw Ben's life being destroyed."

"And yours. And Robert's."

"All right, I felt threatened. Everything I had worked so hard for could have been destroyed by this uncaring bitch. I didn't have a movie star for a mother, Diana. I had to create my own life the way I wanted it, with no help from anybody."

"If you let people cut in front of you in line, you'll never get ahead."

"What?"

"That's what you said to me when we first met. We were waiting to get in to see one of my mother's movies. You're the one who reminded me of it when I was holding frozen peas to your bruised face thinking a man had beat you up."

"Killing Jenny was an accident."

"Was Zackary Logan an accident?"

"I didn't kill him. I swear to God. He called me and said he wanted to meet me at Bella Casa. But I didn't go."

"Why should I believe you?"

"No reason, except it's true."

"What about Ryan Johns?"

"Robert told me that Parson was a madman. That whoever killed his daughter would face an awful death. He told me he had Leo Heath working on the case, and I remembered him from Bella Casa. I panicked. I assumed Heath knew what had been going on at the house. So I thought if I sent him and Parson the video of Ryan. . . ."

"He'd be the perfect scapegoat. Except Ryan turned around and gave Parson your name. That bit of irony must've stung."

"It did."

"How did Ben find out you were his mother?"

"After you called to tell me to leave my house, that I might be in danger, I phoned Ben. If I was going to die, I wanted him to know the truth. And that I killed Jenny for him."

"You left him with the burden of all that?"

Ignoring my question, she asked "What are you going to do?"

Disgusted, I stood and walked to the door. "You can save your-self. I won't stop you. But I'm keeping the memory card."

"You can't." She got her feet. "You can't leave me like this. You know what Parson will do to me. Even if I did mean to kill Jenny, it was to help everyone involved."

"And now you want the card to bargain with Parson. And you don't care if he uses it to continue his daughter's blackmail, even if he hurts everyone you were supposedly trying to help. Christ, Celia. It's over."

We stared at each other. Then the TV in the next room suddenly turned up to full volume, filling the tense silence between us. As we glanced toward the booming noise of the chattering Spanish women, the breathless soft sounds of *pop, pop, pop* splintered the common wall. I lost sight of Celia as I dove for the floor. My gun flew from my hand. The muted gunfire continued. The TV turned off, and the room was quiet. Neither of us moved.

Seconds later, the motel room door crashed open, and a man stepped over me. My hair had fallen across my face, and I was lying on my right arm. I opened my eyes just enough to see Rubio take the camera from the bed. Rubio . . . I had forgotten about the son-of-a-bitch. Then I saw Celia on the floor, blood pumping from her chest. He knelt down next to her.

"Gotcha," he said, like a hunter to a deer.

Then Rubio was beside me. He pushed the hair from my face and we looked at each other. My throat went dry.

He flashed his thick white teeth at me and aimed the gun between my eyes. "Gotcha."

But another gun went off. His grin froze, then vanished, and he fell heavily to the side. I lifted my head to see what had happened. Celia was on her knees, the Glock in her hand. She smiled at me the same way she had when we were young. Then she dropped the gun and collapsed. The room tilted. I laid my head back down.

"What the fuck?" It was Bruno's voice.

I felt him standing behind me. Tensing, I lay still.

"Parson's not going to like this," Gerald rushed into the room, stopping near Rubio.

I tried not to breathe. I opened my eyes just enough to see him peering inside the camera Rubio had dropped.

Gerald frowned. "There's no memory card. Maybe the actress has it."

My need to survive kicked in, my mind began to work. These two men were my one little area of power. Without trying to show any movement, I edged my right hand up between my breasts and pulled the card out, holding it in my palm.

"Is she alive?" Bruno kicked my thigh with his foot.

My body recoiled.

"Yeah, she's alive." Now standing in front of me, Bruno grabbed me under my arms. I let myself go limp and heavy as he dragged me up the front of his body to my feet.

His sweat reeked. I went into my madwoman act, except I wasn't acting. I screamed. I punched and kicked. Moving my right hand down his chest, I slipped the memory card into the handkerchief pocket of his suit jacket and shrieked louder.

"Shut up!" Gerald yelled from behind me.

Then something hard slammed into the back of my skull. I fell to my knees.

CHAPTER FORTY-THREE

opened my eyes. Slumped in a worn maroon-velvet seat, I raised my head, breathing in the odor of dust, mildew, and forlorn emptiness. Putting my hand to my head, I felt a lump. Nausea swept through me as I leaned forward, gripping the back of the seat in front of me, and peering at a movie screen. A velvet curtain draped the proscenium. Light fixtures sculpted like bent arms with hands holding dimly lighted torches lined the walls. I looked up at the ceiling, blinking it into focus. The Hollywood version of the Sistine Chapel mural had been painted on it. The angels, movie-star sexy, had faded and chipped into decay. Gerald and Bruno sat still on either side of me as if we were at a private screening waiting for the movie to begin. I was in Parson's theater.

I sat a few moments, gathering myself. Swaying, I stood up. "I'm going for popcorn. Want some?" I quickly squeezed past Bruno. Just as I reached the aisle he stuck out his foot, tripping me. I went down on the carpet.

Gerald snickered. I got to my hands and knees then sat back on my haunches, waiting for the nightmare room to stop tilting. "I thought you and Gerald weren't allowed in The Rock. At least that's what Mrs. Parson told me."

Bruno shot up out of his seat and leaned down, putting his face in mine. "You keep your mouth shut." He jerked me up to my feet.

"Ms. Poole," Parson greeted me as he came down the stage steps and walked up the aisle to us. "I'm glad you're alive. Rubio had such a need for drama, the need to create his own special effects. Not a good combination for a hit man. I won't miss him."

"How did he know Celia was at the motel?" I asked, as the room finally righted itself.

"I had Bruno, Gerald, and Rubio following you. Bruno and Gerald tailed who they thought was you to the hospital. So I ordered Rubio to wait at Bella Casa in case someone else went in or out. And you did. In a bright red convertible. Rubio followed you to the motel and of course informed Bruno where he was."

"I didn't see his bike."

"He wasn't on it, just in a regular plain sedan. I didn't order him to rent the room next to Celia's or fire stupidly through the wall. But that was Rubio's way. He too loved the movies. Did you tell them where the memory card is?"

"No."

"We searched Celia, the room, and Ms. Poole," Bruno explained. "Nothing. It was a quick search. We had to get out before the cops arrived."

"Where's Heath?" I asked Parson.

Parson assessed me. "You said you didn't tell Bruno and Gerald where the card is. Does that mean you know?"

"Yes."

"We're making headway."

"I want to see Heath first."

"Bring her upstairs," he told the two men.

Parson led us backstage. Bruno's hand gripped my arm as we made our way up the circular stairs. I didn't have a plan. But I had one goal, the card in Bruno's pocket. Other than that, I was improvising, and like all good actresses I knew I had to follow my instincts. Wait for the moment.

Parson opened the door to his bedroom. I braced myself for what bloody condition Heath might be in.

"Sit, Miss Poole."

Bruno shoved me onto the bed. Then he and Gerald leaned against the wall opposite me. Now Parson opened the door to the cement-lined room. Heath was tied to the wooden chair. His shirt hung open and his head lolled down, chin resting on his bare chest.

Luis stood next to him, his black hair glistening like a gigolo's.

"As you can see, we've kept Heath under control," Parson said. "I could play the torture game to make you tell me where the card is, but that's tedious, don't you think?"

"Let him go. I'll tell you where it is."

Luis grabbed Heath's hair and yanked back his head. Heath's face stretched in a grimace of pain.

"You know I can't do that," Parson said in his most reasonable tone. "You tell me its location, and I'll send Bruno and Gerald to get it."

"Let Heath go first."

"Luis." Parson spoke his name but it was really a command.

In one balletic movement Luis pulled a knife from his pants pocket, flipped the blade from its sheath, and pressed it to Heath's throat.

"Stop it!" All eyes were on me. I had my moment. I had my audience. "I don't want to watch any more people die. I saw Celia die. I saw your wife die. I can't take it . . ."

"My wife?" Parson looked as if he'd been shot. "What are you talking about?"

I glanced at Heath, still with the knife at this throat. He was watching me closely. And I realized he was more alert than he'd first appeared.

"What about my wife?" Parson demanded.

"I was there in the penthouse when she jumped. I tried to prevent her. We all did. Ask Bruno. Ask Gerald."

"She's lying!" Gerald said. "We checked on your wife every hour, like you said. The last time we did, she was gone."

Bruno stared silently at me, his eyes filled with pure hatred.

"Go on, Ms. Poole," Parson said.

"She was on the balcony when Bruno and Gerald broke in."

"Broke in?"

"Yes. She'd stolen the key from Bruno and had locked the door from the inside."

"I don't know what she's talking about." The blood had drained from Bruno's face.

With a small, hard smile, Luis moved to the doorway, the knife in his hand, his back to Heath.

"I was with her," I said to Parson. "You have pre-Columbian art in your penthouse. The glass wall automatically folds back into panels. You have a private elevator with a door that looks like all the other office doors. Your wife had auburn hair, she was wearing jeans." Parson's eyes were beginning to glaze over with rage. I glanced at Heath. He was working his hands trying to loosen the ropes on his wrists.

"She said you took Jenny to the Rock, and Jenny came home wanting to be an actress. She said you used the theater for solace. Or to kill."

Parson's stone-like eyes narrowed, his cadaverous body went rigid, and he jabbed a finger at me. "Enough of this bullshit. I want the card *now.*"

"I saw Bruno take it."

Parson turned slowly toward the big man.

Bruno pulled himself up. "I don't have it, sir. She's screwing with us."

"He put it in his handkerchief pocket. Look for yourself."

Bruno's left hand flattened against his chest. His eyes widened as he felt the card. Instantly his other hand jammed inside his jacket and pulled out his gun. But Bruno wasn't fast enough.

With a flick of his wrist, Luis hurled his knife across the room and into Bruno's neck. Bruno's mouth gaped open. Dropping the gun, his hands grabbed for the knife. Blood spurted from his jugular. His legs buckled and he dropped to the floor. The Aubusson rug soaked up his blood.

Heath had worked his hands free. He was grappling with the ropes on his legs.

"Stop!" Gerald yelled. "We didn't do anything. It was her. It was all her!" Backing up to the bedroom door, he waved his gun at me, then at Parson.

Parson was motionless, standing as if he were in a trance. I knew Gerald was waiting for an order to shoot, for someone to tell him what to do.

Heath had freed his legs. Silently he rose, turned, lifted his chair, and crashed it down on Luis's back. Luis flew forward, his chin up, surprise on his face. He belly-flopped onto the floor next to Bruno. Gasping for air, he reached for Bruno's gun.

Gerald fired, somehow missing all of us. Heath ducked, moved in, and seized Bruno's weapon from Luis. With a quick twist of his body, he aimed and fired.

A round black hole appeared in Gerald's forehead. He dropped to his knees. Shoulders slumping, he keeled over. I moved to him and grabbed his weapon.

Parson sat down on his bed and asked calmly, "Are you all right, Luis?"

"*Si.*" Luis's hand moved to take the knife from Bruno's neck.

But Heath stood over him. "Give it up, Luis. Go sit with your boss."

As Luis silently joined him, Parson looked at Heath with calculating eyes. "If you were a cold-blooded killer, Heath, you'd shoot Luis and me. Obviously, you're not."

"Don't be too sure," Heath said.

I stood next to Heath, holding Gerald's gun on Parson and Luis. "Heath's going to the call the police."

Parson tossed me his bony Pasha grin, but spoke to Heath. "Are you?"

Heath didn't answer.

"Heath?"

He had a look of not knowing me on his face. He turned and walked back into the cement room and scooped up his wallet, cell phone, flashlight, and coins from the wood table.

"Your mother," Parson told me in an amused voice, "would figure a way out of this mess so nobody got hurt, especially her. That's what Heath is doing. He's the best fixer there is."

My voice rose. "You can't do this, Heath!"

Heath stepped back into the bedroom. "He'd walk right out of the police station, Diana. He knows too much about too many people."

"He should at least be arrested."

Parson pursed his lips and stroked his goatee. "She has a point, a little too moral for this situation, but a point. You must be very disappointed in Heath. Your mother would have loved him. Come on, Luis."

Luis, his perfectly pressed Polo shirt drenched in Bruno's blood, got to his feet and opened the door for Parson.

"Wait a minute," Heath said, "I've changed my mind. I think I will have you arrested."

"I've never seen a woman sway you before, Heath."

"You don't know people as well as you think you do, Parson." He gestured with his weapon to the cement room. "Get in there. Now."

Parson gave a world-weary shrug. He and Luis entered their torture chamber.

Parson turned and stared at me. "Did my wife intend to kill herself? I need to know."

"Yes, she said it was the only power she had over you."

He hesitated, then nodded. "Bruno was a trustworthy man, in my world that is. Did he take the card?"

"No, I put it in his pocket."

"You are impressive. Perhaps more impressive than your mother."

"Did you want the card to protect Jenny?"

A sad, distant smiled formed on his grim lips. "We spend too much time protecting the dead."

Heath shoved him all the way in and bolted the door.

CHAPTER FORTY-FOUR

The stench of blood filled the room. Heath turned from the bolted door and took his cell from his pants pocket and punched in a number. Placing Gerald's gun on the nightstand, I stood by the bed, my arms crossed, holding myself. As Heath waited for someone to answer, I looked at his shirt, the buttons ripped off. He was breathing as if his ribs hurt. Finally he spoke into the phone. "Hey, Spangler, this is Heath. I'm in an old movie theater called The Roxy. Two of Parson's men are dead. I've locked up Parson and Luis. They're all yours if you can hold 'em." He gave the address. "Diana's with me. I'll tell her." He disconnected and peered at me, questions in his dark eyes. "They found Celia at a place called the Larchmont Motel."

"I know." Swallowing hard, I crouched beside Bruno and slid the memory card from his pocket and put it in mine. Needing to get away from the smell of death, I went out to the landing and stood by the spiral staircase.

"Diana? Are you all right?" Heath asked, moving next to me.

"Rubio shot Celia. Before she died, she killed him. She saved my life."

"I'm glad she did." He put his arms around me, pulling me to him.

"I owe you a new shirt," I said.

"I owe you my life. Parson was right. You are impressive."

Taking a deep breath, I moved away from him. "Were you really going to let Parson go?"

"If you weren't here? Yes."

"Why?"

He heaved a sigh. "In the Army you were ordered to do things you knew were ineffective, even useless. And arresting Parson is the same thing to me. He'll be let go. He has too much on too many important people. Why waste everybody's time and money? Why go though the process?" He paused, looking at me. "You're disappointed."

"I guess I am."

"You were right, Diana. I'm a fixer. I see a problem, I try to take care of it for the people involved. The people who pay me. Sometimes I take shortcuts, even skirt the law. It's what I do. It's who I am. Let's get you some air."

"What about Parson and Luis?"

He gave mirthless laugh. "They can't get out."

We walked down the stairs to the area behind the movie screen and out the service doors. It was dark now. Parson's limo was parked in the alley. Behind it was the blue van.

Not talking, not touching, we walked down the sidewalk past stores closing up for the night. Hard-working men and women pulling the gates across their properties, trying to protect what little they had inside. The cold night air felt clean on my face.

"Tell me how you found Ben?" I said.

"After I left you early this morning . . ."

"God, it was only this morning?"

"I sat in the car outside your house. I wanted to make sure you were safe."

I looked at him. "Thank you."

"Later in the morning I decided to stretch my legs. I walked down to Celia's and let myself in. I thought maybe I'd find something connecting her to the murder or to Parson."

"But Ben tore the place apart."

"He did. My job is to search without anyone ever knowing I've been there. When I left, I walked back up PCH and saw Ben's Jeep drive past. I watched him park in front of Celia's, and I waited for about an hour. Keeping an eye on the house waiting for him to come out, so I could follow him."

"I was there talking with him part of that time. He ran away from me."

He nodded. "I saw the two of you on the walkway. I followed him north as he drove up the coast. After a couple of miles he made a fast U-turn and sped off south. I thought he might be going back to Celia's. Just then I got a frantic call from Gwyn that Robert had been drinking and was threatening to kill himself, and that Ben had discovered Celia was his birth mother. That was a big surprise. Hell, this has been a day of surprises." He rubbed the back of his neck. "So I pulled off the road and tried to calm Robert down over the phone. He said Parson had been there, threatening them and searching for a camera. Gwyn took the phone back, and I couldn't get her off, so I hung up on her." He stopped. "I need a drink. Would you like one?" He gestured across the street to a bar next to a vacant lot.

"I could use one."

Waiting for a few cars to pass, we hurried across the street and into the tavern. From a radio on the counter, a male voice sang forlornly in Spanish. Men, their jeans and shirts grimy from their labor, lined the pock-marked bar.

On the opposite wall were three stiff-backed booths made of dark wood. Maybe because of Heath's appearance, or maybe because we were *gringos*, the bartender gave him a stern look as we took one of the booths. A few of the men turned and assessed us, then went back to their conversations. The bartender wandered over. "No problems," he warned Heath.

"No." He tried to tuck in his shirt and gave up.

"Senora?"

"Martini."

"Beer, tequila."

"I'll have a shot of tequila then."

"Dos Equis," Heath said.

We stared out a small window at the emptying street. I could see the battered marquee of Parson's theater.

"Do you want me to go on?" Heath asked.

"Yes."

"I hung up on Gwyn and drove back to Celia's and saw Ben's car in her driveway. I parked, blocking it. I didn't want to lose him again." He shook his head. "Little did I know I already had. I couldn't find Ben anywhere in the house. I checked the deck and the beach. When I returned, I noticed there were only five chairs at the kitchen table. When I was there earlier there had been six. So what happened to the missing chair?" He leaned back and closed his eyes. And I remembered the chair lying on its side in the faded oil stain.

Now he looked at me. "That's when I opened the garage door and saw Ben hanging. I righted the chair, got on it, and felt his carotid artery. He had a faint pulse. Then the chair was kicked out from under me."

"He was alive," I said.

"Yes."

We stared out the window again. The bartender returned with our drinks. Heath took a long swallow of his beer. I sipped my tequila. It was warm and smooth. I fought back my tears, saving them for later when I would be alone. Then sirens filled the small bar as the black-and-whites, the emergency vehicles, converged on The Roxy. The night sky was lit up with their flashing lights. A few of the men at the bar paid and ran out the back door. Illegals? Criminals? Scared of the cops? Or just scared.

"We should be going," I said.

Heath set his bottle down. "You put the memory card in your pocket. What are you going to with it?"

I looked at him. "Give it to Spangler."

"The LAPD is a giant bureaucracy with some good management and some bad. Some good cops and some not so good. There are people who would pay a lot of money to get that card. One of the highest bidders will be Parson."

"Are you saying I shouldn't give it to her? She's corrupt?"

"Not Spangler. But this all happened out of her jurisdiction. She'll have no control over the card once it's put in as evidence."

"What do you want, Heath?"

"I'm going to cut another corner. I need that card to protect my client, Diana."

I sucked in my breath and felt the distance between us widen. "Is he the governor of the state? The mayor? The police commissioner? Head of a studio?"

"He's P. J. Binder."

"What?" I sat back.

"Binder was afraid Pearl had made a copy of the Bella Casa key and had given it to Zackary Logan. He'd seen them together and knew he'd been her pimp in the past. He was worried about her safety, so he hired me to find out what was going on. Then Logan showed up at Bella Casa when he was cleaning the pool and said he had a meeting with Celia. P.J. got angry and told him he knew what was going on. Logan pulled a gun, they struggled, and it went off."

"Celia didn't kill Logan then."

"No."

"And that's why Pearl didn't want to give me the card." I explained what had happened at Bella Casa. "She wanted it to protect P.J. What will you do with it?"

"Make it unusable. Another moral dilemma for you, Diana."

I downed the last of my tequila, took the card from my pocket, and slid it across the table to him.

"And you're all right about covering up for P.J.?"

"Yes."

"Why?"

"My mother helped him to reenter the world when he came back from 'Nam. I guess I'm helping him to stay in it."

"If Celia hadn't died, would you have let her go?" he asked..

"But she did die."

"And you still see my wanting to let Parson go differently."

"Yes."

Heath's eyes burrowed into mine. His voice was husky when he spoke. "What am I going to do with you, Diana?"

"What am *I* going to do with *you*?" I could feel the energy our bodies created dancing between us.

His cell rang. "Heath," he answered. "I'm across the street. Christ, Spangler, can't you guys ever arrive with just a *few* cars?" He disconnected. Then he threw some cash on the table and we walked back across the street to the theater.

A long hour later, inside the movie theater, I had told Spangler and two Central Division detectives what had happened. After many questions, they asked me to wait and left.

Spangler lingered, handing me a Snickers. "Something to remember me by."

"You're not the kind of woman one easily forgets," I said.

"So I've been told. Mostly by the bastards I've arrested. I'll get you a car to take you home."

After she left, I found my purse on the floor next to my seat. I opened it, dropped the candy bar in, and discovered I still had Celia's gun. Christ, was I never going to be unarmed again?

A few minutes later, Heath walked me back outside past all the patrol cars, still flashing, past the ambulances to the waiting black-and-white.

Heath opened the back door for me. "I'll see what I can do to keep you out of all this, Diana. The media doesn't bother much with this side of town. I've got to get back."

"Aren't you being driven home?"

"It seems I shot a man between the eyes. They want to take me downtown."

"I told them it was self-defense."

"Don't worry, I have an excellent lawyer. Almost as good as Parson's."

"Oh, I forgot." I reached into my purse and took out the gun. "It's Celia's."

"For a moment I thought you were going to shoot me." He took it.

"That reminds me. Who's Collette?"

"Who?"

"I accidently called your home phone number when I was trying to track you down today. Collette answered. She was there gathering some things that belonged to her. Bra, panties. . . ."

He cocked his head. His index finger stroked the bump on the bridge of his nose. "Would you believe she was my sister?"

"Yes."

His eyes widened. "You would?"

"Yes. Because you're such a charmer, such a good liar."

Now serious, he cupped my cheek in his hand. "Would you ever want to see me again?"

Without waiting for an answer he turned and walked quickly away, his white shirt stark against the night. Was he afraid of my answer? I wondered, getting into the car. He knew I wasn't sure of him or his world. Did I have an answer? As the car pulled away from the curb, I wondered how Heath and I would feel about each other after there was no more violence. No more adrenalin rushes. No more dead.

Even though I knew Parson was under arrest and I was heading toward Malibu in the back seat of a black-and-white, I glanced several times out the rear window to see whether a Mercedes limo was following me. Or the ghost of Rubio on his bike. I'd be looking over my shoulder for a while.

When I finally arrived home, I found a large manila envelope leaning against the front door. There were no television sounds from the kitchen—I must've forgotten to turn it on. I stood, listening. Yes, the silence was bearable.

In the living room, I turned on the light and placed the envelope and my purse on the coffee table. I walked over to Colin's Oscars and my mother's urn on the mantel. Gathering them in my arms, I carried them into Colin's office and set them on his desk. When Ryan was healed, I thought, he and I would scatter her ashes in the ocean. I closed the door quietly behind me and went back to the living room.

I opened the manila envelope and took out a script. It was from Pedro Romero, the director. In a note, he asked me to read for the costarring role of Elena in his film, *A Long and Happy Death*. I sank onto the sofa, clasping the script to my breasts, and looked at the empty mantel and thought of Celia and Ben. The confusion and pain of Zaitlin. I thought of Heath. I let my tears flow freely.

Not now, but tomorrow, I would feel that powerful surge of hope, of possibility, that keeps all actors going.

ACKNOWLEDGMENTS

My deep gratitude to the team at Pegasus, especially Claiborne Hancock for his belief in Diana Poole; Helen Zimmerman for her faith in the book; Gayle Lynds, not only for her friendship, but for taking the time to read and reread the manuscript and share her invaluable observations with me; Jane Heller and Kathleen Sharp for their support and dark humor. Also, my thanks to Deputy Sheriff Mark A. Ward and Michael Williams for their knowledge of the real world of police, guns, and army. I hope I didn't go too "Hollywood" on them.

And always, Bones.